AUTHOR	CLASS
	P
TITLE	No
	18446022

ADVENTURE OF STATE

By the same author

Cheyney's Law
The Three Colonels

Non-fiction

The Public Poetry of Robert Lowell
Churchill at war: alone
Margaret Thatcher: a Tory and her Party
R. A. Butler: an English Life

ADVENTURE OF STATE

by
Patrick Cosgrave

ROSS ANDERSON PUBLICATIONS

Published in 1984 by
Ross Anderson Publications
22 Higher Dunscar
Egerton
Bolton
BL7 9TE

British Library Cataloguing in Publication Data

Cosgrave, Patrick
    Adventure of state.
    I. Title
    823′.914[F]   PR6053.0775

    ISBN 0–86360–016–6

Photoset in Times Roman by
Northern Phototypesetting Co., Bolton
and printed in Great Britain by
Billings of Worcester

In August 1977 I spent ten days in the National Heart Hospital as a patient. The care I received was exceptional, and I owe gratitude not only to the staff, but to my fellow-patients.

I wrote the early parts of this book in hospital. I was encouraged to do so by my doctor, who came to see me each day. He was bullying and kindly by turns and became my friend. So this story is for

JOHN HUNT

CONTENTS

CHAPTER ONE

DEATH

There was no great distance between death and Sir Harry Richmond on the day he asked to see Allen Cheyney. The rain was falling in London in needles. It was not a decent sheety rain. It was not that dribble from the sky, that compound of water and gas, to which Londoners have, over generations, become accustomed. It was a thoroughly horrid, slanting, driving collection of malignant drops, beaded together like the serrated edge of a Kurdish dagger. Even those who had umbrellas cursed; for shoes and trousers and tights and even skirts were all marked by mud and water.

Of all this – though it was to matter a great deal – Sir Harry knew nothing. He was lying in the cocoon of his bed in the National Heart Hospital. He was propped up on his pillows. There was nobody in the room except himself, an anxious nurse, watching, moment by moment, what was likely to happen to him, and a television set which would have been showing a cricket match, had not that been rained off, too. His hands, though veined, frail and still white, lay either side of the book he had strength neither to lift nor to read. He looked at the television screen – music across a picture of Old Trafford – and hoped very much that they would come out to bat again so that he could luxuriate in his memories and not have to use up the tiny little bit of energy he had left in a request and a statement. Feeble though he was at seventy, and after three strokes, he could still put his thoughts in that way; the civil service way of a lifetime.

1

But he had only the tiniest bit of energy left. He could understand what was going on around him and he could speak quite well. At least, he could speak, but he could not be bothered to do it. True, it required much more effort than it used to; and from the often puzzled faces of nurses and doctors he gathered that the words as heard were not always the same as the words as formed, or even uttered. Still, none of that mattered very much, and indignation at their stupidity consumed so much of his remaining energy that he had decided, a day or two ago, not to be indignant. His mind now moved fitfully between the cricket match and his request and statement. On this grey day and at this moment Sir Harry still had presence of mind enough to notice, with alarm, how much more circumscribed the range of his mind had become: it was a couple of days at least since he had noticed how attractive this Malaysian nurse was. Now, when he tried to kick his mind into some interest in her austerely sexy figure and her dark and lively face, he could not do it. And, besides, it would take energy away from his request and his statement.

The habits and discipline of an orderly lifetime came to some extent to Sir Harry's rescue now. He could almost see the life ebbing from him, and a tear rolled down his cheek. The nurse was instantly on her feet to wipe it away, clucking softly to herself and to him. She dabbed at his forehead, tidied his hair, straightened his bedclothes, and was, for a moment, all over him with her nicely starchy smell, her warm concern, and her kindness. It distracted that tired and over-burdened mind, and his left hand came up for a moment to flap at her to go away: here was more distraction, more ways of taking up the little bit of energy that was left.

After all, he thought when, worried, she had sat down again and automatically taken up her Mills and Boon romance while keeping an eye fixed on him, he didn't have to do the statement and the request together. The request could – probably, should, probably would have to – come first. Then he could rest, gathering some strength from the consciousness that he had done, at last, the right thing, for perhaps a few hours, or a day at the most, and watch the cricket, and take more fully on board the fact that the nurse – the nurses – no longer interested him. Christ: he had to have a few days left at least. The nearness of death struck him suddenly and for the first time; and his acceptance that he was going to die struck him at the same time.

Paradoxically, this new consciousness added to his strength and resolution. It may, of course, have been that his protective mind flitted quickly away from what was going to be the inevitable and drastic conclusion of his time in this neat, clean, aseptic bed, surrounded by the hushed care of the devoted staff of a really first class hospital, noticing the cloying smell of detergent and disinfectant that is inseparable from even the best run of hospitals, and turned instead to what had been in his mind since, at the latest, his second stroke. Perhaps, though, it had been there for years; for all the years.

So, anyway, he started to say what he wanted to say, to make the request, if not the statement. He ran his feathery old tongue out over his cracked old lips and he resolved that this time there would be no gap – no gap whatsoever, no fissure, no distance – between what he was going to say and what was apprehended by the human being on the receiving end. Lips damp now, hands feebly bunching, a touch of sweat on his forehead, he tried to fix his washed out old blue eyes on the nurse's breasts – the most convenient point of reference – so that he could concentrate. And then, after a moment, he was ready to speak.

But she got up. So intent had he been that he neither heard nor saw the door opening. She, of course, was trained and conditioned to come to attention when a doctor entered the room. Besides, she had been forewarned that at twelve thirty the consultant – Mr Mason – and an old friend of Sir Harry's – the Permanent Under Secretary at the Treasury, no less – would call. Some part of her mind had been, even while she was attending to Sir Harry, and giving notice to the latest Mills and Boon heroine, constantly fixed on this forthcoming and august visitation all morning.

Mason, a man of great medical skill, and enormously self-satisfied with it, came in first. Like his companion, Sir Richard Fleming, he wore grey striped trousers and a black jacket. Unlike Sir Richard he wore both hair cream and after shave lotion. As his jowls wobbled – they invariably did so, because he walked with his head bent forward, in an attitude of scowling and concerned attention, and they shivered and jumped against his collar – they seemed, by their movement, to give off waves of *Aramis*. Around his neck Mason wore a stethoscope (he put it on as he climbed out of his car, and removed it as he came down the hospital steps) even though he rarely used it. In truth, in everything except the exercise of his scientific skill, Mason was a *poseur*. He had, of course, no doubt about Sir Harry: the man was as good as dead. But Mason was pleased enough to have so distinguished a former Civil Servant as his patient; even more pleased at the trickle of distinguished visitors to that gaunt bedside; and happy today that his old school friend, Fleming, should have called. He was not impatient with the dying Sir Harry. Few doctors were more conscientious. But he knew it was all over, and he went through the motions of checking on and tapping the stricken man in the bed while keeping up a constant patter of cheer, and thinking about his lunch.

During the performance Fleming stood apart. Tall, thin, ascetic in appearance and a man who pursed his lips, he felt uneasy in this room of death. But he did notice, as Mason hovered over Sir Harry, that his respected and even revered former colleague – five years retired now – seemed to want to say something. Or did he? Those faded eyes were fixed on the nurse. They swivelled as she moved around Mason. And they were, Fleming saw, constantly fixed on a rather embarrassing part of her body.

Why had he come? What a wretched business this was. Harry and his wife, to Fleming's certain knowledge, had not got on for fifteen years, perhaps longer; and Lady Richmond made only the barest and most formal visits to the hospital. Not that Harry had seemed to care, one way or the other.

Certainly he had not cared during this last illness. Yet the colleagues, like himself, had rallied round. Even Harry's old minister – and the opposition spokesman as well – had come along. Was it, he wondered, a form of superstition? Did they all think – did he think – that by coming here when Harry was dying, by paying their respect to death, they were putting the inevitable visit to themselves off? Still, as he felt uneasy in Harry's presence, he felt discomfited by Mason's ritual, and when the doctor finally pulled back, blowing out his cheeks and whistling softly, he came forward.

'Ah, Harry. Good to see you. Anything I can do? Anything I can get you? I gave the sister some flowers.'

He sat down by the bedside, being unable to think of anything

4

else to do. Conversation was impossible. At this stage even Mason had nothing more to say, no cheery message, no bonhomie however false, no advice to give, no comfort to impart, no prospect to hold out.

Sir Harry's eyes left the nurse for the first time and settled on Fleming. For the last time his verbal co-ordination was perfect, and he said with clarity what he meant to say.

'Get me Cheyney. Allen Cheyney. Ask him to come to see me. Please.'

A few moments later Sir Harry was again looking at the television. An announcer was reporting expert opinion on the prospects of play for the rest of the day. Mason and Fleming were walking down the corridor together, the former unruffled, the latter subdued.

'How long has he got?'

Mason shrugged. 'Any moment now he should go. A few days at the most. It's not his age so much. It's just that his heart is very bashed about. You know . . .'

Mason stopped, thoughtful suddenly, in the hospital hall, ignoring a passing sister anxious for even a glance of recognition from the hospital's most famous consultant.

'You know,' Mason repeated, putting his hand on Fleming's arm, 'if I was sentimental I might think it was a broken heart. Ha.'

Then he swept Fleming along with him and they faced the weather outside.

'Oh Christ.'

Mason looked at the rain as though it were some deliberately recalcitrant houseman.

'Sent my car away, I'm afraid. Still, got to be back in an hour or two. So I picked a little bistro close by. Manage the walk?'

'Oh yes.'

They picked up their umbrellas and went out into the driving rain.

Two minutes later, umbrellas dripping in the restaurant foyer, both uncomfortably wet around the feet and ankles, each with a drink by his right hand, Mason and Fleming sat in some comfort.

'Thank Christ for that,' said Mason, and took a swallow of his gin.

They had left, but not really parted from, Harry Richmond,

and Mason therefore said:

'Who's this Cheyney fellow? Relation? Old friend? Should you do something about it?'

Fleming frowned. He, too, had been puzzled.

'Not a relation. He was a very high-powered security *wallah*. Retired now. Lives in Scotland. He's a younger brother of Invermuir. You know Invermuir. You'll have met him at White's. Funny, I didn't realise Harry even knew him.'

'Well, I suppose you'd better give him a tinkle.'

'Oh, I will. When I get back to the office. Tomorrow, that is. I'm not sure of his number. I don't think he has a London address now.'

'Well, I should do it. Nothing's going to help old Richmond now. I doubt if he really recognised you. Still, must do the best one can by the dying.'

Mason then fell on the menu and, grunting and gurgling away to himself, considered the dishes, commented on them, and ordered.

'Ah,' he said as the preferred wine was poured, 'now, *that's* a claret.'

As he was sipping it, the head waiter came over.

'Mr Mason' – he spoke with a Mediterranean lilt – 'a call. You're wanted back at the hospital immediately.'

'Oh. Shit. Did they say what?'

'No, sir.'

'Hell. Dick. You eat. Charge it to me. We'll do this again, soon.'

He left at speed, and Fleming was abandoned. He felt low and dispirited. He toyed with a piece of veal and, deprived of his company and affected by what he had seen of old Harry Richmond – also, perhaps, still touched by the superstition that had visited him in the sick room – he decided he would do right by Harry Richmond, and call Allen Cheyney. Depressed, he was also impatient. He summoned the head waiter, asked about a telephone, got his office, found Cheyney's number, and dialled it there and then. Cheyney seemed as puzzled as he was himself. Nonetheless, Fleming felt he had done his duty; and putting up with the peremptory Cheyney even over the shortest of telephone conversations was, surely, more than duty.

Irritated by Cheyney he nonetheless felt, having called the man, entitled to enjoy his solitary lunch. His only complaint was, Mason having gone, that he had nothing with him to read over the meal.

Mason, of course, was doing other things. He had been recalled by the most terrifying noise a heart hospital knows. It was the unearthly howl — ringing through every floor of the building, reaching every ward and frightening the patients, driving into the kitchens and making even the cleaning women stand for a moment in fear — of the klaxon that signals a cardiac arrest.

CHAPTER TWO

CHEYNEY

In the year since his retirement Cheyney had been in London only twice; and on one of those occasions he had been in transit. Now, as he had promised young Tommy Graham he one day would, he had put down his roots in heather. Still in the full vigour of his middle fifties, tall and bony and, somehow, leashed, any slight decline there had been in his physical powers with the onset of middle age and a life that, however often interrupted by time in the open, was nonetheless mainly sedentary, had been more than repaired by a year's hard work and hard play on and around his land in Galloway. He could still outlast much younger men in a hard day's hill walking, as his friend and successor in Whitehall, Tom Morgan, had found the day before Fleming and Mason lunched together in rain lashed London.

Over the year he had declined attempts to draw him back into the business, even in various consultant roles. As he withdrew further and further he still did not abandon old friendships. Such knowledge as he retained of the dark world in which he had lived all of his adult life after the Army came from casual gossip when Morgan, or Pierce, or Robert Davies made the smooth rail journey from Euston to Dumfries to stay for a weekend at Loch Hill; or when one or other of them – or others like them – took part of a holiday there, fished the loch or the river or took part in the fairly easy shooting the estate offered. Even then, since his friends came to get away, and since Cheyney became daily more absorbed in a life that was to him at the same time both very new

8

and very old, there was no great indulgence in shop talk. The magic of the hills and the trees and the rivers and the heather, and perhaps above all of the house, Loch Hill, seemed easily to keep sordid cares and troubles at bay. All agreed that Cheyney's career was over.

The first period of withdrawal had not, naturally enough, been without its difficulties. Cheyney had taken some time to recover from his wild night battle on the heights of Masada; and Rachel had been in hospital for a long time before their marriage. It took months – and more than a lazy honeymoon in the sun – before he stopped waking, sweating, in the night, or could cross his own land without the burden of a nervous vigilance.* His mind, too, took months to unwind after years of cogitation and suspicion and strain: for all the dreams he had had and all the plans he had made, becoming a full time farmer rather than a part time squire was not an easy transition to his surprise, and, causing him annoyance with himself, he had not found it at all easy to settle into a daily agricultural routine. The intermittent bouts of intense work on the estate, he now came to see, had been, more than he knew, a relief from other things, rather than fully satisfactory experiences in themselves. Besides, apart from his contacts, and the (though diminishing) calls from Whitehall, there was Rachel's injury to remind him of other days: it was only a month before Fleming's call that she had thrown away her stick. And even on that happy day streaks of fear and hate and effort and blood and sacrifice scoured across his memory.

That morning, and after their tramp of the previous day, Tom Morgan had cried off Cheyney's visit to the other end of the estate, and announced his intention of spending a peaceful morning fishing, without much hope of success, the loch. Cheyney took the Land Rover and drove his factor off to inspect progress on some cottages that were being rebuilt and, leaving the car with Cooper, set off for home – some ten miles – with his wolfhound, Bruce. They loped along happily, and it was an indication of the completeness of Cheyney's retreat that those parts of his mind not spent in satisfied contemplation of the land were engaged in rumination on his now nearly completed study of

* See Patrick Cosgrave, *The Three Colonels* (Macmillan, 1979).

occasional bird migration into Galloway. For all his hospitality to his guests Cheyney himself neither shot nor fished nor hunted. But he spent hours in bird hides or, from the breakfast room one part of which had rapidly been transformed into a study, sweeping the loch ceaselessly with his glasses, examining the rich variety of birds which, according to the season, found temporary purchase there. He had been particularly careful, during the restoration of the house, while he was trimming and cleaning and dredging the long neglected edges of the loch, to preserve as much as possible of the decadently lush water greenery there, so that the wild life which had found sanctuary when humans had retreated from Loch Hill a generation before would be disturbed as little as possible. The result was that a stranger looking down from the house could easily be misled into thinking its borders still wholly wild: he would not readily see the small jetty and the concealed boathouse. Cheyney allowed no motors on the water, but there were a couple of dinghies, and from these guests could fish the deep centre of the oval loch. The house itself stood on a gentle eminence in the very centre of the bottom of the glen. As Cheyney and Bruce reached the lip on the other side, at about a quarter past one, he stopped and lit his pipe, looking forward with immense animal satisfaction to his lunch – his last for some time with Tom, who was returning to London the following day. That afternoon he would spend on estate paperwork, and even the thought of that drudgery gave him a sort of tranquil delight. As he came down the slope he saw Morgan beginning the trudge up to the house from the loch, and even at a distance reckoned he could detect disappointment and frustration in his friend's gait. He shouted and waved his stick, and Morgan altered direction and came around by the side of the house to meet him.

'No joy?'

'Not a damn thing. I think I'll take up golf.'

Morgan scratched Bruce behind an ear and the two men turned to make their way up the new road Cheyney had laid to the great oak door of his home. Cheyney was a tall man, but Morgan topped him by an inch or so, and was much more obviously rugged, with great broad shoulders and hands like young hams. Fifteen years Cheyney's junior, he had a big and deceptively open face with a dimple in the centre of his chin, a nose flattened in some forgotten Rugby engagement, and a shock of black, curly hair, untainted with grey.

'Never mind. I'll come back soon and get some of the bastards, if you'll have me.'

Cheyney touched his shoulder lightly.

'Any time.'

Rachel opened the door as they reached it. As always, Cheyney stopped for a second, to marvel at his fortune. Much smaller than he, and slight, she never ceased to captivate him. She grinned, pushed back her hair, and put up her face to be kissed. His hands were rested only lightly on her shoulders for that moment, but all his happiness and joy were in it.

'I saw you coming. But, look, Allen, there is a telephone call for you. Don't be long, please. Lunch is nearly ready. I'll take Tom through for a drink.'

'Telephone?' Cheyney asked irritably. 'Oh hell.' He saw the instrument lying on the table in the hall and went towards it, saying, over his shoulder, 'Who the devil is it?'

Rachel and Tom had already started towards the living room door.

'Someone from London,' she said, carelessly, over her shoulder. 'A man called Fleming.'

They had not quite reached the door when Morgan heard Cheyney say:

'What? Harry Richmond? Dying?'

Something in his tone made the hairs on Morgan's neck prickle him and he stopped Rachel and turned back to listen. Hearing only one side of a telephone conversation when one is anxious, or curious, to know the whole exchange, is intensely irritating. Rachel's mind was divided; she did not like Morgan's detaining hand on her arm, because it implied that there might be something of consequence from the old world in Cheyney's call. But after a moment she found her attention divided between Tom and Cheyney, simply puzzled, as well as slightly worried. Morgan, for all that the warning signal had sounded in his head with Cheyney's second sentence, could make nothing of it either.

'Wants to see me? What do you mean?'

'I see. So he's far gone?'

'Hm. Couple of days. What did you make of it?'

There was a longer pause here, and Cheyney's left hand fidgeted with the telephone cord.

'Oh, well. But I scarcely know the man. Things still bad with his wife?'

'Hm. Oh, very well. I suppose I'd better come down. Tell them, will you? G'bye.'

He turned away from the telephone looking, Rachel was relieved to see, neither tense nor worried, but puzzled. He stood for a moment in thought, then looked up, grinned, advanced on them both, swept them into the big, airy living room and went to pour drinks. As he began Tom Morgan spoke.

'Harry Richmond. That's the old Home Office puss, isn't it?'

'Puss?' Rachel asked, bewildered. 'Is it a cat?' She could accept almost any sentiment on her husband's part for animals.

Cheyney laughed as he handed her a pink gin, turning back to pour whisky for himself and Morgan.

'No, darling. It's a set of initials, P.U.S. for Permanent Under Secretary. A Permanent Under Secretary is the top Civil Servant in any government department – what you would call a Director in Israel. Because enough of them are feline and most of them are pretty damn ineffective at everything except stopping people doing good things the police and the Security Services have always called them pussies. Just a bit of office slang.'

Still, he went and put an arm round her and squeezed her shoulder. Such little gestures, never automatic, were nonetheless now habitual whenever he thought or felt that any little detail of her new life was incomprehensible to her.

'Oh. I see. But this man is dying. He is a friend of yours?'

'Or he has some other reason.' Morgan was suspicious, as he had been from the beginning.

'Well,' Cheyney began, but Mrs Burns came through just then to announce lunch and he did not resume until they were sitting down in the big, high-ceilinged dining room which was Rachel's favourite. She and Morgan sampled the clear soup while Cheyney addressed himself to opening a bottle of Bernkastler. When he had poured for them all he stopped, sitting thoughtfully.

'Well?' asked Morgan.

'What are you thinking, Tom? Senior Civil Servant on death bed wishes to confess treason?'

'It could be.'

Morgan looked stubborn. Rachel looked apprehensive.

'No.' Cheyney shook his head and laughed. 'There's more to it than you heard me telling Fleming – my caller, dear, was the puss from the Treasury – but I think I may know what he wants. Harry Richmond was one of the most cold-hearted old buzzards I ever met in my life. It's true I scarcely knew him, but we had one meeting that may well be on his mind now. I hope so. And if he's troubled about it – and I hope he is – it's no more than he deserves.'

'That doesn't sound like a happy brief for a deathbed visit.'

Cheyney shrugged. 'I'll do it for Charlie.'

'My God. The puss is Charlie Richmond's father?'

Rachel rapped her spoon on the polished table surface.

'May I be told what this is all about?'

Cheyney instantly covered her hand with his, long, thin and brown both of them, Morgan noticed. He felt a pang of envy as, for a few seconds, they went back into their inner world. A damn sight different, he thought, from whatever half world the old buzzard Harry Richmond was now occupying.

'Let's eat,' said Cheyney, lifting his hand. 'And I'll tell you both about it afterwards. I do think, though, that I'd better go down to London. I'll go with Tom in the morning. I can't stand that bloody sleeper, so I'll put up with Charles and come back on Friday, first thing. I'll collect that tapestry after I've been to the hospital, so that'll be a useful bit of business transacted.'

Without a thought for, nor knowledge of, Richmond's condition, the hospital's concern, Mason's pomposity, Fleming's annoyance, or the weather in London they tackled a sole, sampled a Stilton and finished the Bernkastler. They complimented Mrs Burns on a perfect lunch, light and tangy and leaving them satisfied but not replete, in the mood to gaze out of the big picture window on a perfect cold Galloway day and the trees in the orchard – which was set ten feet below the level of the house – stirring in the sharp breeze. Rachel had long ago arranged that, after meals, people did not repair to the living room, but sat round the table for conversation. She rarely drank after meals and now took just a glass of mineral water. Cheyney gave himself and Morgan a glass of whisky and his friend the cigars. Normally he

after a meal, but today he took the cigarette box
ble.

en. The story, please.'

d at her, but his mood, it was clear to them both, was
hearted. He shifted round in his chair so that, for a
, he looked like the chairman of a meeting, and startled
Morgan with memories of days long past, and never now to
return, in which he struck just such an attitude at departmental
meetings.

'Some of this even Tom doesn't know. I'll tell you the whole
story one day, Tom. A lot of it is not to be found in the files.'

He looked directly at Rachel.

'Charlie Richmond was just about the bravest man I ever met.
He was what we called, in the jargon, a penetrator, that is, he
specialised in temporary missions behind enemy lines. When he
was operational that meant in Eastern Europe. He was, oh, I don't
know, in his early 'thirties I suppose, when he went over for the
last time.'

Cheyney lit another cigarette.

'But that's not the most relevant part of the story. In the
beginning Charlie was rather a layabout. Broken with family and
home and that sort of thing. Had a small legacy from an aunt
which he blew all over the place. All in all, he was quite an
embarrassment to his father. Not in the sense that he might have
hindered the old man's rapid upward progress. The times had long
arranged that the sins of the children should not be visited upon
the parents: if they had been there'd have been precious few old
Harries left. But Charlie's behaviour bit into something deeper in
his father, something much more fundamental. He was outraged
that *his* son should go on like this. And, although Sally Richmond
didn't get on with her husband she agreed with him on that.
Neither parent was the type to tolerate a rakehell.'

'Just a second, Allen,' said Morgan as Cheyney got restlessly
up from the table and walked over to the window, 'You said
Harry's upward progress. I know Home Office puss isn't a bad
job – good pension, honours and so forth – but it's not exactly the
top either. In fact, it's a bloody dreary backwater, if that's where
you finish. You talk about old Richmond as though he were some
sort of tough high flier. What happened?'

Cheyney put his backside on the window ledge and looked back at Morgan.

'Shrewd as ever, Tom. Harry Richmond's genius was – sorry, is – a mixture of ruthlessness, dedication, hard work and a quite extraordinary insight into committee politics. I'm sure he expected to end up at the Treasury, and probably as Head of the Home Civil Service.' He paused and grinned at Rachel. 'That's the super-puss. It didn't happen. Maybe the climb was too hard. Maybe they found out that he was missing something extra. I don't know.'

Rachel, as usual when she was attentive, was sitting with one hand cupped under her chin and the other holding an opposite elbow. She was not smiling now. She was very grave and her big eyes were fixed. 'Allen,' she said, further diverting him from the path of his original story, 'You speak with great confidence about a man you scarcely knew.'

'The little I did know of him was pretty intense. It took, I suppose, about forty minutes. But I knew him by reputation, of course, as I knew every senior Civil Servant. And I sat in his company at umpteen meetings. But let me get this story straight, both of you.'

He pulled his thick brows together, poured himself another drink and gave Morgan the bottle. While Morgan got up for his splash of soda Cheyney sat down again at the table and lit another cigarette.

'Bob Davies recruited Charlie for us. You know, Rachel, that Davies's reputation is based on his work in pure intelligence – assessing incoming stuff, trading it off for other stuff we – that is, Tom now – need, and sometimes getting better stuff. That's why he's called the trader. But he's also a first class recruiting sergeant. Nobody better at assessing the basic things in a man – or woman, if it comes to that. When he put Charlie Richmond up to me I thought he'd begun to lose his touch. Charlie's reputation was against him. So was his father. We'd always tried to avoid recruiting the children of people important in government; too much potential embarrassment. But Bob persuaded me to see Charlie, and Charlie persuaded me that he and his family no longer recognised one another. We trained him and tried him and, by God, he was brilliant. There's no other word for it. He'd never have made a desk man. He could never collate – like Tom or Bob Davies, or even, God help us, me. But he had every conceivable technical potential – five languages, total ability to melt into a background, first class shot, top class fighter – honestly, there is no superlative that, applied to him, would be an exaggeration.

'But there was one huge drawback. His operational intelligence was extremely limited. He had to be briefed very carefully. He would interpret the brief with brilliance. But he could never really go beyond it. Oh, sure, he could run a fire fight with genius. He could get close to that seedy lot of boozers and cardsharpers in the Sofia cafés and talk their language, swing their women, break their safes and come home by Rumania on a *laisser-passer* from the Bucharest Security police. He did exactly that just twelve years ago. But he could never see a big picture. Only the particular job interested him.'

Cheyney seemed slightly lost in a long ago and far away world. Rachel's face, as she watched him, gave nothing away. Morgan was nodding with understanding.

'That posed the problem of what to do with him. Even for somebody like him, working in the field presents enormous strains. We let him do more jobs than he should have done, simply because he went on being so good at them, and every trial of him at base in London was a disaster. Anyway, and to cut the story short, a tiny crack appeared in Charlie one day in Zagreb and I had to fly out there myself. It was too dangerous to abort the mission – which was back to Sofia, by the way – and too late to bring anybody else in, not that we had anybody remotely as good as Charlie. I sent him on his way. He ballsed it up. He was killed.'

'Kill confirmed,' said Morgan quietly to Rachel, as he saw the question in her eyes.

'Now, I've always taken a dim view of the system that says people in our line of business can get honours and rewards after a spell behind a desk, when they can be given the gong for something they're supposed to have done, rather than what they've done. That's why I don't like the things myself.'

'Allen,' said Morgan, surprised by the extent to which he was perturbed by his friend's sudden vehemence, which had been gathering force in the course of his story, and which seemed to be applied more to the peripheries of that story than to the short life of Charlie Richmond. 'I think there's something Rachel may not know.'

Then, to Rachel:

'You know, of course, that your husband left the army as a Colonel. He may not have told you that he has turned down everything since.'

'He hasn't.'

To lighten it Morgan grinned, and said:

'I'm not one for self-denial. This job carries a knighthood and I crave it. But they'll never offer me the VC.'

'Anyway, I thought something was owed to Charlie. I don't know. I was very likely wrong. But there had always seemed to me to be too much passion in Charlie's story about his break with his family. Purely on impulse, after some bloody committee, I asked Harry out to lunch. I thought he'd like to know how his son died, and what he had died doing. We had ten minutes chit chat and then – since Harry was certainly cleared generally on past security operations – I started to tell him a little about Charlie. The buzzard was drinking Martini – the rubbish from the bottle, not the serious drink. I can't remember exactly what he said, but I know he started with 'Colonel Cheyney'. Then he said that he thought Charlie's work for the Department was certainly no more praiseworthy than what he had been doing before Davies recruited him. But he didn't walk out. Not him. He suggested we change the subject and might profitably go over some of the points of the last meeting we had been at, the one where I invited him to lunch. I said 'No', and then he did leave.'

'And this man you will go to see?' asked Rachel, outraged.

Cheyney looked weary. The account books of the estate no longer looked so alluring. Nothing did.

'Yes. In Zagreb Charlie and I talked about things in general. Nothing specifically about his father. But I think he'd have liked me to go. Let's take a walk.'

Pointedly, Morgan refused to move. He poured some more whisky both for himself and Cheyney, got up, fetched the mineral water, filled Rachel's glass, to his delight saw that she was going to let him stay, and not indulge Cheyney.

'No security factor, then?'

'My dear Tom. No. Check if you like. If Harry Richmond was

a spy I'll give you Loch Hill. He could have played lots of cards differently – and he had the intelligence to do so – if he was working for the other side. He needn't have wound up as Home Office puss. He's been gone over like the others, and he's one of the dozen or so I'm sure of. No. He wants to see me because of Charlie, and I'll go down and see the bastard.'

They sipped their drinks for a while and then Morgan said:

'What about that walk?'

The three of them went around the little orchard and Cheyney explained to Tom what he had been doing in the way of new plantings and new grafts. He and Rachel aired before their friend their little disagreements about sitings and choice of trees and contradicted one another's expertise on growth potentials. After an hour, the account books neglected, they walked around the loch and back to the house.

'Some day you must tell me about Zagreb.'

'I will, Tom. I will.'

CHAPER THREE

FLEMING

Fleming finished his veal in the same state of concealed irritability that he had begun. The weather was the cause of most of it – that accursed, bloody, rainy weather. But there were many other things which went to make up his discomfiture. There was Mason's departure and the fact that, left alone, he had nothing to read. There was this *bloody* restaurant, not his sort of place at all. Damned tables too close together for a start. Damned food too oily. Damned checked tablecloths. Damned noisy crowd in jeans and chains and beads and so on and so forth. *Damned*, twice damned, waiter hovering around and rubbing his hands and pressing things on Fleming and telling him it was all on Mr Mason.

'Waiter.'

The man came over.

'Would you be so good as to send out for an evening paper for me? Mr Mason having left, you see, I have nothing to read.' Fleming was conscious of having added a word too much of explanation.

'Certainly, sir.'

Bloody man, thought Fleming as he went away. And why was it still bloody raining? Little chance of a taxi just yet. Didn't suppose this bloody place would run to getting him one.

Fleming had this thought just as the waiter returned with his paper. For the moment he saw no illogicality in the run of his mind; and he was not humorist enough to notice the difference between his thoughts – and their inward expression in words – and his politely authoritative manner with the head waiter, which was such as to give that good man enormous pleasure, have him tell his underlings that here was another real gentleman – he had always been disappointed that the distinguished Mr Mason invariably seemed to bring tedious young girls to lunch at his place – and allow him to hope that the pattern of custom was changing. It was perhaps just as well for Fleming's temper that he failed to notice the head waiter beaming benevolently on his dark jacket and striped trousers, thinking the while even more benevolently of the bowler, the Crombie overcoat and the umbrella waiting in his cloakroom. For, at almost that very moment Fleming noticed that a girl, leaving with a young man, both dried out by the heat of the restaurant but still marked in their straggly hair and damp-patched clothes by their earlier passage through the rain, pointed him out in his prim outfit and giggled. Really, why on earth had Mason chosen this bloody place? And what was he thinking about, leaving?

Once this point had been made, however, Fleming's natural reasonableness reasserted itself. Mason, after all, had gone back to the hospital. He had work to do. Saving some poor bugger's life, like as not. Fleming was instantly shocked by this unspoken and even unconscious lapse into an idiom long thought forgotten, long overlaid, long vanished into a forgotten past. To be sure, there were senior Civil Servants – not as senior as he was, perhaps, but senior nonetheless: Fleming was a fair-minded man – who made something of a parade of their origins. Botham at Trade, for example – a perfectly *bloody* man – who spoke such broad Yorkshire that nobody could understand him. Send Botham to Social Services, thought Fleming, in a brief burst of megalomania. Exile the shit to the Elephant and Castle.

At this moment Fleming realised two things. First, he had not yet opened his paper. Second, he had had one large gin and the bottle of claret was empty.

He took out his watch and checked the time. God, it was only a quarter past two. How had all this happened in the time? He then took out his diary. The afternoon was blank. That was an enticing thought. He suddenly remembered that he had expected a long and leisurely lunch with Mason and had planned to go home, by taxi and train, immediately afterwards, to Henley, that he had cleared his desk in anticipation of a jolly chat over old times, reminiscence about old friends, and that, conscientious man that he was, there was already in his house a fat file to be gone through that evening after dinner, as a result of his notes on which a great number of people would hop rapidly about from place to place for the next week or so.

'Waiter.'

'Sir.'

'Ah. An excellent claret this. I haven't drunk it before. Don't even know it.'

'You are very kind. Mr Mason drinks it sometimes.'

'He may be back.' Fleming was very pleased with this lie. 'Look. Bring me another bottle now. And, do you think you could put a dozen together in some sort of safe box or something for me to take away when I leave? I'll pay you for that separately, of course. Cheque all right?'

'Of course, sir. It will be a pleasure.'

The head waiter hesitated.

'If Mr Mason does not come, sir, will you want a taxi?'

'Oh, how good of you. Probably.'

'Whenever you wish, sir. It takes about ten minutes.'

'Very good of you.'

Baulked, thus, of his deepest potential resentment against the restaurant, Fleming fell back inside his armour. Rather ostentatiously he flicked through the newspaper until he got to the City page, and set himself to read the Neil Collins column. He always read it anyway, usually with interest and pleasure. Today, however, he had to grit his teeth and force his mind. Wine was poured, his coffee pot replaced by a fresh one, the crumbs apologetically swept off his table; and it was only half past two.

Even drunk, even irritable, even still touched by the ghostly finger he had felt in Harry Richmond's room, Fleming was a fair minded man. He put Collins down, lit a cigarette – he was a careful smoker, and saw with horror that he must have taken at least ten since the beginning of lunch – and looked around the restaurant. He no longer found the clientele objectionable. To be fair, the staff, however tediously obsequious, did not merit the ascription bloody. They did their best, poor souls. It was a bloody

21

place to eat, perfectly true, bloody inconvenient, bloody out of the way. But not all the people there were bloody. The coffee was very pleasant and the claret – light, dry, just a little nutty – was really very good.

'Sir.'

'Ah. Yes.'

'I have packaged your wine, sir. It is waiting for you when you are ready.'

'Ah. Very good of you.'

Not a bad chap at all, really, Fleming thought, giving himself another glass as the waiter moved away. Botham probably ate in pubs. It was not that Fleming was a snob: his origins were at least as humble as Botham's. It was just that he thought a Whitehall manner and a Whitehall voice and a Whitehall attitude were proper parts of the equipment for the job. They were like the component parts of a uniform for a soldier or a sailor or an airman. The offence was not to be born ill or, for that matter, born well: it was to fail or refuse to adapt to the disciplines of the service, the required, the necessary disciplines. The only things that kept the show together. Drunk or sober this was Fleming's faith. He cared nothing for a man's school, not even – despite myths about the Civil Service – for his university. He cared deeply and long about the man's commitment – or, in the case of a recruit, potential commitment – to the service, and his style in discharging that commitment.

But the repeated and steadfast refusal of the restaurant to provide evidence to fuel his resentments, and his growing feeling of kindness towards the other clients, caused him to wonder why he still felt so angry and irritated. Probably it was this bloody weather, he thought, looking out of the window at the needles of rain still stabbing down. It was certainly the bloody weather. The *bloody* weather. His shoes – he looked down at them – were mud splattered. He surreptitiously rubbed the toes against the backs of his calves. The ends of his trousers were wet. It was a bloody day.

'Do you mind, sir?'

The junior waiter wanted to sweep away crumbs, replace his coffee pot with a fresh one, pour another glass of wine – with alarm he saw that there could not be more than a single glass left. Choking inside he suddenly found the focus and cause of his resentment and, since it was only a quarter to three, he asked, in an even and civil voice, for a large brandy. He never knew how much admiration he had excited in the head waiter who saw, with that order, how gentlemen could hold their drink and keep their poise.

It was that *bloody*, that truly and pluperfectly *bloody* man Cheyney. No: Cheyney hadn't said, 'Do you mind?' he hadn't said exactly that. He hadn't even been that courteous. He had said . . . Fleming looked for it, looked for the words, willed himself to recall them. They were somewhere there, at the very back of his head. They were there, though. They were. They had to be. He couldn't get them, though. They were there, but he couldn't get them. There was something, though. It was definitely Cheyney who had insulted him. No: he hadn't said, 'Do you mind?' He hadn't said that. He definitely had not said that. He had not been that courteous. The bloody waiter was more courteous than Cheyney.

On the strength of this insight Fleming ordered another brandy and asked for his bill. There was a polite dispute between himself and the head waiter which ended by the meal and ancillary drinks going on Mr Mason's account, Fleming writing a cheque for the wine, the head waiter receiving a five pound note and a taxi being summoned (and required to wait until Sir Richard was ready to leave).

Suddenly Fleming found himself presented with a further large brandy, on the house this time. He thought how unfair he had been earlier to the head waiter. Good chap, after all, he thought, looking at two large brandies and a third already half consumed. He realised suddenly – and this was true – that he would never have drunk as much or brooded as much in any eating place where he was known. After all, Mason's little bistro served a purpose. And, in a few minutes, a taxi would arrive to take him to the station from which he would go to Henley. He would lie down for a while, he thought, or perhaps garden, and then he would have a light dinner with his wife – who, all things considered, was a pretty ideal woman – before settling down with a lot of black coffee – he would *need* a lot of black coffee – to go through that file.

He thought he had better look at that *Standard* again. It

wouldn't do to appear preoccupied all the time. He thought he had better have a pee. He did so, calmly, sedately and in a manner which provoked further admiration from the head waiter, who expected most of his customers to stay until at least half past three, to find those who remained somewhat drunk, and to have difficulty in ejecting them. Fleming did not even look flushed.

When he returned to his table he still faced two large brandies. He sipped one and read his way through the Collins column. Only when he got to the end did he realise that he had read it before. He sat back, and lit another cigarette.

Cheyney. What was it Cheyney had said? Cheyney was certainly the fountainhead of his surely justified annoyance. Suddenly his mind pounced on the words. 'Will you? G'bye.' Those were the words. No waiting for a response. No courtesy, such as the head waiter had displayed in getting him a brandy on the house. Could he recall all the words? Perhaps he could. He had trained himself for years to remember whole passages of direct speech. Surely a few lines from that curt bastard were not beyond him. Yes. He had it. No. It was gone. He started his last brandy. It would not come. He had forgotten even what he had already remembered. He read Collins's article for the third time, and then the brandy was gone.

He rose and went to his taxi.

'Thank you very much, sir. I hope you enjoyed your meal. I am sorry Mr Mason was called away.'

What a splendid fellow. How considerate he was. How thoughtful.

'I enjoyed it very much. Excellent veal. I'll bring my wife here one evening. After the theatre, if that's convenient?'

'Certainly, sir. We receive many theatre parties.'

'Good. I'll do that then.'

He took the card offered him.

'Ah. Thank you. I'll ring to book. Oh. The wine. Thank you.'

This, as the waiter managed to hold his umbrella, carry the case of wine, and shepherd him into the taxi:

'What perfectly *bloody* weather. I don't expect it's like this where you come from?'

The waiter looked puzzled. 'I come from London, sir.'

'Ah. Oh. Well, thank you very much. Victoria.'

In the taxi he suddenly remembered the full sentences.

'I suppose I'd better come down. Tell them, will you? G'bye.'

He supposed. He was a truly bloody man. He expected, clearly expected, Fleming to telephone the National Heart hospital and arrange for them to receive Colonel Cheyney, ex Security *wallah* and bloody gentleman farmer. Well, Sir Richard Fleming had better things to do. Having lunch at that nice restaurant, for one. But he thought he would not bring Pamela there. It would remain his secret, shared only with himself. But he would *not* ring the hospital. Cheyney could make his own bloody arrangements. He could see bloody Richmond if he bloody well wanted to. Fleming was not his go-between, nor his messenger boy. Damn the man.

If Fleming had telephoned the hospital he would have found that Sir Harry Richmond was dead. If he had found that, and if he had been sober, he might have telephoned Loch Hill. If he had telephoned Loch Hill Cheyney would have shrugged and not come to London. But, that day, and perhaps largely because of the weather, Fleming telephoned nobody.

CHAPTER FOUR

MORGAN

Tom Morgan was a morning mutterer. When Cheyney ran the Department he normally arrived at the office at eight. Morgan rarely appeared before half past ten. If brooding time for Cheyney was the night, brooding time for Tom Morgan was made out of all those hours between waking up and noon.

It was a penance for Morgan, therefore, to have to catch, with Cheyney, the Glasgow–London express at Dumfries at the absurd hour of eight in the morning. He had barely managed to shave and – with a consciously weary cackle at his wickedness – avoid either a bath or a shower when Rachel rang the breakfast bell, at a quarter to seven, for God's sake.

Morgan muttered away to the mirror about that. He was not bad-tempered early in the morning, just grumbly and a little soporific. This morning he still, as he got out of bed and shaved, had an odd little worry tapping quietly away at the back of his head. Morgan was a very efficient young man, and he had once read a book about mnemonics – tricks for remembering things one did not want to forget. The book he had read suggested that when you did not know what to do with some worry or problem or difficulty; or when you came across some beautiful aphorism or barbed saying, or maxim of conduct, you should think of your mind as a storehouse, a sort of attic, and you should put the worry or the problem or the difficulty, the aphorism, the saying or the maxim, away on a shelf in that attic. The practice – it was not just a theory – was devised in an age when there were no printed books, or video tape machines, or tape recorders; and Tom Morgan found it very useful for storing away impressions and suspicions, doubts and problems which could not be filed anywhere else. So, as, with the first two fingers of his left hand, he levelled out the dimple in his cheek and, with his right, he used the razor to scrap the hairs out of the little cavern the dimple had formed, he stowed away, on a medium high shelf in the left hand corner of the attic of his mind, the thought that there was something odd about Sir Harry Richmond's dying desire to see Cheyney; and something inadequate about Cheyney's hypothetical explanation for Harry's request, and Fleming's call.

He stowed the thought away, up there in the attic, because he did not want to forget it, even while he accepted there was nothing he could do about it. He could do nothing with it unless Cheyney was interested, and Cheyney's interest, such as it was, seemed to run to things long ago and far away. Often – well, perhaps not often, but once or twice – in the old days Morgan had come to Cheyney with an argument – supported by, at the maximum, one sheet of quarto paper, typing one and a half spaced – which had made Cheyney change his mind. Once upon a time he, because of some inexplicable equation of comradeship, or followership, or, damn it, hero worship, had, having received a priority message, left the office very late at night, and telephoned Cheyney from a public call box and warned him that the roof was about to come in on him. (That was the first occasion, Morgan recalled, when he had called Cheyney 'Allen'). What Tom Morgan was telling Allen Cheyney that night was that the cards suggested that Cheyney was about to be fired and an operation aborted. All Cheyney had said – Morgan had been so furious and so admiring at the same time that he had stowed the words away in one of the pigeon holes in the upper right hand corner of his mind – was:

'Very good, Tom. Thank you for calling. I'll remember it.'*

But Cheyney was wrong about this one, Morgan thought, inspecting his dimple and finding it satisfactorily clean. There was something *else* here.

The trouble was that Morgan now was Cheyney. Tom Morgan knew perfectly well – even while he was putting a thought away

* See *Cheyney's Law* (Macmillan, 1977).

on a medium high shelf on the left hand side of his mind – that he held the job only because Cheyney had cast his vote and his weight on his, Morgan's, side and, therefore, against Bob Davies. Here, at Loch Hill, Morgan found it very hard to take action against the institution of a man who was first a hero, second a boss, third and most formidably, a friend. Things Allen Cheyney had taken in his stride, Tom Morgan shied at. That was one of the reasons why Morgan woke every morning wondering what had made him, every hour and minute of his day, responsible for security, wondered what force had given him Allen Cheyney's chair. That sense of wonder, allied to an indefatigable Welsh stubbornness, was, very likely, what made Morgan a better head of the Department than Cheyney.

Old men, old times, Morgan went on with his mutter, as he came downstairs in response to Rachel's second bell. Cheyney simply didn't see it. There was something askew with or about Harry Richmond's request. It wasn't Charlie Richmond, it wasn't just that. He couldn't say precisely what it was, but he would be happy to have a long look at it. Anyway, it ought to be checked.

He almost took the thought off the medium high shelf on the left hand side of his mind when he saw them together in the breakfast room. They were both eating away. Rachel jumped up when he came in. She had her hair tied back in a *bandana*. She was wearing jeans and boots. She gave him a kiss and, then, looked at him with some concern.

'Tom. You have not slept well.'

Embarrassed, Morgan sat, muttering, at the table. The breakfast room, in the bow of the house, gave the most perfect view of the loch. From it you could see a perfect fall of land, dipping quickly and then flattening out to a hard sheen of water.

He looked at it.

'You'd better have eggs scrambled,' said Rachel, 'if you are to catch that train.'

Ten minutes later, Cheyney, at the other end of the table, looked up from his second piece of toast and the local paper.

'Come on, Tom.'

It was a beautiful and clear morning: one of those mornings on which Morgan deeply envied (though without hatred) Cheyney. The fields glinted with dew. The ripples of the loch water shifted in

28

strands to and fro. The hills, still lightly shrouded in mist, looked down on the house with kindness. The odd animal raised a head, the rabbits scurried back behind the heather above the house, the birds scolded furiously in the trees, as Rachel swung her new Range Rover out into the main road, Cheyney puffing away at his pipe, Morgan striving not to yawn and reminding himself of the thought put safely away on that shelf in the attic, and of eggs eaten in three minutes. Behind the human passengers there decorously sat the great grey-blue figure of Bruce with, beside him, Rachel's brave, brown, flirtatious standard poodle, Shana.

'Bloody hell,' said Cheyney as they reached the edge of the village. 'Look at those road edges, Rachel. Mention them to Cooper, will you?' and, then, to Tom:

'I can't stand that kind of untidiness.'

Perhaps, thought Morgan in a sudden depression, there was no way of waking Cheyney up now. And he could see why not. All this was quite different, so very different, from Tom Morgan's own past. True: he knew that the Loch Hill estate made very little money. Its prosperous appearance deceived only the ignorant. True, he knew that just breaking even had cost Cheyney untold sweat and ingenuity. On the other hand he also knew that Cheyney enjoyed the benefits of a more than comfortable legacy from his mother, and the advice of his reportedly wizardly brother. Then Morgan realised how unfair he was being in expecting Cheyney to respond to that hidden away thought up in the attic. Cheyney had given years of his life, when he didn't have to, with all this available to him, to the security job he, Morgan, now held. If he had now chucked it in, and had the advantage, not only of the land, but of this strange and lovable and loving woman, what else could he have done; especially if he was tired? And he had been, Morgan thought, very tired, a year ago.

Morgan shared nothing of Cheyney's simple pleasure as they trundled down the road to Dumfries. His muttering was now entirely in his head, and he allowed himself to counterfeit a yawn or two, and even a droop of the eyelids – such as confirmed Rachel in her view that he was a dear old sleepyhead, and elicited a joke or two from her, and a head-twisting glance from an amused Cheyney – while he brooded away to himself.

It was always difficult to think in a straight line in the morning,

Morgan thought. That was the time, after all, when he let his mind ramble where it would. Now, when he wanted it to operate along a straight line, it quite simply refused. He was still sure, though, that there was something he should say – something he should be able to say – to Cheyney during their journey to London, and before Cheyney went over to the National Heart Hospital. But he needed to have it crisp and clear – like those old single quarto sheets, one and a half spaced – before he tried to use it to take Cheyney by the scruff of the neck and shake him out of whatever other world he had retreated into.

And, to Tom Morgan, it was another world. Morgan loved his visits to Loch Hill. He loved them even more since Rachel had arrived, though he had been there only twice since she had married Allen. But he never thought of them as other than holidays in the purest sense. He was an urban animal, Morgan, the son of an Army sergeant, who had fought his way through various staff courses – and sometimes, always winning, fought his fellow cadets – before he had been recruited into Cheyney's service by Sir William Downing. For all its frustrations what had delighted him about that service was its combination of Army discipline and the encouragement of the oddball. Never until now, though, had it occurred to him that he could not put a point over effectively. And he was miserably aware that he was now least effective of all in putting it over to Cheyney.

Several moments the previous night he had thought of how it might be done, how he could swing Cheyney away from this Elysium, away, perhaps, and only for a time, even from Rachel, and back into an awareness of *something wrong*. He had thought, as first the three of them, and then the two of them, sat around the fire and when Rachel, as always, left her husband alone with any visiting friend, and then when the two men again walked around the loch, that he might ask Cheyney to tell him about Zagreb. But, somehow, he hadn't felt there was ever a right moment. Their conversation was very light, and gently gossipy. They had not returned to Harry Richmond, and certainly not to Charlie. And Morgan had never got round to asking about Zagreb.

Now, as he looked at the backs of their heads, Morgan remembered to remind himself of something. He looked at the male head that was fair and streaked with grey and the female head that was dark and simple, and reminded himself that he had been allowing his mind to go off at something of an inaccurate tangent. He had been thinking of how to detach Cheyney from present things in order to get his mind applied to the problem of Harry Richmond's request; and he had thought, much as he liked her, that Rachel Cheyney might prove a hindrance to that. But Rachel had suffered more in big causes than Allen ever had. She might cosset a little or play a little or hesitate a little, but she would never hinder. His problem – his evasive, annoying problem – was with Cheyney alone. For, whatever there was, it lay far back in the past, and though he had access to all the files, as Cheyney said, it could not be found in files.

But there was nothing to be said on the train either. Rachel kissed him warmly, urged him to come again, and departed: Cheyney hated being seen off. They bought separate sets of newspapers and sat opposite one another at an angle, Cheyney with his back to the engine, Morgan facing it, partly because these were the directions they preferred, partly because both men liked to exercise the first class passenger's privilege of putting his feet on the seat opposite. His heart sinking slightly Morgan watched Cheyney fishing for the sports page of *The Times*. Really, the old boss was dead to everything of general interest. They couldn't talk now, anyway, Morgan realised, as a plump and pink male figure in middle age came and sat between them. What was worse, Rachel having fed them at that ungodly hour, there would be no later excuse to go to the restaurant car. Morgan opened the sports page of the *Telegraph*.

He was fast asleep when they reached Euston, and Cheyney had to shake him awake. Even getting on for lunch time the new Euston is a dreary place to arrive at, and the two men showed no haste as they ambled down the platform towards the main concourse. Morgan, having been a few days away from home, was carrying more gear than his friend and Cheyney, having only his single bag, relieved him of one suitcase. Perhaps it was that that gave Morgan his idea.

'Allen. What are you doing now?'

'Oh. I thought I'd go straight to the hospital. Fleming will have told them to expect me. Haven't you got your car? Do you want a lift?'

'No.' Morgan was thinking furiously. There was one thing his mind would still not let go of, and that was connected with Harry Richmond.

'Look. I wasn't planning to go to the office today anyway. But I'd like to give them a ring. Let me do that, and then I'll tool along to the hospital with you and we can have a late lunch at the Arches. I don't suppose you'd made a plan for lunch.'

Cheyney stopped.

'Good idea. I thought I'd better discharge the duty quickly. And I hadn't thought about lunch. I'm staying with my brother, as you know. Yes. Let's do that.'

'Good. I'll just call the great Miss Levison, if you find a taxi.'

And that, Morgan thought as he went to the telephone, was the first clever thing he had done for a long time.

CHAPTER FIVE

HOSPITAL

Morgan telephoned Miss Levison — who had once been Cheyney's secretary — explained that he would probably not be in that day, told her where she could reach him, asked her to acquire numbers for the day for Robert Davies, and made his way back to the taxi rank where Cheyney had booked a cab.

'Did you see Richmond again, after that lunch of yours?'

'What? Oh, from time to time.'

'But not for a long time now, I suppose?'

Cheyney pulled his brows together.

'Not for a pretty long time. Peter Haley was the last Home Office puss I dealt with. Silly little man. Not in Harry Richmond's class. I think Richmond's been retired for four or five years now.'

'I can see him, of course I can see him, remembering Charlie over all those years. I can't see him remembering you that clearly.'

'You didn't know Charlie Richmond, did you?'

'Only by reputation.'

'Well. I find it very easy to see anybody who knew Charlie remembering him, and especially his father. I even find it easy to think of them remembering people around him.'

Then Cheyney sat rather hunched for a moment.

'You're still a bit bothered about this, aren't you, Tom?'

He was rather grave and Morgan was suddenly taken aback; astonished that Cheyney should have asked the question he had been trying to bring himself to pose for a full day.

'I am, rather.'

'Well. Look here. We'll find out what the old buzzard has to say. But I do assure you that there's nothing for you in Harry Richmond's record.'

He took his case out and lit a cigarette.

'Do you think I may have gone terribly soft?'

Cheyney was sitting on Morgan's right. When Morgan looked at him after that remark he seemed to be paying attention to a point somewhere over the taxi driver's right shoulder. Morgan saw, then, the untidy and cropped hair, the heavy eyelids, the beaky nose. He also had a deep feeling inside that Cheyney was just doing tricks. After all those years, and even after a year of retirement, Cheyney could not have forgotten how to pick up instincts and motives, how, simply, to notice what the people around him were about. But, since Cheyney never deliberately played tricks on his friends, Morgan interpreted for himself that long look out of the window. Over the years he had worked with Cheyney he had made one little rule for himself about interpreting the business conversations they had. When Cheyney looked straight at him, Morgan reckoned, he was interested, and paying attention. When Cheyney looked somewhere else he was either convinced that the point Morgan was making was weak; or he was uninterested.

Therefore, Morgan concluded, although it was gratifying to observe a little stir, a little bit of noticing going on, there was nothing to be optimistic about.

'Here we are.'

Cheyney turned to pay the taxi and Morgan therefore had a few seconds to think. Their luggage was scattered somewhat on the pavement when Cheyney turned and looked up, as though to check, at the modest frontage of the National Heart Hospital.

'Allen,' said Morgan, taking the thought down from the attic of his mind and giving it another look, 'let's hump this stuff inside first. Then you go and see old Richmond. Meanwhile, I want some cigarettes, so I'll trot over to that pub' – he indicated the pub directly across the road from the hospital – 'and I'll call an office car from there so we can get comfortably to lunch. I'll wait for you in the pub.'

'Good idea,' said Cheyney and they brought the four bags inside the hospital door. Then Morgan left Cheyney alone and went across the road.

He asked for a large Scotch and the location of the telephone which was, as usual in pubs, away at the back. Not muttering now, but slightly febrile, Morgan hunted in his pockets for change. He had a sufficiency. He got the Department's number and asked for Davies. He was pretty sure Davies would be there: the trader rarely went out for lunch, preferring to sit over cheese rolls, bottled beer and some of his files, for the couple of hours during which his colleagues were relaxing or dealing or working or just eating and drinking.

Morgan went straight through to Davies.

'Bob? Good. Look here. Could you do something pronto please? Could you look out all the Charlie Richmond files? You remember them? Good. And anything on old Harry? Could you do that, too?'

Davies had one or two faults. He had a tendency to slightly heavy humour. And he was a bit over-willing to display his knowledge.

'I take it you are in London, Tom? I suppose you have Colonel Cheyney with you?'

'How the hell did you know that?'

The ham actor in Davies gave a quiet sigh. He had once almost given up the habit of showing off his knowledge when he had told Cheyney something he knew about him and was frightened for a moment or two afterwards. But he liked and got on with Tom Morgan, and he had no resentment against Morgan for taking Cheyney's job. Still, he could allow himself a sigh and a tease or two. Still, again, there was an edge in Tom's voice that he didn't like very much.

'I knew you were staying with Allen. And I heard in the canteen that the Treasury pussy cat telephoned to find Allen's number yesterday; and mentioned Harry Richmond.'

'You're a clever old thing yourself, Bob. Now, do this. Send a car round to the National Heart Hospital and tell it to wait for me. Then get those bloody files out. I think I'll probably want to read them this afternoon.'

'Done.'

'And, Bob? Hang around, will you? I may want to get hold of you this evening.'

35

'Certainly.'

Morgan put the telephone down and went back into the bar. It might well, of course, be nothing at all. But this business was very largely about hunches, and he couldn't see that he had caused any damage by lighting a flare or two here and there. That could certainly do no harm. It used to be one of Cheyney's favourite moves, unearthing old files and asking people to take a look at them again. Nothing happened most of the time, after the look through, but once or twice quite big things had happened. And, certainly, Cheyney had spoken about Charlie Richmond with a warmth that was unusual. Even from the historical point of view, Tom Morgan told himself, that Zagreb file would be worth a *shufti*. He could recall those one or two occasions when Cheyney was found by him sitting alone in that bare room that he, Tom Morgan, had livened up a bit, a sort of half grin on his face, after some dive into the archives had brought up a bit of gold. No: decidedly his instruction to Davies was no mistake. He stopped in the bar, and before he turned the corner to where his drink was waiting, in the other leg of the L, made a decision – to keep in contact with Cheyney for a day or two yet. That was a decent obeisance to the thing stowed away in the attic. Christ, he thought, he mustn't begin to think of the lumber up there as a collection of household gods.

And then Tom Morgan began to get just a bit angry. When he came around the corner of the bar he saw, first, his drink standing by itself and, second, Cheyney sitting at a table glancing through a newspaper, and tasting a drink of his own. For all his regard and even love for the man Tom Morgan, after his troubled night, his troubled journey, and his slightly frantic bit of business on the telephone, found it irritating if not intolerable that Cheyney should calmly have assumed, since they were to meet in the pub, that Morgan would find him, and simply not bothered to ask for his friend.

But the irritation had passed in a second. What was Cheyney doing here that early?

Morgan picked up his drink and dropped down in a vacant chair opposite Cheyney.

'What happened?'

Cheyney looked up.

'He died. Yesterday afternoon.'

'You weren't told?'

Cheyney shifted in his chair, annoyed.

'I can't say my heart bleeds for Harry Richmond. But I've no love for that bloody man Fleming. He was supposed to arrange things at the hospital. He didn't even telephone again. And he was supposed to be a great pal of old Harry's.'

Here was another fact to be taken out, looked at, wrapped up, put in a box, and stowed away on a shelf of the mind.

'Was he, really?'

'What?'

'Fleming was a great pal of Harry Richmond's.'

'Yes.'

'Well, let's have lunch. You can collect your tapestry, and get back tomorrow morning. Saved trouble really, now that the old buzzard's dead.'

'Oh. Damn. I'm sorry, Tom.'

They had another drink, and by then the car was there and they went to the Arches.

'Leave any message?'

'What?'

'Did Harry Richmond leave any message for you?'

'Lord, no. So far as I could learn from the sister he pushed off within about half an hour of that fool Fleming calling me yesterday.'

Morgan thought he had better leave it. But, when they got to the Arches, a peculiar club much frequented by people of their kind, with huge and forbidding Victorian portals which lead to a surprisingly small and rather seedy basement entrance, he excused himself, telephoned Davies again, and asked him to make sure, discreetly, that Sir Harry Richmond had left no interesting papers behind him.

Unruffled, Davies undertook the commission.

Curious, Morgan asked:

'How will you do it?'

'Well. The National Heart Hospital employs a large number of nurses from agencies. Highly skilled, wholly admirable people. Assuming that Richmond's effects have not been removed already – you say he died yesterday and I would therefore think that unlikely – I can have one of our people in there tonight.'

'I see.'

Davies was then ruffled.

'Tom. Is somebody else on to this? If so I can't guarantee anything. If we have competition . . .'

'Not as far as I know.'

'And you don't want it formal? Search warrants and that sort of thing?'

'God All Mighty, no.'

'Tonight, then.' And then Davies said:

'And I also assume that his relations with his wife have continued bad recently? So she won't have rushed down to claim anything?'

Tom Morgan suddenly felt very battered and very weary. He knew that recently, somewhere, he had heard something about this ancient old puss and his undoubtedly bloody wife. But how the hell did Bob Davies know it? Whatever he had heard had not been recorded and stowed away in a place in his head because, it seemed, he had not thought it significant at the time. How many things was he now going to have to store away in his head? In the attic? Anyway, he suddenly knew that he had heard about Harry Richmond and his wife when he was standing in the hall at Loch Hill with his hand on Rachel's arm.

'Assume what you bloody well like.'

'The files you asked for will be in your safe this afternoon. The report on the Richmond effects will be on your desk, ah, I should think well before midnight.'

'Thank you, Bob.'

'Have a nice lunch.'

Morgan went from the telephone to wash. The Arches being blessedly free of lavatory attendants, he could loosen his collar and cuffs, rinse his face, neck and wrists, and plan what he was going to do next.

Now he did not want Cheyney's company. He wanted to get away by himself, take various things down from their shelves, and see if they made any sense when looked at together. Meanwhile, though, since he was convinced that the clue – if there was a clue to anything, if anything that had been going on in his head was important – lay in the past, and perhaps even in a dead Harry

Richmond, he did not want to let Cheyney get back to Scotland.

'What's this tapestry which will justify the visit to the metropolis?'

'Fascinating thing. Sub-Bayeux. It's a part, really, of all the eighteenth century frauds. You know, for all their purported rationalism – formal anti-religion and all that – the Enlightenment people were suckers for just about anything. No century more credulous until our own. The interesting thing – or, at least, the thing that interests me – is that the forger craftsmen of that age worked so brilliantly and so hard, solely to convince well-off patrons that they had done no work at all.'

He saw Morgan looking puzzled and explained:

'Rachel got hold of an eighteenth century tapestry that purports to be medieval. In the eighteenth century it was sold as medieval. In my view the quality of the work in it is superior to the medieval. The fact is, some johnny made his money not out of his work, but out of selling that work to somebody who thought it was done by somebody else, ages ago. We both like the piece enormously. Got it for nothing. We've been having it repaired by a twentieth century craftsman who doesn't have to pretend.'

Cheyney enlightened Morgan for a little longer on the mysteries of tapestry weaves.

'You're staying with your brother?'

'Well. In his house. I rang yesterday. He's away. Now that old Richmond's dead I thought I might pick up the tapestry and get back tonight.'

'Don't do that. Look. I checked at the office and there's something bothering me a bit. Let me go back and look at it and then let's have dinner together. You told Rachel you'd get the morning train.'

'That's a good idea, Tom. Fine. Look, I'd better get along now. Can you drop me in St James's?'

So. The moment was postponed. Tom Morgan had not yet lost sight of Allen Cheyney. But he had nothing very much to go on either.

CHAPTER SIX

BURGLARY

'Is this fucking well all?'

Morgan rarely used coarse language; but on this occasion frustration and consternation wrung the vulgarism from him. He was sitting behind his desk. Davies, legs crossed, fingers steepled over the bridge of his nose, sat across from him. On the desk top lay, in different order, a substantial collection of files. On the edge to Morgan's right were three thick personnel files on Charlie Richmond. To his extreme left three separate heaps of files lay closely together: each file referred to a particular operation Charlie Richmond had taken part in. Morgan's right hand rested on – or twitched at – a bulky file on the Sofia operation in the course of which Richmond had been killed. His left fist, though, was bunched on top of a file that was very thin indeed, a file marked AC/CR/Zagreb 249(BLM), to which obscure signal was added a date. It contained two sheets of foolscap paper, double spaced, one and a half covered; and half the material on the sheets described Cheyney's travel arrangements to and from Zagreb. Morgan had not expected – Cheyney had warned him – to find the full story in the files. But he very clearly expected to find a great deal more than he had. He swung his head from side to side in irritation and glanced hopefully again at the personnel files.

'That's all. Allen was never the most prolix of report writers. That tells us that Richmond called him in London and that he went out to Zagreb; found that a minor agent of ours in Bulgaria had been blown; saw that Richmond was under some strain;

decided he could neither abort the mission nor replace Richmond; talked to him; and sent him on his way.'

'Damn.'

Morgan took a swallow of Miss Levison's coffee, lit a cigarette, and ruffled his thick hair. He suddenly felt the lack of a proper wash that morning. His collar was open and the knot of his tie pulled down. His jacket had been tossed on the sofa against the wall. He looked and felt both ruffled and crumpled. The thought on the shelf in the attic had been taken down and taken apart, and pretty insubstantial it looked.

'Tom, it might help if you could tell me more precisely what you're looking for, or hinting at, or whatever it is you're doing. I've got several points, and I'll summarise them, if I may. Sir Harry Richmond, former P.U.S. at the Home Office, for a period a director of some minor companies and member of one or two government committees of inquiry, is dying. He asks to see Allen Cheyney, also retired, formerly our boss. Cheyney hotfoots it from Scotland, having told you Charlie Richmond, late brilliant – smart, neurotic young thug, actually – member of this establishment, is son of Harry. Cheyney gets here, Richmond dead. Bore for Cheyney, much heat, worry and suspicion in your head.'

During the dry recital, put across in so dusty and dismissive a tone that another man could have felt humiliated by it, Morgan's head was coming slowly up until, at the end, his eyes were riveted on Davies.

' "Smart, neurotic young thug" ', he quoted, slowly. 'That a considered view, Bob?'

'Certainly.'

'You recruited him.'

Davies shook his head. 'Bill Downing recruited him, same as he did you. I introduced him, and I assessed him.'

'You regularly introduce smart, neurotic young thugs to the Department?'

'Not often. But we need a certain proportion of them – baggage carriers, protectors, bodyguards, smugglers, charmers. Men of essentially shallow and egocentric feelings, but brave and clever. Not many of them about, and we do need a proportion. The difficulty for any controller is to assess before it happens when the neurosis is going to take over from the sheer excitement and pleasure of the work. That's when they crack, start feeling insecure, let down other people.'

'Allen seemed to think very highly of Richmond,' said Morgan mildly, 'he was rather a legend to my intake. I mean the people I came in with.'

Davies shrugged, not exactly with distaste, not exactly dismissively, but as though the point put was one of very trifling weight when weighed in the balance of a discerning judgment.

'Every intake needs a few heroes. Young men like yourself, straight out of the Army, need to be convinced of the excitement of the job – which is there anyway. The instructors know this, and feed it. As for Allen. Well. It was all quite a long time ago. He's retired. He's human. He's always had a romantic streak.'

'Good God, man, he's not senile. He's only fifty-five, and it's only a year since he pulled off the greatest coup of his career. He's not a Barbara Cartland reading schoolgirl either.'

Davies put up a placatory palm.

'Don't explode in my face. I like – all right, admire – Allen as much as you do. But he's not perfect. And there's something else you ought to know.'

Davies sat forward in his chair and put his long and bony hands on his knees.

'Allen Cheyney is in many respects a very hard man, and a very remarkable fighter. He's killed in firefights without hesitation, probably could still do so. But there's a – I won't say soft, let's say conscientious – side to him. He undoubtedly felt deeply and bitterly responsible for Richmond's death. And there is no question in my mind that he was: Richmond was not competent for that mission.'

'Allen said something like that.'

'Well, to a man of a certain kind of temperament – a man of Cheyney's temperament – there is a temptation to exaggerate the virtue of the chap you've lost in circumstances like that. I'm not saying Allen tortured himself about it: he's too good a battle commander to agonise over mistakes. But there is, in a case like this, a very understandable tendency to magnify one's mistake, and also to magnify the virtues of the lost man.'

Davies gave a dry cough, covering his mouth for a second.

'And now Allen's retired. He very likely hasn't thought about the matter much for a year or more. But be sure – at least I've felt this when I've seen him – the elastic slackens when a man retires from a job like ours. A funny glow comes over the past, and it's not always warm. I find it human and even endearing that Allen should think more of Richmond's capabilities than any of us really thought at the time, especially now that he's retired.'

'I find it hard to believe that you even know the meaning of the word endearing, Bob.'

'Well, for certain one of us has got to be wrong about Charlie Richmond. I think that if you glance at the early documents in his first personnel file you'll discover that I, at least, am saying the same thing now as then.'

Morgan picked up the file and spent some minutes on it.

'You are,' he said eventually.

A shadow passed over his face.

'And Allen agreed with you.'

Implacably Davies went on:

'And if you look through the Sofia file you'll find that I was against giving the job to Richmond.'

Morgan obliged, and after a few more minutes he lifted both hands palms outwards.

'You win.'

'Understand, it was a very nice judgment. And there wasn't anybody with remotely as good a track record as young Richmond. I say it without any self-satisfaction, but I was the only one against sending him. I wanted to call it off.'

Morgan looked at his watch.

'God. It's six thirty. I'm seeing Allen for dinner at eight and I wanted to shower and change. But let's have a drink first.'

He picked up his telephone, called Miss Levison and told her to go home. Then he yawned, rubbed his eyes and stretched. Then he went over to the cupboard, picked out a bottle of malt, glasses and Vichy water and returned to the desk. Neither man spoke while he poured and they sampled their drinks.

'Was all that relevant at all?'

Morgan got up, holding his glass and rubbing the small of his back with his left hand. He went over to the window and stood there staring out, still rubbing.

'Damned if I know. It's unveiled a weakness in Allen's account of things. But I don't know if that matters.'

'It certainly distracted us from my question. I gather it is your contention that Richmond wanted to see Allen to confess something, and Allen's that his wish was merely the deathbed sentimentalism of a man who had been a very hard father?'

'More or less. Hey.'

Morgan swung back from the window and dashed to his desk.

'I've just had something from that cold-blooded analysis of yours. Allen found Richmond's sentimentality perfectly understandable, even though he said that Harry had been a bastard – buzzard was the word he used – all his life. But if you're right about Allen – and the evidence suggests you are – that would explain why he was uncritical about it all.'

'It might. *Do* I understand you to say that you believe Harry Richmond wanted to confess to Allen Cheyney?'

Slowly, reluctantly, Tom Morgan shook his head.

'That was the original idea. But I find it a bit hard to believe in it now. He could have, probably would have, sent for someone else. There's nothing that connects him with Allen. It's not even as though they were friends.'

'Charlie connects them.'

'Yes. That's why I still feel there's something there, something I'm not getting, something Allen is certainly not getting. But I can't believe any more in the original idea that Richmond was a traitor.'

'No. That won't do at all. When he went to the Home Office he actually started pulling out of a lot of committees, sending deputies and so forth. He was bloody fed up he didn't get the Treasury, you see. He was number two there about the time Charlie was killed. Pretty bitter, he was, I think, took it out on the Home Office people, sulked a lot until he retired. No intelligent or committed spy or traitor would have done that.'

'You think I'm being a damn fool too, do you?'

'Oh. Does Allen?'

'I don't think Allen's thinking at all,' said Morgan, finishing his drink and pouring another. 'He finds the whole thing a tedious chore. He doesn't want to be in London. He's cross with Harry Richmond for being dead, and he's irritated with old Fleming for not organising things better.'

'Cheyney and Fleming never liked one another.'

'Well, do you?'

'Do I, what?'

'Think I'm being a damn fool?'

Davies gave this question some thought. He also gave himself another drink and lit a cigarette.

'No. I don't. I think there is something odd about Harry Richmond asking for Cheyney *then*. I'd have been less surprised if it was when he fell ill. His doctors gave him no hope nine months ago.'

'You have been doing your homework.'

'I thought I'd do a general check. Anyway, I think there is something odd. And when there's ever something odd we ought to check it thoroughly. In my book nobody can cry wolf too often in our line of business. I've put out traces on everything about old Richmond. And, if it's all right with you, I'll stay in this room this evening and go through those files again. Best not to let things slide.'

'Be my guest. You're a wonder Bob.'

Morgan got up and went over to the wardrobe where he kept a spare set of clothes. By the time he left the room on his way down the corridor for a shower Davies was already behind his desk and was deep in the first of the operational files. Later, of course, he would descend to the computer room to cross check anything he wanted, call up much more detailed material, re-analyse doubts, press questions home. But for some time he would sit there, methodically reading and sifting, calling up memories and impressions from the very age and kind of paper he read, the type faces that recalled vanished secretaries and junior officers, the turns of phrases and notes of human excitement that a file could contain and a computer could not. He might stay there for hours, all night even, and he would be the same dry, detached, inexhaustible, academic, expert in the morning.

Morgan had a delicious hot shower, followed by a medium length burst of icy water all over his frame. Revived, he shaved and brushed his teeth and combed his hair. He had a vague feeling of guilt that he had not showered that morning: perhaps that was why he had been feeling low most of the day, out of touch with things, not grasping points in his usual way, below par. He put his head around his own door and called goodnight to Davies, around whose head there were wreaths of pipe smoke. He got a lifted hand in acknowledgment and went on out past the security guards and into the street. Time had not, he realised as he glanced at his watch, passed all that quickly, and he still had more than half an hour to his date with Cheyney. He strolled along between St James's Park and the Horse Guards, therefore, revelling in a fine and clear night. In the Mall he hailed a taxi and arrived at Brennan's a few minutes later than Cheyney.

Cheyney was sitting at a corner table reading a book and smoking his pipe. He looked up and grinned.

'So,' he said, 'you've been getting Bob Davies excited too?'

'What?' Morgan dropped into the chair, dumbfounded.

Cheyney laughed. He called the waiter over and insisted that Morgan had a drink by his hand before he would expand on his opening comment.

Confused, even bewildered, Morgan waited impatiently. When he had tested his drink Cheyney looked grave.

'Bob telephoned just before you arrived. I took the call. It seems that for the last three days Sally Richmond – Harry's wife, that is – has been staying with her sister in Sussex. I'm surprised to hear that she was that much grieved by Harry's illness, but there you are. The thing is, the Richmond house in Chelsea was burgled – or is it house-broken: I believe there's a distinction according to the time of day it happens – earlier this evening. And Bob thinks you'll have some reaction to it.'

CHAPTER SEVEN

DAVIES

Morgan had lots of reactions. He had come to dinner, primed and fresh and clean, prepared not to mention either of the Richmonds, and certainly not the mysterious Sally, Lady Richmond. He had planned, with a certain innocent guile and a good deal of chatter, to make his way towards detaining Cheyney a bit longer in London; longer, even, than the following morning. That, he knew, would be a difficult task, since it would mean keeping Cheyney in London over the weekend. But he had thought, as he walked along by the park, that it might be done; and that there were ways of doing it. Keep Cheyney here, if only for as long as it took for Bob Davies to go through the files, and perhaps even come up with a guess or two. That was Morgan's plan.

It would not do, though, now, to bounce around with the kind of firecracking enthusiasm Cheyney's little speech excited. That might well put Cheyney off. Never advance *too* far ahead of your information: that was one of Peter Hannay's great maxims; and Hannay had taught Cheyney damn nearly everything. Cheyney was like a wild bird now: he might get up and fly away from this table suddenly, and back to Loch Hill. If he did the thought stowed away on the medium high shelf in the left hand corner of Tom Morgan's mind, like a forgotten flower in a pot, tattered and bereft a couple of hours ago, now suddenly blooming happily away, might well go with him.

So Morgan said:

47

'Well, that's interesting.'

'I thought you might find it so.'

By God, Tom Morgan thought, eyes do twinkle. How was it done? How did it happen? He had, of course, seen girls do it. But that was usually a trick with their eyelashes. If you liked them, it was a twinkle. If you did not like them, it was a flutter. Allen Cheyney was now looking straight across at him. He was not smiling. Morgan had never seen his smile get higher than his mouth before he married Rachel. But his eyes were twinkling. No doubt about it. It marked a stage on from their conversation in the taxi, at any rate. Then Morgan had managed to create a little bit of interest on Cheyney's part. Now there was – how to put it? – perhaps a little bit of excitement as well. Morgan liked what he hoped had been Cheyney's irony.

Cheyney's head dipped suddenly, right down into Brennan's menu. He's giving me, Morgan thought, remembering the great days again, time to think.

'Steak *Diane*, I think,' said Cheyney, 'rare. And a mixed salad. I'll do the dressing myself.'

'Same. French dressing, though.'

'And wine, sir?'

'Oh, yes. A bottle of my usual.'

'Thank you, sir.'

'By the way, Tom. I asked Bob to come over and join us later. I hope that's all right?'

Morgan wanted to say something like yippee.

'Sure. I left him ploughing through files.'

'I wondered if there might not be something from the hospital.'

'I don't know whether there can be,' Morgan said, directly. 'It seems unlikely. If there's anything Richmond wanted to say to you – or ask you to do – other than mooning about over his son, it's highly unlikely that we'll find it neatly packaged under hospital effects. What would they be anyway? Wallet and watch? Handkerchiefs. Two. Old Harry being a gentleman. Smoking gadgets if he's a smoker. Razor. Tooth brush. That sort of thing. An engagement diary but not, I think, a diary. What he came in with in his pockets – *if* he didn't come in in his pyjamas. And what he acquired while he was there, which can't have been much, in his condition. Half a bottle of Lucozade, a few shrivelled grapes.'

In speaking at such length Morgan was very largely letting off the steam he had contained when Cheyney had given him the initial promising news that Harry Richmond's house had been burgled. Perhaps, though, like Fleming, he had been visited by the superstition of death. He remembered how, over the lunch table at Loch Hill, he had made a contrast between the momentary enjoyment of Cheyney, Rachel, and himself and the momentary half world of Harry Richmond. By the time he had finished, however, two steaks were being grilled and tossed by their table and, given the matter of their business, they had to remain silent, or simply chatter.

'I'm sorry you didn't catch anything in the loch, Tom. I've been meaning to get around to having it cleared and restocked. But there's so much else to do.'

'Oh, I'm sure there is. I had better luck in the river, last time I was up.'

'But that's been maintained. The loch hasn't been fished for, I suppose, twenty years before I took over the place. Full of predators, I'm told. Pike, that sort of thing. The bottom's very deep, you know; and full of filthy weed. It's still perfectly situated and protected for birds. So, I suppose, I've been very content to watch them, and I've thought about other things to do with the place.'

'How long have you owned it?'

'Fifteen years or more. Charles, my brother, gave it to me. He knew I was keen on the house, you see, though the estate was part of *his* inheritance. It made a fairish loss, even with rents because we were being robbed blind by the people we employed. Natural and reasonable, you see, when you think that nobody in the family had paid any attention to it for years. I'd always said I'd like to make a go of it, and Charles challenged me to do it. I did the work on the house myself.'

'Allen, one thing I've always wanted to ask you. Forgive me if it seems a class thing. You don't shoot or fish or – do you – hunt in your part of the world? Why?'

'Oh, as to that ...'

They were interrupted by the presentation of the steaks. The silence was prolonged by the addition of the salads. Then the wine waiter brought over a bottle which Cheyney sampled and voted excellent.

'Tom. What do you mean by treason?'

'What do you mean by the question?'

'Don't fence with me. At Loch Hill I scouted your idea that Harry Richmond was a death bed traitor about to confess. Did you mean traitor or spy?'

Morgan had just about started on his steak, and now wondered whether he could get through it. He took a leaf of lettuce from his salad while Cheyney was conscientiously mixing his dressing, and chewed it. He had another mouthful of the steak. Cheyney did not seem to be pressing for an answer, was not even looking directly at him.

Cautiously, 'I meant traitor.'

'What's the distinction?'

'Well, a spy is like us. I mean, he's a professional. We send, oh, say, Charlie Richmond, to Bulgaria. If they catch him they find out he's Charlie Richmond. A traitor is just a traitor. He's one of us, and betrays us.'

Cheyney munched steak and salad, and Morgan got mad.

'Allen, you said don't fence with you. All right. Don't fence with me. I'm doing a job, a good job. The best job I've ever had. I wasn't aware, when you backed me for it, that a degree in metaphysics was a requirement for doing it.'

'Not at all. But answer me this. What did you make of Penkovsky? I know, we've had traitors inside Russia whom – which – we've bought, for lots of money in Swiss and Danish and Finnish bank accounts, money for them to enjoy when they made a break. But there was never any doubt that Penkovsky would stay as long in the Soviet Union as he lived. He was a Russian. Was he a spy? Or a traitor?'

'Or.' Munching, Cheyney held up his hand, 'Brandt? What about Brandt? Stout fellow. Left Hitler's Germany, though he wasn't a Jew. Came back with the allies and made Prime Minister, or Chancellor, or whatever they call it. They were honourable men, Tom. Or weren't they?'

'You're playing some game, Allen. I'll indulge you for five minutes. No longer.'

Following Cheyney's earlier example Morgan took some time to eat steak and salad.

'Penkovsky I give you. He was a traitor with real convictions. He didn't run. Brandt ran. He should have stayed, and died. I will just add that I know of no British traitor who stayed, and suffered more than a few comfortable years in prison. Lots did better than that, a damn sight better than that.'

'You think we should kill them?'

'Yes, oh yes.'

'Umm. What about de Gaulle, then? Ran like hell. Only managed to get on the 'plane out because our chap — Spears — helped him on board.'

This was, Morgan thought, a dirty trick, for Morgan was known greatly to admire de Gaulle. But he rallied:

'He was in uniform. He was retreating to fight. Any commander can do that.'

'Mind you,' Morgan added before Cheyney could speak, 'I don't object to working with traitors from the other side. Interesting fellows, some of them. And I have a lot of liking for some of the ones who've come over from Eastern Europe.'

'Traitors or — what's the new word? — dissidents?'

'I'm not sure what you mean.'

'You know what a dissident is, Tom. It's just that he's not in your world. He's not a spy, nor a traitor, in the sense of conveying political information across borders. He's just a chap, often a brave chap. He has particular ideas, about his own life, or religion, or culture of some sort. It may be poetry, or painting, or whatever. Anyway, he says it out loud, and takes the consequences. Perhaps he's making a testimony to something a great deal bigger than your world, or what used to be mine. I don't know. But I do know that I like him. In principle, I mean. I've met, of course, a lot of the Jewish dissidents, through Rachel. They're not spies, nor traitors.'

'Allen, your five minutes are nearly up.'

'I think you are quite sympathetic to traitors from the other side. Or, at least, you're prepared to consider them individually. But you have no sympathy for traitors from your own side. Also, you have prejudices — preferences, if you will. You like de Gaulle, you don't like Brandt; you like the French, can't stand the Germans. I have the same tastes myself. In practice that's one of the things that makes you good at your job. Trouble is, you sometimes, not too often, but sometimes, pretend to a principle

51

when you're expressing a preference. Don't.'

Morgan saw that he had half a steak left. He took a piece and chewed on it.

'Allen. I'm beginning to think that Loch Hill has made your mind soft. What the hell are you getting at?'

'Only this. You have a hard mind, Tom. You cut things out and chop 'em. But you're a bit – forgive me – limited. You divide the spy from the traitor. I wish to God that I had killed that distinction. I was wrong, you see, in what I said to you the other day about honours, and so forth, for spies. A spy should be hanged or degraded or given exactly the same treatment as a traitor, however judged. It shouldn't matter to the spy. If it did he shouldn't have taken on the job. The battle is really about systems of politics, as you have just implied. Shooting spies and hanging traitors is a nineteenth century distinction, and a false one. What I'm getting at is this: if you're looking for a traitor, Tom, think of him sympathetically. Think of him the way you would think of Penkovsky. Or the way *his* Russian spymaster thinks of him.'

Cheyney looked at his watch.

'I've got thirty seconds of my five minutes. One question. If you found a traitor, and liked him, and sympathised with him, what would you do with him?'

'I would kill him. I see you wouldn't, though.'

'Wrong. Of course I would. *I would have to.*'

Then the blaze seemed to go out of Cheyney. Their plates were taken away. Morgan picked at some celery. Neither man wanted cheese or a pudding. Coffee came, and some Calvados. Morgan wasn't sure whether he had got somewhere or nowhere. He retired behind his coffee cup to think about it. He reached a tentative conclusion or two.

This was the first time, in however bizarre and pointless a way, that Cheyney had talked about the principles of the profession to him. That was a plus. Cheyney had deliberately switched the conversation that way. That was also a plus. But Cheyney was giving a Socratic lecture. That was distinctly a minus. Cheyney was raising hares – no, rabbits, because rabbits ran more wildly into different burrows than hares did – because he sought to instruct Tom Morgan in some rules and difficulties. Cheyney was philosophising: that was a very big minus. That was the biggest minus of all. That showed Cheyney was not really engaged in the business. The business was about work, and the old man was just going on and on. Interesting, no doubt, and lovable, but not serious.

'Here's Bob.'

Davies came over, sat down, seized some cheese, accepted Calvados and coffee. He looked and Cheyney, and Morgan began to stir himself.

'The hospital,' he said.

'The hospital,' Davies confirmed.

'What?' asked Cheyney.

'Should I go through the list of possessions?'

'No,' said Morgan.

'All right.' Davies was put out.

'Our girl in there says that the possessions are short one item. There were – oh, sorry, I won't go into them. A small engagement diary. Usual size, she says, two and a half by four inches, is gone.'

'Well, then,' said Morgan.

Cheyney swallowed the last of his Calvados.

'Would you like me to take a hand, Tom?'

CHAPTER EIGHT

HOSPITAL AGAIN

'Yes.'

Cheyney leaned back in his chair. He lifted his cigarette and drew in deeply. He let the smoke drift quietly out of his mouth for some seconds. Then he came back to put his elbows on the table.

'If you're right, Tom, it'll be a damnable business.'

This was the moment, Tom thought, to ask about Zagreb. But, somehow, Zagreb seemed inappropriate now. What Morgan said was:

'Whatever is here, Allen, it's away in the past. That's why I want you to do it. You know the past.'

Morgan was conscious of having said a word or two more than was necessary. But that was understandable. He felt the hairs creak again at the back of his neck. He thought of Cheyney now as an old dog, not as a wild bird, not as a cosseted landowner. The old dog had taken a long ago scent and was savouring it and wondering about it, and meditating, if not a gallop, then a romp, over his old ground. Morgan felt, with a real onrush of pleasure, that it was he who had released the dog.

'You're sure this is all right, Tom?'

Typical of Cheyney, Morgan thought, so to attempt to clear the lines of authority first. He was asking whether Morgan had the authority of the Minister to bring Cheyney in. But that was only the first question. The more important question, the much more important question, was whether Morgan would really let Cheyney go. In effect, the question was whether Morgan would let Cheyney be boss again. However considerate Cheyney would be from now on he would – it was his way – be difficult. Morgan's huge hands lay on either side of his coffee cup and, as he looked down at them, he saw authority oozing away. Suddenly, and in spite of all his thoughts over days, and hours, and minutes, he did not like it.

'Of course, I haven't talked to my Minister.'

Morgan tried to say it lightly, but it came out through his lips like rubber.

'But, no trouble there, I should think.'

Cheyney was still prodding. How, Morgan wondered, had this thing turned over so completely? A few hours ago he had been trying to wake Cheyney up. Now the animal threatened to run at him. Still, Morgan thought, in the biggest and most generous act of his life, there was something important to be done.

And then he realised that, after all, Cheyney was not prodding, merely doing a job. It did not weaken his generosity, nor diminish him.

'The police, Tom. The police.'

'Are you dreaming?'

'Asking around the hospital is going to be difficult. It would be a damn sight easier if we had their help.'

'I haven't talked to the police.'

And then:

'Get on with it, Allen.'

Cheyney looked at his watch again. He called the waiter over and signed his bill.

'Well. Bob. Is Pierce available?'

For some time Davies's head had been moving to and fro between Cheyney and Morgan. Impatient, acerbic, scholarly, and the discoverer of the fact that a two and a half by four inch diary was missing, he knew his moment would come.

'Because ...'

Davies cut across Cheyney's assumption.

'Pierce is in Australia.'

'Damn. We want a first class interrogator. Bob. You're looking at the files? Good. Now, who's the panjandrum at that hospital? I don't mean the Princess, of course. Who'll line up everybody who saw old Harry from admission to death? If I can't have hard

55

questioning I'd like to do my own gentle kind.'
Davies thought.
'You mean somebody secret?'
'Yes.'
'Give me a night to think about it. But I imagine Lord Hobart will do.'
'Good. You know what I want?'
'Lists of everybody who saw Richmond in hospital. Staff and visitors. Number of times. Length of visits or, if professional, overall likely duration. D'you want this done secretly?'
'What do you advise?'
'Oh. Tom should do it. To Hobart, if we think Hobart is the best man. Use the hush hush way of going about the business.'
'Will you do that, Tom? In the morning?'
'Of course.'
'We can't do this like a police investigation, Bob. It's got to be more careful and subtle than that. We haven't got a crime to detect, yet. Certainly there's no body, no murder. But . . . hang on. How long will it take you to put the hospital visit dossier together?'
Davies thought for quite a time. Morgan could see him making all the calculations in his head, working them out minute by minute, making allowance for human failings, making further allowance for diplomacy, making the biggest of all allowances for the fact that nobody knew precisely what he was looking for. Then:
'Monday morning. That's pushing. Do you want me to push?'
'Certainly. Meanwhile, don't excessively interrupt staff weekends. I mean nurses and sisters and so forth. This, I repeat, is not a police investigation. But, gentlemen, we will need the police.'
'I understand that.'
'Don't be impatient, Bob. I'm feeling my way back into things.'
Cheyney grinned quietly. He stretched and pushed out his hands across the table.
'Tomorrow morning, though, I'd like to see whatever police officer they sent round to investigate the Richmond burglary. And I'd like to see Harry's bank pried loose to find if he's got a box there.'
They got up following Cheyney.

'If you're back to the boxes, Bob, I'll take Tom along to Chelsea with me.'

So Davies took the office car back to Whitehall and Cheyney and Morgan took a taxi back to the house in Chelsea – his brother's house – where Cheyney was staying. All the way Cheyney was completely silent, and Morgan was silent too. Somehow the old man seemed to be getting down to business. And just as Morgan had that thought – the thought that included giving Cheyney the affectionate ascription – he realised how much thinner and fitter Cheyney looked than he did himself. Let us hope to God, Morgan thought, that he is intellectually fitter as well, for this I swear, that I saw it before Allen Cheyney did, even if I have to confess that I have no idea what it is. The omens, Morgan concluded, as they turned into a little private road off Chelsea Square, are not good; not now that we are getting down to the details.

However, certain things were done. The taxi was paid off. Charles Invermuir's housekeeper let them in. They went up stairs to the big L-shaped living room that Cheyney's brother loved. Cheyney opened the french windows onto the tiny balcony which overlooked the handsome rectangular garden which all of the houses had in common. Then he walked back. 'Drink?'

'Whisky, Allen, please.'

Cheyney went around the corner, into the other leg of the L, and came back with a bottle of whisky, glasses, soda, and water. He put them down on a glass coffee table between two sofas and gestured Morgan, uneasily examining the flowing abstracts which distinguished the walls of the room, to sit down. This uneasy and neurotic activity on his part was, for Morgan, and again, a signal that the old days were back.

'Just call Rachel,' said Cheyney.

For the second time in a day and a half Morgan heard one side of a telephone conversation. This time, though, as he sat there, nursing his whisky and wondering what move he could make next, he was not as puzzled by the side he heard as he had been the last time. He was first comforted and then amazed. He was comforted – it so much seemed to recall the domesticity of Loch Hill and the magical comfort that was there – to hear Cheyney ask Rachel to send some clothes down, and to arrange for his brother's housekeeper to pick them up. He was even more comforted because he could detect no splutter on Rachel's side, of annoyance, or anger, or fear, once Cheyney had told her there was a job to do. He was comforted, finally and somehow restored in his esteem of himself, when he recalled that, in the car on the way from Loch Hill to Dumfries, he had realised that Rachel, for all her Jewish protectiveness, would never stand in the way of anything Allen thought of as duty.

And just as he was getting himself very comfortable with all these comfortable thoughts – thoughts that rather restored the self-confidence and authority that he had felt oozing away from him earlier, as Cheyney seemed to be taking over completely, thoughts that arose from the fundamental conviction *that he had seen it all first* – Morgan was amazed. He was amazed because he heard Cheyney tell Rachel in the firmest of tones that he would be no more than ten days in London. They were not reassuring tones. This was not a wife who had to be reassured. Morgan's comfort had grown from the fact that he had realised she was not such a wife. His comfort, guessed at a day or so ago, had been confirmed by hearing Cheyney's side of the conversation. But, now, 'Ten days at the very outside,' he heard Cheyney say.

Cheyney came away from the telephone and stretched himself on the sofa opposite Morgan. He took up his whisky.

Morgan was now angry, very, and very bloodily angry.

'It may take a damn sight longer than ten days, Allen.'

Cheyney pressed the glass against his forehead. He put it down on the table. He lit a cigarette. When he spoke his voice, which Morgan had expected to find strong and vibrant and arrogant, was tired and quiet and soft.

'I don't think it will take ten days, Tom. Don't you see? This hunt, on our side, has gone on for a generation or more. We have suddenly been given clues. Clues you saw, Tom, and I didn't, God help me. I never thought the hunt was over. But I thought I was too old to be in on the final chase. And now, because of somebody's Goddamn folly I am.'

'For the second time this evening, Allen, I haven't the faintest idea what you're talking about. You compliment me. You talk about folly. You natter away. Say something sensible, man, for God's sake.'

'Sorry.'

Cheyney lay there on the sofa, looking his age, and still looking the way he had looked in the taxi. Then he swung up and sat up, and drank some whisky.

'First, given the clues, if we don't solve the problem in ten days it's unsolvable. The instinct that there was something there was yours, Tom, and you'll come out with instincts as good and perhaps better in the next week or so. The trouble with you at the moment is that you're so damn pleased with your instinct that you're neglecting the clues.'

That was too close to the bone. Morgan did not like it.

'And the instinct's half wrong anyway, Tom. Harry Richmond's no traitor. Sorry, *was* no traitor. It's the clues, Tom.'

Cheyney looked almost exasperated.

'Look, Tom. Answer one question. How professional, how technically professional, was the Richmond burglary? By how technically professional I mean as recognisable by the police, not by people like us? Can you make any deductions from the fact that it was noticed, Tom?'

'No.'

Morgan spoke disconsolately.

'I can. And you should have. You would have if – before me – you weren't just trying to pull me in.'

'Either it was genuine. So to speak, an honest break in, chap knocking off an empty house. We suspect it's not because of, oh, I don't know, because Harry asked to see me, because of the diary missing at the hospital, because of all sorts of signs. But if it was professional in our sense, Tom, there would be no signs at all. Right?'

'Right.'

'But you and I and Bob are all bothered by some of the clues. You by Harry. Bob by the diary. Who could tell us whether there was anything odd about the Richmond burglary?'

'Who the hell?'

'The local police, you fool. The only objective witnesses in this charade. We'll see them and Sally tomorrow. We'll do a little work over the weekend, and we'll see the hospital folk on Monday. That make you happy?'

'Richmond was a traitor, then?'

Cheyney was now standing up.

'No. He couldn't have been. Tom. Spend the night here. Sleep on it. Review the evidence in your own mind. Consider it this way. Either Harry's request to see me, the vanishing engagement diary, and the burglary are coincidences ...'

'They're not.'

'Of course they're not. Or, as I was going on to say, the first caused the last two, and the last two are the product, not of professionalism, but of panic. Who panics, Tom?'

'People who are frightened.'

'Certainly. But, do spies panic?'

'Some, but, look here ...'

'Who panics?'

'Traitors,' said Morgan, outmanoeuvred.

'That's it.'

Alive, suddenly, Morgan said:

'Tell me about Zagreb.'

Then Cheyney looked his age again.

'Maybe tomorrow, Tom. Let's go to bed now. Ask this, though. Who knew the buzzard wanted to see me?'

CHAPTER NINE

SARAH

'What I find extremely hard to understand is why I have to answer all these questions again. Mr Lewis was most searching in his questions yesterday and now I find that you, Mr Cheyney, want to question me all over again. I really do find it all very trying.'

Lady Richmond looked at them both. She did not look at them as a pair, but individually. They sat, perhaps a yard and a half apart, on small and delicate chairs in a drawing room that was gloriously light, large windows looking out on a private garden square, pale grey carpet, walnut cabinets containing a small fortune's worth of china, and dominated by a handsome Georgian mantelpiece topping a fireplace so blacked and polished that one could see that, like the room itself, it had never been used, was designed to be nothing other than a spectacle. She sat some distance from them, dead centre on a sofa upholstered in the same intricate silken material as their chairs and, when she addressed them, moved her head very slightly the required inch or two to meet first Lewis's, and then Cheyney's, eyes directly.

Good for you, thought Cheyney of the young Inspector who, having been given the thankless task of questioning Sarah Richmond when she had reported her burglary, had been handed on by rather graceless superiors when a second stage of the investigation had seemed advisable to Tom Morgan. This man was not going to be fazed easily. And he had got a point Tom Morgan had missed.

For some seconds she gave Lewis, at thirty eight not much more than half her age and, probably, in difficult interviews, to be regarded as younger still, her full attention. Then she moved her head the requisite inches, and her eyes were on Cheyney. She was a tall woman, though it did not appear so when she was sitting, for all that her back was stick straight. She was neatly, though not fussily, nor mannishly, nor aggressively, dressed. On a less angular figure, even of her age, the dark suit might well have been becoming. There was no skill about the grey hair – no artificial curls, no rinse. Nor had she made any effort to conceal the wrinkles around her neck or on her face. Indeed, she wore a limited and decent amount of makeup. Even the pale grey eyes now turned at Cheyney were not in themselves formidable or challenging. The only thing about her that had such characteristics was her harsh and grating voice.

'Do I understand, Mr Cheyney, that you were a colleague of my husband?'

'No.'

At this stage Cheyney was most keen to give Lewis whatever backing he needed. He did not want to get into the argument himself, not just yet, at any rate. He had no great skill in this kind of affair, which was where Pierce was at his most formidable. He had no means of outfacing a basilisk. This woman was a basilisk, frozen and hardened and dried. Everything there had gone a long time ago, and it was hard now to see what there had ever been. Perhaps there had been nothing. Anyway, as Cheyney had told Lewis an hour earlier, the policeman was to make the running, and Cheyney would chip in when he could, or thought it advisable.

She moved the slight lines across her forehead closer together. It could not be called a frown exactly, for a frown implies concentration, inquiry, depression, misunderstanding. It was more like a mechanical reaction of some kind, a car halting at an obstacle, its engine revving somewhat, hoping to get over whatever little hump was, inexplicably, put in the car's way.

'You are Lord Invermuir's brother?'

She's a snob, thought Cheyney. But then, inside, he brightened a little. Snobbery meant vulnerability.

'Yes.'

Not, though, it seemed a moment later, on this occasion.

She went on speaking directly to Cheyney. She made a movement or two with her hands as she did so. They were long, thin, heavily veined hands. She wore three rings, he saw, a wedding and engagement ring, and another – a garnet – on the opposing finger of her right hand. The grate in her voice altered slightly, as though she were counterfeiting distress. But she was not forging, he saw: she was mimicking, or recapturing, what distress was. There was a flutter somewhere there; but there was also armour.

'My husband is dead. My house has been broken into. My jewellery has been stolen. Mr Lewis says this room has not been touched: but my bedroom has been destroyed. My husband's study has been wrecked. His silver has been taken. I was staying with my sister when all this happened. I have been co-operating with the police as much as I can. I am anxious to return to the country as soon as I can. But you have come and asked me the same questions again. I cannot understand why.'

In another woman that would have been an appeal, an appeal, perhaps to their masculinity, an appeal from her female weakness. But, again, not here. It was more nearly a piece of bullying on her part than it was a demonstration of weakness. Cheyney felt – as he was sure Lewis did – uncomfortable on his delicate little chair, unable to find a decent purchase for his backside, scarcely daring to shift himself from a posture the maintenance of which required a distinct measure of stoicism. They were not, for God's sake, here to harry or trap or embarrass or distress the blessed woman. But he could see as little prospect of a successful appeal to her intelligence or her better nature as he could of discovering her with a spool of top secret microfilm in her handbag.

The truth was, he thought, that she was not merely unintelligent, not merely stupid. Certainly, she was stupid, implacably, immovably so, stupid from the very grain of her personality. But she was stupid, implacable, immovable *with training*. The younger daughter of a well-to-do country gentleman – Cheyney was remembering her file – she had been noted at school for nothing except a certain skill with horses. She had married the much poorer, but flintily ambitious, young Harry Richmond – with, oddly, her father's blessing – when she was twenty two. The old man had stumped up a decent *dot*. They had had the one child and, as Harry proceeded steadily up the Whitehall ladder, Sarah had added to what home and Roedean had taught her the impeccable and impenetrable discipline of a good Civil Service wife. Within himself Cheyney drew a long and despairing sigh.

But Lewis, young and ambitious himself, seconded from his force for an intriguing and potentially exciting – if still rather obscure – job, and conscious of Cheyney's eye upon him, was not prepared to give in as easily as Cheyney himself might at this stage have done.

'Madam,' he said, 'Lady Richmond. When I was here yesterday we made a list of valuables that were missing. But I was concentrating on what had most of the appearance of an ordinary burglary. Now I want to ask another question. Were any of your late husband's papers missing? Diaries, things like that?'

She looked back at him, unmoving and unmoved.

'I would not know. I never took any interest in such matters.'

Then she moved her head, again slightly, to take in Cheyney.

'Are you suggesting, Colonel Cheyney, that this burglary was carried out by enemies of the country?'

She had not even dropped her voice to accommodate the conspiratorial flavour of the words she had chosen: it was the same grating monotone.

Demanding, insisting on, her attention, Lewis said:

'We think it possible, yes.' It had been clear, it should have been clear to the meanest intelligence, that they thought it possible from the moment Cheyney had entered her drawing room.

'Yes.' Cheyney added his affirmative once it became clear that she did not intend to shift her eyes from him until she had had an answer from him: Lewis would not do.

'In that case,' she said formally, 'I must obviously do anything I can to help. But I must say I consider the whole thing extremely unlikely. Henry had been retired for five years, you know.'

And she had a fair point there. It was hard to justify any species of interrogation with the slender things they already had and, anyway, they scarcely knew what they were looking for.

Cheyney thought he ought to help Lewis out a bit.

'Well,' he said, 'we are only at the very beginning of what

certainly will be an intricate, and perhaps even a protracted, investigation.'

He was conscious, as he spoke, of his undertaking to Rachel and Morgan to polish the whole thing off in ten days.

'At this stage,' he added, 'we must cast about rather. It's hard to be as definite as we – or you – would wish.'

This time she did frown, a real frown. The ridges and furrows on her dry old forehead were suddenly concentrated in vertical lines between her eyes, driving downwards towards the bridge of her nose. And she held the frown for several seconds, concentrating, perhaps even thinking.

'The funeral – cremation actually – is tomorrow morning. I wish to return to the country immediately after that. Shall I be able to?'

'Certainly.' It was Lewis this time, pleased to be able to give her something, pleased to have an apparent concession to offer, hoping that the concession might soften her somehow.

'Excellent.' The frown, Cheyney realised, had been the result of her concern that their investigation, which she had professed a willingness to assist, would keep her in town. There had, he now realised, been no sense of drama, however suppressed, in her reference to enemies of the country: it was merely a manner of speaking, a generation old. There was not going to be much for them here.

'May I ask,' Lewis pursued, 'what your intentions for this house are, Lady Richmond?'

And, as he saw her frown gathering again, he added:

'We would like to carry out a very thorough search, for papers, that sort of thing; and we're anxious not to discommode you.' The pompous flavour was infectious when she was there.

Her forehead cleared.

'I shall sell it,' she said, 'soon. I intend to live with my sister.'

'Well,' said Cheyney, frustrated and despairing inside, 'I think that Inspector Lewis and I should – if we may – look through Ha – Sir Henry's study now, and this afternoon – again, if that is convenient – we will have a squad go over the whole house. I assure you they won't damage anything.'

'As you wish.' She was indifferent and escorted them to the study.

Half an hour later she saw them to the door and closed it firmly as they started down the steps. She had not offered them coffee and she did not now offer her hand.

When they reached the bottom of the steps Cheyney let out his breath in a long whistle and the two grinned shyly at each other to mark their recognition of that conspiracy of maleness which comes into existence whenever men escape from the company of difficult women.

'Time for lunch,' said Cheyney, as they got into Lewis's car. 'There's a decent pub not far from here.'

In the few minutes it took them to drive there Cheyney recalled to himself their fast, thorough and polite dissection of Harry Richmond's study. His widow had left them to it. No gesture of hers – and certainly no remark – dissociated her from their work. But none suggested aid either. She left them in the study and she was there when they came out of it: but there was no suggestion, no hint, that she had been waiting for them on the half landing outside the study. She was just there – as, Cheyney suspected, she always had been, always in place, never intruding, except when she spoke in that voice.

And there had been no haul in the study. It was a small room, ruined, now, by the burglars. Three cabinets had been emptied of their contents, and the glass in one had been smashed. The books, once hauled out of their cases, had been replaced in a somewhat higgledy-piggledy way – by Sarah? The papers that had been in the drawers of the neat, small, elegant pedestal desk, pulled out and thrown around, had been, before they came, put back on the desk top. But they were trivial enough, in all conscience. There were a few bills, a few letters, a wad of Richmond's own stationery, some envelopes, a Lett's desk diary. The only oddity had been a postcard – unsent, uninscribed, clearly saved from some trip – of Bruges. It was possible that the search squad that would come later to the house would find something, but Cheyney doubted it.

The pub that Cheyney had suggested for their lunch was one of those pleasant inner London pubs that boasted a small garden. When they arrived there was the usual sweaty, office-based, half-dressed lunchtime crew. It took some minutes to get food and drink – and Cheyney shuddered to see Lewis, at the self-service salad counter, load a plate with bread and cheese and horrendous pickles – a little longer to find a place in the garden, and longer still – until two o'clock – to have a chance of private conversation.

'Well,' said Cheyney.

'Not much from her,' said Lewis. He put the last pickle in his mouth and, without invitation, picked up their mugs and went off to recharge them.

When he sat down again Cheyney, clearing his lines, asked: 'If I understand correctly, we're working together until this business is finished?'

'Yes, sir.'

As he said it Lewis had his face in his mug of beer. But the eyes came sharp and clear and brown and ambitious across the edge of the glass to meet Cheyney's. Cheyney had an urge, not so much to berate Lewis as to try to tell this much younger man something. He had seen that look too often in the eyes of young policemen and young soldiers, the look that told of an interest in, a fascination with, the secret world, the world he had been, unwillingly, pulled back into. Cheyney had seen that look so often that what he wanted to do now was warn Lewis off.

But, speaking slightly pettishly, he said:

'Not sir, for God's sake. I'm retired. Let's not be formal.'

Lewis grinned and ducked his eyes. Cheyney saw neither the puzzlement nor the potential mutiny there. That's all very well, Lewis was thinking, but, if I don't call him sir, am I allowed to call him Cheyney? In a brief moment, as the sun from over the wall of the little pub garden shifted and hit him Lewis saw a world in which the man opposite might be called Allen. It was a new world for Lewis. He had felt strong and well backed that morning when they were questioning Sarah Richmond, much stronger and more effective than he had the previous day, when he was just a policeman investigating a burglary. And he wanted to know more about what he was doing: he liked it.

But he strayed a moment too long. Cheyney was asking a question. 'What now? What do you think?'

There was a bit of delight in Lewis's mind as he grasped, by that question, that Cheyney was casting about, was guessing, genuinely wanted to know Lewis's opinion. Lewis felt he had value. He also, and more importantly, felt that he *knew*.

But he wasn't one to risk things, or to rush fences.

'I went through the Richmond file. But I haven't any, any, any — what do I call it? I haven't any grasp of him. D'ye know what I mean?'

Lewis was suddenly absorbed in his analysis, forgetful of Cheyney, forgetful of protocol, forgetful of class, forgetful, almost, of ambition. Lewis was doing his job. He had a question.

'Did you know him at all well, Colonel?'

As he said it Lewis was pleased. The word 'Colonel' popped out of his mouth automatically, and it seemed to Lewis, once he had spoken, the nicest and most diplomatic compromise between 'Sir' and 'Allen' and 'Cheyney'.

He was, therefore, surprised to see the veiled irritation spring quickly to Cheyney's eyes at the use of his Army title. Once he saw that look he was, of course, on the verge of being mutinous again.

'Not well.'

In for a penny, thought Lewis. But Cheyney had risen, and invited Lewis to have a stirrup cup and, while he was fetching large whiskies for them both, Lewis had time to think again. And the more he thought the surer he was that he was right. In the three or four minutes that Cheyney was at the bar he phrased and rephrased what he wanted to say. He also thought of abandoning the whole line his active brain had led him to. He thought that would be safer, by a long chalk. However right he was this implacable man might not see it his way. Oscillating between confidence — inside him — and lack of confidence Lewis saw Cheyney sit down across from him and say:

'Why do you ask?'

Well, in for a pound this time, thought Lewis.

'Was he normal?'

'What on earth do you mean?'

'Was he' — this took a plunge, a very big one, and it took a gulp as well, and Lewis still could not get it out casually, or in any sort of slang — 'was he homosexual?'

Cheyney laughed.

'Harry a queer? Certainly not. A bastard, yes. You've read the file. But in the sexual department I'd've thought as straight as they come.'

Then Cheyney suddenly came together. Tom Morgan and Robert Davies and Rachel and others had seen that happen. They had seen the nose of the dog come up as he caught a scent. They would have recognised the way he hunched his shoulders, the way the heavy lids moved back from his eyes, the extra care with which he found a cigarette. They, Morgan especially, would have known that Allen Cheyney was on to something. And, just at the moment when Lewis, convinced that he was right, was however still flickering within himself between what he thought wise and what he thought good, Cheyney said:

'Go on.'

'Well. Was he normal? Did he ...'

It all trailed away suddenly. Lewis, on the edge of something, started to lose heart. Cheyney saw it going from him and leant over, across the table, across their drinks and, fiery-eyed, with the curious strength he had, did not assert but asked.

'What would you do now, Lewis?'

Lifted, Lewis put all his courage together, and he even added a little humour to it:

'After seeing that old biddy' – he smiled – 'I'd say, find Richmond's woman, *Cherchez la femme*, I believe it's called.'

'That's a policeman's view?'

There was a moment, then, of real intimacy.

'That's a policeman's view.'

Cheyney sat and thought and looked again and got up and said:

'God. You're right.'

69

CHAPTER TEN

LEWIS

As they travelled back to Whitehall after their scratch lunch Cheyney wondered about Lewis in a more considered way than he had hitherto. He had been given no more than a sentence or two of background on a man who had, under modern and streamlined police training procedures, reached a far higher rank than would have been attained by somebody of his age during most of Cheyney's own career. He had seemed to his police masters a suitable secondment to Cheyney and Morgan, since he had opened the investigation into the Richmond burglary. Like most policemen his superior clearly disliked, feared and even suspected the activities of such as Cheyney and Morgan – that Cheyney had gathered from the Superintendent's somewhat grumpy contribution to their brief conversation. Yet he had given them a man who, on the face of it, was one of his high fliers.

As for Lewis himself, Cheyney thought it would be unwise to try to form too many conclusions about him too quickly. Determined, intelligent and quick – he was clearly all of these things. His dark face, beetle brows and self-contained air – they all went well with the steady, rather hairy, hands on the steering wheel of the car as he threaded their way back to the Department's offices. But there was about him something Cheyney could not get yet. For all the initial suspicion of nearly every policeman – even, and sometimes especially, the Special Branch – for the secret world you usually found that a man seconded for a particular operation nonetheless showed a trace of pleasurable excitement.

Indeed it was often a problem at one and the same time to cauterise the disgust and dampen the excitement of such a recruit before he could be useful on his operation. In Lewis no disgust, no hesitation had been evident: there had been nothing wrong with his intellectual footwork when Cheyney and Davies had briefed him that morning; when they had talked to Sarah Richmond; or when they had lunched together. Nor had there been any particular excitement. Of course, Cheyney reminded himself, for the moment the affair had all the appearance, all the feel, of a straightforward police investigation: that was why he had insisted, somewhat against Tom Morgan's wishes, on having a policeman on the strength. And it made a good team now, he thought with some satisfaction – himself and Lewis, full time; Tom and Bob Davies part time; Davies supervising the Department's questioners and search teams.

This led him to leave speculation about and evaluation of Lewis for a moment and drift on to Lewis's guess about Harry Richmond. It could be the wildest red herring or the most brilliant insight, and Cheyney was inclined to feel it was the latter. The hours had moved on so fast since he had discovered that Richmond was dead that, Cheyney realised, he had really given very little time to a considered and structured attempt to recall and examine the dead man. He started in on this now, and was in a brown study, from which Lewis had to stir him, when they arrived in Whitehall.

'Right,' said Cheyney. They climbed out of the car and showed their passes to the porter, who greeted the Colonel with a salute which conveyed a delighted warmth. Cheyney led the way briskly down a maze of drab corridors to the airy room that had been set aside for him and the adjacent and smaller one that had been provided for Lewis. He introduced them to the compact and capable looking young blonde in the outer room: she would act as secretary to both of them for the duration of their stay. Now she was sent for large pots of coffee while Cheyney inspected both rooms and, with various grunts of satisfaction, noted that they had been efficiently cleaned and dusted – it was clear that neither had been occupied for some time; the shelves empty of everything but the occasional dog-eared Government report bore witness to that. On each desk were pads, freshly sharpened pencils, ballpoint pens in various colours, ashtrays, paperweights. Somebody (Miss Levison, Cheyney guessed) had seen to it that his long preferred taste in matters of desk organisation had been pandered to. He opened a cupboard and found that in the matter of drink, too, he had been supplied as of old. The set up was not, of course, quite as comfortable, nor quite as warm, as his old room. But it was close enough; and for the first time a faint pinprick of nostalgia tapped at his heart. Partly to dispel it, he spoke slightly brusquely to Lewis:

'Park yourself here. I'll go and indent for all the Richmond files for you. Just go over and over them again. By close of play we should have a lot more on him from other sources. So we'll all foregather in my room at about six and assemble what we've got. All right?'

'Yes,' said Lewis and, greatly daring, added, 'Cheyney.'

Cheyney did not seem to notice the familiarity which, after all, he had invited, and went off to arrange the delivery of the files, to check on Davies's progress, to have a word with Tom Morgan, to thank Miss Levison for her prevision. Then he came back to the bare room, nodded to the girl, saw that she had indeed provided the coffee, and sat down behind his desk with that, a large malt whisky, and his thoughts.

Harry Richmond and a girl. Try as he would he could recall no evidence, not even a rumour, of any extra-marital involvement on Harry's part throughout at least that period of his career when he had, from time to time, come under Cheyney's eye. What, though, had made his wife into what she was? Was it merely the maturing of something inherent in her? Could it have been caused by Harry? He began to review what he had told Rachel and Tom Morgan about Richmond, what he had felt when he was talking to them to be the truth; and yet, he now felt, it was a truth which clashed conspicuously with the ready assent his instinct had offered to Lewis's outsider's guesswork about Harry Richmond. Slowly, as he took alternate sips of whisky and coffee, and as cigarette followed cigarette, the true, the considered, the rounded, picture he had in his deepest mind of Harry Richmond began to take shape.

He had been wrong, he now realised, in the description he had given to Rachel and Morgan of Harry Richmond on the occasion of their aborted lunch. (And, he remarked to himself, if his memory had played him so false for that searing occasion, how many other falsehoods had it already perpetrated, and how dangerously, in this affair that would depend so much on reading the past correctly?) The point about the lunch – the effort now made, he was able to bring the shadows forward from the very back corners of his mind and make them reform into solid shapes in its foreground – was that, at Loch Hill he had made Richmond bloodless, unfeeling, callous, pompous. He had been all of those things except, possibly, the last. But there was also about him, Cheyney now thought, a crude and overbearing and distinctly aggressive power – a bloodfulness, if he could make a word for himself – that was a central feature of Richmond's personality and which, if one accepted its existence, bore sharply on Lewis's hunch.

Cheyney brooded on. In trying to recollect everything it would not, of course, do to be too obsessive about Lewis's hunch; and Cheyney therefore started taking that hunch to pieces. There had never, he repeated to himself, been a hint of scandal about Harry Richmond that he could recall. He was familiar – surely Lewis must be too? – with many marriages in which one or the other partner atrophied: the fact of atrophy did not justify conclusions about the other partner. Lewis was a policeman: he was accustomed to sifting among, to dealing in the coinage of, the crudely base among human motives. Here their investigation would have to be subtler, just as the material they were dealing with – of loyalty and treason and twisted motivation – was subtler. But then, thought Cheyney with a sudden rush of despair, were they in truth dealing with anything at all? The rush of confidence and, more important, of knowingness, that had come to him in the restaurant with Morgan and Davies had passed on in that second: the blazes on the trail were, surely, too trivial for all the weight that was being put upon them, the whole scheme of things the four of them – and the teams they already had at work – were creating was altogether too fantastical.

He got himself another whisky and went with that and a cigarette to stare out of the window, rubbing the small of his back with his left hand, just as he used to do in the old days. He forced his mind away from the gloomy charms of speculation about the uselessness of the task in hand and back on to the clear tracks of the job he had given himself for the afternoon – recalling and defining everything he could about Sir Harry Richmond. His mind was no longer used to bending itself meekly to his will in such matters of introspection as it once was, and he had something of a struggle. Eventually, though, it gave in, and he found himself back at the desk, another cigarette between the fingers of his left hand, his right holding a pencil, used to make the occasional note on the pad in front of him.

Leave Lewis's hunch, plausible or implausible, aside for the moment, he instructed his brain, and concentrate on building up a picture of Harry as he was. Another little incongruity suddenly popped up. His widow had called him Henry. Cheyney himself, while talking of the man to Rachel and Morgan, had spoken of him as Harry: he thought of him as Harry. He never thought of him as 'Henry', or even as 'Richmond'. Come to think of it, everybody in Westminster and Whitehall – and everybody in Fleet Street except *The Times* – had, during his days of prominence, called him Sir Harry. The portrait Cheyney had drawn for himself and others of a paragon of Whitehall coldness, ruthlessness and stuffiness did not go with that kind of familiarity. Yes, he recalled with surprise, there was a certain bluffness, a certain crudity, about the man which went with 'Harry' and definitely did not go with Henry. He himself had got it wrong, Cheyney now realised, because he had in the last couple of days concentrated too exclusively on Harry in relation to Charlie, and his subconscious had been trying to justify in terms of Harry's personality Harry's treatment of his son's memory, the memory of a son whom Cheyney had held in high regard, had even, perhaps, betrayed.

Unless he could get it all right now, Cheyney thought, taking a restless turn around the room, the whole investigation could easily go askew. Morgan and the others had brought him in because Richmond had asked for him at that late moment in his life; and because whatever was there came from the past, and because Cheyney himself was from the past. If the past could not be unearthed and reassembled with mathematical accuracy and strict honesty he might as well throw his hand in.

He sat down at the desk. So, now. He had disinterred and tested for accuracy within himself two further strands of Harry Richmond. There was that raw power of character, checked, but certainly not overwhelmed, by the style and polish of Whitehall. And there was that bluffness, that something or other that got him called Harry, that was harder to define. Cheyney suddenly recalled Richmond at a dinner telling a dirty story of some violence. It was more a barrack room story than a Whitehall one. That was another little piece to be put down on the jigsaw now assembling more rapidly before him. As the afternoon wore on and the time for his staff meeting approached Cheyney suddenly understood that the dead man coming to life again here in this bare room – itself made to live and function only for a temporary purpose – under the shaping and moulding pressure of his, Cheyney's, thoughts, was a more formidable being than he would have – than, damn it, he *had* – admitted forty eight hours before. He was not only a more formidable figure; he was immensely a more human one.

That brought him sharply up against something else, up against another gap in his hitherto far too casual reasoning. He remembered having lightly over-ridden Morgan's question about why Richmond had not risen to the very top in the Civil Service. But he had not, he now saw, really answered the question. As Richmond became less bloodless, less controlled, more basic, more formidable, the question posed itself more forcefully. Of course, there could be a thousand or more good reasons, including what was very probably the true one, that events had not conspired for Harry Richmond as they must always conspire for any man who is to reach the top in such a profession. Still, the point was there.

It was certainly true that in his last years at the Home Office Harry Richmond had not been the man he had been in earlier years; and most people put it down to disappointment. Did it . . .? Cheyney's mind leaped eagerly on the date of Charlie's death, and he regretfully had to haul it back. Charlie had been dead for a year before his father had begun to show that disillusion and grumpiness that had made his closing years a minor hell for those under him. However, thought Cheyney, rallying, there was something here, and he jotted down a note.

The door opened and Tom Morgan strode in.

Cheyney glanced at his watch and spoke irritably.

'Tom. I believe I said six o'clock.'

Morgan shook his big head and sat down in the chair opposite Cheyney's desk. His brusqueness suddenly reminded Cheyney that Morgan after all was the boss.

'There's something I wanted you to know now, Allen, before we assemble.'

He lit a cigarette.

'OIS and HIS* have both been on to me. They want to know what the devil I'm up to *re* Harry Richmond, and what the hell you're doing back here. Harrison and Matthews have both been screaming at me since lunch, and the two bastards have clearly got together. Matthews called me twenty minutes ago and told me they and Brown – he's head of Special Branch now, you may not know – want to convene a meeting of the Joint Intelligence Committee *instanter*.'

Cheyney whistled softly. Morgan, seeing the bottle on the desk, got up to fetch a glass and pour himself a drink. He spoke over his shoulder.

'We're recovered for the moment,' he said. 'I spoke to the PM this morning. Told him the lot. Told him you were back. Spoke to Patterson, too. That's all O.K. But Matthews is gurgling away at Bob's request this morning for HIS files on Harry Richmond. All my instincts tell me this has got to be a very tight operation. It's gone out as far as it should already. But I don't know how long I can hold off. I'm worried about it, Allen.'

'Isn't this just the usual inter-departmental jealousy?'

'Could be. Hope it is. But what you don't know is that we had a hell of a scrap half a year ago. HIS wanted whole responsibility for treason investigations, leaving me simply with counter terrorist intelligence. Since Harrison and OIS wanted to cut down my activities abroad, they were willing to support Matthews as a

---

* As was mentioned in *The Three Colonels*, the various intelligence services were re-organised in the mid 1970's, although the powers that be decreed that they should be known to the Press only by their familiar names – MI5, MI6, SIS, DIS, etc. Of the new departments only that headed by Colonel Cheyney was not given a designation. The exact nature of the re-organisation, and its consequences, are described below in Chapter Twenty. OIS is Overseas Intelligence Services, HIS is Home Intelligence Services. Neither acronym implies full authority, as this story makes clear. – P.C.

first step. One or other of them wanted to transfer Bob as well. So it could all be rather more of a problem for the Department than the usual Whitehall squabble. Frankly, Allen, I've just realised what a risk I've taken.'

'Well,' said Cheyney, 'it's certainly true that this Department has always had rather a ragbag of responsibilities. So for that matter has Bob Pierce and his lot. But we exist because successive Prime Ministers wanted a check on the other lads, and God knows history shows one was needed. Still. Is it because I'm back that the wolves are gathering?'

Morgan grinned for the first time.

'I expect so.' Then:

'Don't worry Allen. I'm not pulling out. I just wanted you to know. And to tell you that if parallel activities start we may not have all the resources or all the access we want.'

Cheyney looked very pale and for a moment very frightening.

'You can leave that to me. Now, look here.' He scribbled for a moment.

'I'm going to send that charming lassie of yours out for some shirts for myself. Then I'll grab your shower and we'll foregather as planned at six. Meanwhile, I think you should warn both Bob and young Lewis. Lewis at least must be given a chance to pull out. Bob, of course, will stay in. I'm set now, Tom. I'll do this damn thing our way whatever happens.'

He got up and went out. After a moment Morgan realised that he had been left with the responsibilities of command as well as the pleasures and got up to go and talk to Lewis. As always, he mused, the sharp definition of Cheyney's will heartened him.

CHAPTER ELEVEN

REVIEW

At six, a refreshed, damp-haired Cheyney lit his pipe and looked around at his little circle. Lewis had been unable not to raise his eyebrows when, coming into the room, he had glanced curiously — almost censoriously — at Cheyney's desk and seen nothing but the ashtray, the bottle, the glass, the forgotten coffee and a single sheet of paper with several scribbled notations. No files, no confusion (the ashtray had been emptied and wiped), no disorder or evidence of any kind of hard work. Now Lewis sat, flipping back and forth among the pages of his spiral-topped notebook, wondering whether he had got anything from three and a half hours scrutiny of the Richmond files, and worrying as well. Beside him there was the curiously reassuring and lanky figure of Davies, a pencil between his teeth and another stuck behind an ear, a sequestered small table beside him on which rested an untidy bundle of files, various parts of each one marked by paper flags. In his hand, though, was a buff folder containing, as Lewis could see, a dozen or so neatly typed sheets of yellow paper, one and a half spaced.

Tom Morgan sat a little way back from the trio, beyond the centre of the room, indicating by the position that he adopted that he did not consider himself to be a fully functioning member of the team, but by his presence at the meeting that he would guard their lines from encroachment. At the outset Cheyney formally asked both Lewis and Davies if Morgan had told them of the new interests that had manifested themselves during the day, and both men affirmed that he had. Cheyney went straight on to the main business, but he was gratified to note, as he moved his mind on, the slight tightening of Lewis's lips and the hardening of his eyes. Decidedly, they had got a good man here, he thought, and he would have been even more pleased had he known of Lewis's feelings inside, the rage at the interference from OIS and HIS which, because he felt it, made him truly a member of the team. The other anger he felt, and, to be honest, the other concern, Cheyney would know about shortly, for Lewis interrupted the opening paragraph in which Cheyney was describing their visit to Sarah Richmond.

'Colonel Cheyney,' he said, clearing his throat, 'gentlemen.' He had decided earlier that this would be the best and most mannerly form of introduction. 'There's something else I want to say.'

'In a moment, Lewis,' said Cheyney, 'I'm just going to review what we did, and then Bob will fill us in on his work, and we'll be able to have a useful discussion.'

'No,' snapped Lewis, 'not about the main meeting. About what Mr Morgan was telling us.'

The other three were suddenly still. Lewis explained:

'I should begin by saying that I don't get on particularly well with my chief. We're not exactly the best of friends. But he's a loyal man, and he wouldn't want to see one of his people get into trouble. Anyway, when I set off to meet Colonel Cheyney I promised I'd keep in touch regularly on how things were going – not on the details, of course, but mainly on how long I thought I'd be away. Anyway, I rang him a few minutes ago, and I found him very worried. He wanted to know if I wanted him to pull me off this job. He said he'd been chatting to some pal on high – he didn't say who it was – who was fairly rude about Colonel Cheyney's new operation and' – Lewis grinned here – 'suggested that ambitious young men with careers to make shouldn't get too attached to it.'

He knew that the silence and the stillness that followed his statement were unnatural. For one thing, the other three had stopped dead short in the middle of what they were doing – Cheyney with a hand slightly raised to arrest Lewis, Morgan with a match half way to his cigarette, Davies, in the middle of turning over a page, and with a set frown running across his forehead. For

another, Morgan and Davies, having first looked quickly at
Lewis, transferred their eyes directly to Cheyney, and waited for
him. Lewis immediately felt a lack of air in the place, a constraint:
he felt a touch of claustrophobia. He would not have been
surprised if something had exploded.

Instead, Cheyney spoke in a voice that was mildness itself:
'Well, well, well,' he said. 'And that will be our new friend
Brown, will it not, Tom?'

And Morgan said, through his teeth:
'I expect so.'

It could not be an easy task even for Morgan and Davies, who
had lived some time in the official jungle of names and titles and
acronyms and predators, to proceed quietly to the business in
hand when all the evidence suddenly available told them that
some of the very big guns in the jungle were out hunting. It was
not easy for them. For some curious reason – perhaps it was his
personality, perhaps it was his lack of experience, perhaps it was a
streak of bloody-mindedness – Lewis seemed the least affected by
his own news. But they all waited for a lead from Cheyney.

'Thank you, Lewis,' said Cheyney. 'I think we all now know
what we may be up against. And I think it important that we
should keep one another informed as we go along.' He took a
breath, and continued with his résumé of his and Lewis's work.
He went about it in his most quiet and flat voice, with neither
extenuation nor malice describing their questions, the answers
they had received, their reaction to what they had found in Harry
Richmond's study. He dangled before Morgan and Davies, but
briefly, the little piles of paper on Harry's desk – even the Bruges
postcard – and concluded with Lewis's guess about Richmond.

But while he was doing this – and he was able to do it
convincingly only because he had slipped quickly back into old
harness and old habits – the rest of his mind was screaming at
him. Why, in God's or Rachel's name was he back here, and
doing this? What quirk of mind, what temptation, had led him to
encourage a scheme that could easily end in ruin for Tom Morgan
and the less resilient, much more vulnerable, Lewis? That was the
honest and fair bit of his mind having its say. But there was the
selfish bit as well. Was it for another filthy little Whitehall battle
that he had told Rachel he would be away from Loch Hill for

some time? Just when he had got himself settled there, and properly settled? Who the hell cared anyway?

But his even voice went on:

'Bob?'

'This is, of course, a preliminary report. I've sorted it out into two parts. The first concerns Sir Henry Richmond's life for the period since his retirement from the Civil Service. Earlier files and security files on him you've all already seen. In so far as they are available, of course. There may be more. Am I all right so far?'

Odd, Cheyney thought, the way Davies was jumping about. He was not normally jittery. 'In so far as they are available.' That recognised the already admitted problem of access to Harrison's and Matthew's files. Not something, surely, to trouble Davies, of all men. In the blackness of his inner mind Cheyney began to prepare a plan that would guard them against Davies leaving them: if the Department was to go – and even Tom thought it might – Davies would have a share to claim.

'You're fine so far,' said Lewis.

'Get on with it,' said Cheyney.

'The second part concerns what we have dug out at the hospital. You'll have to deal with a lot of that yourself, Allen. I'll come to it. But I want to concentrate now on the first.'

He pulled his little table round in front of him and moved a paper here and there.

Oh God, thought Cheyney in contrition, he's not nervous, he's not doubtful, he's got something. Cheyney put down his pipe and reached for a cigarette.

'Richmond in fact resigned from the Civil Service a trifle early,' Davies began. 'Nothing significant in that, so far as I can see. All the indications are that he was a difficult and querulous head of the Home Office, and that he was less and less happy there as time went by. The difference between actual and expected retirement was a matter of a few months only and – here's an interesting, though not, I suppose, a significant thing – Downing Street bent the rules so that Richmond could take an outside job. He became a director of a middle-sized concern, Pantax, whose main interest lay in medicine, proprietary drugs, that sort of thing.'

'Excuse me,' said Lewis, looking puzzled, 'what rules?'

Cheyney explained. 'There's a rule that senior Civil Servants

should not, for some time after retirement, take gainful
employment where they might be able to put immediately to use
up to date information from their time in Whitehall. Fair enough,
really, especially considering they've got damn generous
pensions, inflation proofed. I'm afraid, though, that it's a rule
honoured in the breach rather than the observance: most Prime
Ministers break it on application. That's why it's not, probably,
significant in this case. Worth remembering, though.'

'I see,' said Lewis, outraged again by this further glimpse into
the doings of Whitehall.

'Well,' resumed Davies, 'Pantax is a sixty per cent owned
subsidiary of a continental company, Belge-Fabre. In the course
of his duties Richmond therefore went to Brussels, oh, three or
four times a year.'

'Did he hold any other jobs after retirement?' asked Morgan.

'Yes. He was a director of an insurance company which had a
tie in with some of the Civil Service staff associations and clubs.
He lost that after a couple of years when the company was
merged. He was a collector of porcelain and china, and became a
director of a company making and exporting modern versions of
traditional designs. Lucrative little business that, and he held on to
the job until his illness. He also sat from time to time on *ad hoc*
government bodies. No peerage. It's thought, I believe, that his
personality went against him on that.'

'No retirement tycoon, then,' said Cheyney. 'Not like some of
them.'

'Certainly not.'

'Why start with Pantax,' asked Morgan, 'some significance
there?'

Davies frowned and coughed and looked down at his neatly
typed notes. He lit a Gauloise and ran his fingers through his hair.

'I don't know.' He frowned. 'Of course, there hasn't been time
to do a really thorough reconstruction job on Richmond yet. And
if there's opposition to our requisitioning other people's files it'll
take *even* longer than I'd supposed – even working flat out. But
from what I've been able to sort out Harry Richmond lived the
most irreproachably above-board and disciplined life in
retirement. Even now I could practically rebuild his diary for you.
Days for porcelain, days for drugs, days for insurance. Regular

auction visits depending on what's at sales. Lunch at White's once a week, usually with different Whitehall chums. Oh, by the way Allen, it seems he saw a lot of our friend Fleming. There's just a slight oddity in the matter of travel.'

Davies frowned and sighed again. As always when he was giving one of his lectures, or embarking on one of his sessions of analysis, he seemed to grow in untidiness before one's eyes. His hair got more rumpled and, whenever he had a hand free from cigarette or papers, it got on with the business of making a mess of the knot of his tie. The toes of his shoes came up, in succession, to rub the back of the opposite calf and, in consequence, his trouser legs began to ride up and his socks were collapsed untidily around his ankles. Had it not been for the hard eyes he would, by the time he was finished, have made himself over into a lovable picture of academic abstraction. As he worked himself around, and then into, a problem Davies, Cheyney thought, seemed alternately like a swamp and a snake, a swamp when he was wrapping himself all round the thing, festooned by files, buried under scraps of paper, a snake when he had got hold of something and was working from it, holding on to it with his teeth, never letting those eyes drift from it as he squirmed his way into the mass of the problem. Then he was formidable, admirable, but, somehow, frightening.

'Richmond kept the job at Pantax for nearly three years. During that time – we've been on to his travel agent, used the same one for twenty and more years, see what I mean about his regularity – he went to Brussels eleven times. Took his wife on seven of those trips, no pattern to the omissions, that I can see: she didn't go on the last one. Then he left the company.'

Davies took a deep breath, lit another cigarette and rumpled himself some more.

'No particular indication why he left. As it happens, I have a contact at Belge-Fabre.'

Lewis looked impressed. Cheyney sighed. He had years ago given up being surprised at the rabbits Davies pulled from a hat he had had a quarter of a century to fill. And he had given up, too, showing much reaction to the quiet glitter of pleasure in Davies's eyes when he modestly held the bunny up for inspection.

'Nothing particular, again so far as I can see, in the resignation. Richmond said he was getting on, feeling seedy, had too much to do, wanted to get on with hobbies and things that interested him more. He'd worked conscientiously. Pantax gave a party for him, and a cheque for £5,000.'

Davies's eyes now took on a special glitter. He licked his lips and passed the back of a hand across them. He looked ever more like the avian predators he had once watched for a living.

'The thing is, Richmond went on with his Belgian trips. In fact, they became more frequent. So far as my contact knows, he never saw anyone at Belge-Fabre after he left Pantax. But in the twenty months between leaving the company and his first stroke, he went to Brussels nine times.'

'On the other hand' – Davies looked almost hurt – 'he made no secret about it. Went always to the same travel agent, and they always booked him at the same hotel. He never took his wife, though, not after he left Pantax.'

The look Davies gave Lewis was satisfied, even praising.

'I think,' said Davies, 'it was brilliant for someone who has had so little time to study the characters to perceive that there was something – or someone – else in his life. I'm not certain, yet, that it was a woman, but I'm inclined to think it was. And you didn't even know what I've found out today.'

Lewis realised that there was nothing patronising in his voice. It was all congratulation. And, obviously, Cheyney had already told Davies about the policeman's hunch. A glance between himself and Cheyney confirmed that.

He was learning more about these people all the time. He had thought the difference between himself and Cheyney was one of class; or, perhaps, of rank. But it was more than that. There was a difference of perception, or experience, or training, or something. He saw approval in Cheyney's eye, and he was pleased to see it. They were, thought Lewis, gratified, impressed by him.

And yet the inner and critical voice that was an essential part of his personality told him that his guess – as yet unproven, the voice added – was one that any good copper would have made immediately he had the information – such as it was – in his hands. Properly speaking, Lewis the copper ought now to reach out for the judgment that these powerful and secret men were naïve. Sure, Davies had, in the short time available to him, done a remarkable job of ferreting out a scheduled history for Richmond.

But then he had remarkable access and remarkable resources; more and better by far than any policeman would have had, and more quickly and easily activated.

But Lewis did not reach out for the unfavourable judgment. It was not just that he was, as yet, feeling his way. It was that Cheyney and Davies and Morgan and their strange world − perhaps, too, their collective personality − were exerting − had exerted from the beginning − a powerful attraction for him. They were pulling him towards them. They were doing it more and more every moment. And even while level-headed young Lewis realised how gossamer were the threads they were all spinning, he was excited; and that was the paramount fact about him and to him that evening.

Cheyney was speaking.

'Tom. I think Lewis and I had better go to Brussels. I presume we have a contact there?'

'Good man in the Deuxième Bureau,' answered Davies. 'Le Marchand. Inspector. I'm sure he'll cooperate.'

'Right. Well, look here. I think we'll wrap this up now. Have a drink. Get an early night. Get off to Brussels tomorrow. Unless, Bob, you've got something spectacular from the hospital we'll simply aim to review the whole situation here on Monday, as we originally planned.'

'Well,' said Davies very slowly, pulling out two more sheafs of material and dropping one of them in front of Cheyney, 'as I said earlier, you'll have to deal with a lot of that yourself. And we haven't finished all the inquiries we want to make. Can do over the weekend. But in the light of what we've been talking about there is something that may be important.'

'Well?'

'According to one of the four nurses who regularly attended Harry on his last visit, and according to the ward sister, he had a few bouts of talking in his sleep. Usually under drugs, never very connected or lucid. We'll try to persuade them to recall more of what he said. Both of them are having sessions with Greeley tomorrow.'

He turned his head on its long stalk towards Lewis, fully accepting him now as a colleague.

'That's our tame psychiatrist. Interrogator. A first class one.'

85

He went on:

'According to these ladies Harry repeated a woman's name over and over again. 'Anna'. And he kept asking where she was.'

'But that's it. That's terrific.'

'By all that's holy.'

Cheyney and Lewis spoke together, and Tom Morgan gave a piercing whistle.

'You old fox, Bob,' said Cheyney. 'You've held this back, you bastard.'

Davies held up his hand. He grinned, but then he shook his head.

'It's nothing like as good or certain as that, I'm afraid. Of course, as you've instinctively grasped, that could not be a reference to the revered Lady Richmond.'

He paused.

'I think you probably don't know, Allen, that Harry Richmond had a sister. A younger sister. He was devoted to her. She was killed in the war. But by all accounts they were very close, too close for Sarah's liking. He marked her anniversary in *The Times* every year. Visited the grave – she was killed by a flying bomb – regularly. Her name was Elizabeth Anna. Not Anne, of either variety. Anna. Named for a Swedish grandmother.'

He gave a very deprecating grin.

'I don't know what she was called by friends and family. It could be anything. But I'm checking.'

The exuberance went out of them like air released from a balloon. For a few moments they sat in silence, each with his own thoughts.

Lewis's little voice was silent in shame. That had been a formidable piece of checking, or research, or memory or whatever. He realised he was disappointed. He realised his disappointment might itself later be washed away by the discovery that Richmond's sister was called 'Elizabeth' or 'Liz' or 'Lizzie', or even 'Betty'. But above all he was impressed by Davies's having discovered both the fact that she existed and the warmth of her relations with her brother. He couldn't possibly just have known it? Or could he? Lewis wondered, looking at Davies's great domed forehead.

Cheyney's feelings were not dissimilar. He was, of course, not at all surprised that Davies should have extracted this unlikely and buried information from somewhere. He had known Davies too long for that. But he went through the disappointment, and he recognised the hope. And he suddenly felt, like a blow, another shaft of illumination on the character he had spent most of the afternoon reconstructing in the workshop of his own mind.

Harry had a sister. Improbable. Harry *loved* his sister. More improbable still. Harry kept his sister's memory green. Most improbable of all from a Harry who had expunged his only son from thoughts and memory alike. More thought had to be given to this suddenly different, suddenly elusive, Harry. An unknown, an unlikely Harry. A stranger to Cheyney much more than he had been a stranger in Cheyney's memory when Fleming's call had arrived.

'Bob,' he said, 'do a bit more than the name, eh?'

'Find out about her, you mean?'

'Find out about them.'

'Will do.'

Cheyney stood up and yawned and went to get them drinks. Morgan took over his telephone and gave instructions for flights to be booked for the following morning and for contact to be made with Le Marchand. Then the business of the day was over and they sat down again, savouring their drinks.

The next half hour was Lewis's period of unalloyed enjoyment, the first he had had so far, the first in which he was not plagued by doubts and suspicions and tentative judgments. They each came over to the table and Cheyney handed them drinks. But then Cheyney sat on the edge of the desk rifling through Davies's separate reports – one on Richmond's post-retirement life and journeys; the other the first report from the hospital.

Tom Morgan pulled his chair round, so that he, Davies and Lewis formed a triangle, with Cheyney outside it. He gave Lewis a big and friendly grin.

'Well,' he said, 'James, isn't it? What do you make of us, I wonder.'

'Yes,' said Lewis, 'James, well I . . .'

'Tom,' said Morgan, sticking out his great, beefy hand, and Lewis realised that, though they had spoken before they had not met until now.

'Bob,' said Davies, following suit.

Tom was a much less stuffy head of the department than Allen, thought Davies as he shook hands. No, he quickly amended, that wasn't fair. Cheyney wasn't stuffy. Rather the reverse. But there had been — there was — something distant about him, something uncomprehending of human beings in his make-up. It might of course be the Army. Or the aristocracy. But Tom Morgan had been a soldier, a professional soldier, just like Cheyney. It was as though Cheyney did not really understand the workings, so to speak the tactics, of any human relationship short of friendship (or, now, he supposed, love). He had no sense of camaraderie, except with his friends. He assessed people (Davies had seen from Lewis's unease that he had assessed Lewis and that Lewis hadn't known what the result of the assessment was) and assumed they assessed him and assumed that each man knew what the other's assessment was. That was the coldness about him that made people afraid of him.

Davies glanced up at Cheyney, left hand flicking through pages, right hand holding glass and cigarette. People who had been in battles with Cheyney — blood battles or political battles — worshipped him. Once his allegiance or support was given it was given totally; and it felt like having a tank regiment at your back. (Davies, a most unmilitary man, was given to military metaphors). Did he, though, now have the subtlety of mind, behind that crispness, that brusqueness, that curtness of manner and thought, to delve into whatever they were delving into? It sometimes seemed to Davies that Cheyney's so powerful will had, if not invented the world, made that part of it he inhabited over in his own way. He had made things into sharply shining areas of action and decision; and it wasn't always possible to act or decide.

He pulled himself back from the brief and brown study.

Morgan's question to Lewis had not been a serious one. He neither wanted nor expected an answer to it. He had merely been breaking ice. He had broken it successfully; and the interesting thing about him, Davies thought, was that he had forfeited nothing of rank in doing so.

'How big a set-up do you have here?'

'Sorry, James. What's your latest murder case? Whom do you suspect, that you've no evidence on?'

'Sorry,' said Lewis.

'You wouldn't tell me. I wouldn't tell you.'

Morgan gave that big and charming grin again, and neither man had given nor taken offence.

'You know,' said Morgan to Davies, 'I really don't think Miss Levison has ever recovered from Allen's departure.'

Then, to Lewis:

'She was Allen's secretary. Mine now.'

To both of them:

'It took me weeks to get her to put a bottle of Vichy water in my cupboard. Rachel drinks only Perrier, you see. Longer to take out than damn sherry. Now, I see from what Allen's got here that she's reproduced his whole thing exactly. Malt, blended, gin, tonic, soda, dry sherry. No variety. You know, James, Allen used never to offer a pre-lunch drink *in the office* that wasn't dry sherry. You had to get him out to drink beer or whisky. And gin. Jesus. He never drinks gin except on airplanes.'

'He's obviously very definite,' said Lewis. 'Who's the gin for, then? The gin here, I mean.'

'Oh. Drinks before close of play were a different matter. He thought he should provide a choice then. He was aware that some people drank the stuff *off* airplanes. No bloody vodka, though.'

'Because it's Russian?'

This seemed a successful sally. Morgan and Davies laughed in a friendly way. He had meant it as a joke, and they had taken it as a joke.

'No, man, no. Because it's for drinking *with* Russians. There's a story . . .'

Morgan paused and swung himself round in his chair.

Lewis had a moment to take him in, this huge, beefy, *young* man, thick black hair, body of a boxer, looking as though he would be uncomfortable in anything but some kind of sporting strip, huge, truly huge, hands, but with shrewd and glinting eyes. He could, if he did not want to be comfortable, be more uncomfortable even than Cheyney.

'Allen,' said Morgan. 'Come over here. I was going to tell James about you and the vodka and Telnikovsky.'

Cheyney came, but not to talk about Telnikovsky.

He walked the yard between himself and them. He had left his glass and his cigarette behind him. He had one of Davies's reports in his right hand and the other in his left.

'Bob. Have you collated these two?'

Morgan having turned from Lewis found himself looking at Davies. He was surprised to see a flicker of annoyance with self, even irritation.

'No. Not really.'

'Huh.'

Cheyney pulled another chair over. He put the two dossiers on the floor.

'Look here. You point out that he went to Brussels nine times in the twenty months after he left Pantax. Fair enough. Now look at the hospital report. It has a useful preface. Three strokes, the last fatal. Six of your trips are since the first stroke. He was in Brussels twice – or he went to Brussels twice – between his second last and his last stroke. Matter of three months, even though, as I understand this thing, he was virtually under sentence of death.'

They were silent as Davies reached to the floor and picked up his papers. After a moment:

'Hell. You're right.'

'Cremation, isn't it? What kind of cremation? I understand there are differences. Sometimes they scatter the ashes, no memorial. Sometimes relatives take the urn. Sarah won't do that, I'll bet. Sometimes there is a memorial in the crematorium garden. Which is it for Harry?'

'I don't know.'

Davies looked perplexed, cross, caught out.

'Find out, Bob. Now.'

Davies went to sit in the chair behind Cheyney's desk. In a sort of *pas-de-deux* Cheyney went to Davies's chair, glaring at him.

It took Davies four telephone calls and twenty minutes. Then he said:

'The crematorium has a garden. Richmond's ashes are to be scattered there and a stone urn will mark the general area. As I understand it this is a compromise between the dead who don't want to be buried and relations who may want to leave flowers.'

As he spoke of these ghastly things in an almost light voice Davies's skin seemed to have tightened around his face so that the huge bones of his cheeks and his forehead struck out.

'Put a watch on it, Tom,' said Cheyney. 'Now. Twenty four hours a day. I want to know everything that happens there. Everything.'

'Now,' Cheyney continued, 'let's recap. What have we forgotten? We've just – by pure accident – picked up something in Harry's movements just by glancing. Let's get systematic.'

This was an old favourite of Cheyney's. Perhaps because, Morgan remembered thinking once, his instinct was so rarely at fault, but also because it was often so fitful, he was always trying to make it march for him, in a line, in a form of drill.

'Well, look,' said Davies, things rushing quickly past him, still nettled that Cheyney had noticed something he hadn't, beginning to be a little defensive, 'I haven't really had all that much time . . .'

'Fleming,' said Cheyney. 'What about Fleming? How much do we really know about Fleming?'

'Allen,' said Morgan, 'if there was anything for us in Fleming he would never have called you at Loch Hill.'

Cheyney stared at him now. 'True,' he agreed.

Davies spoke in what seemed to Lewis to be a distinctly peevish tone.

'I haven't collated everything yet, but let me tell you what I'm trying to do. All circumstantial, mind you, and I haven't got all the details yet, but I'll give you the theory.'

Detail was what Cheyney was hungry for now, Lewis saw, even if it was theoretical detail. Davies was wise in his way of handling him.

'When somebody falls sick,' Davies said, 'he . . .' His voice trailed off and he went over to the desk and started shifting papers. He resumed:

'When somebody falls *seriously* sick, people react in different ways. Close friends, well, they do what close friends do. For example: I know somebody who was very sick – in the National Heart Hospital, as it happens – and his very closest friend never visited him, because he knew that the sick man hated being visited, or having any notice taken even of the idea that he was sick. Some thought the friend heartless, only a few knew that the friend was doing exactly the right thing.'

Davies looked around at them in his donnish way.

'The patient got better, by the way.'

'Oh get on with it,' said Cheyney snappishly.

'I am,' said Davies, now giving that academic exposition of behaviour which was his speciality.

'However, there is a pattern. It would be more correct to say that there are patterns. Some colleagues or acquaintances will visit. Some will send flowers, some will smuggle in a bottle of the patient's favourite drink. Or, it it's female . . .'

'*She* is female,' said Cheyney.

'I was speaking in the abstract. Anyway, perfume or chocolates. Anyway, again, what I want to do is put together a picture of everything, other than the purely medical things, that happened to Harry in hospital. Who did what, is my fundamental question. To get meaning out of it, however, I have to have a view on how the giver naturally behaves, and how he would expect the patient to respond.'

'You're losing me,' said Lewis.

Davies turned his scrutinising eyes on Lewis.

'I'll give you a concrete example. Fleming visited Richmond with punctilious regularity. He brought flowers every time. It is not common for men to bring flowers to men in hospital. Is there a reason?'

'Oh, come off it,' said Morgan.

'There *is* a reason, to my mind a perfectly satisfactory one. Fleming is a punctilious and unimaginative man – I haven't got your dirty mind, Tom – who would see it as his duty thus regularly to visit an old colleague, and who would associate flowers with hospitals.'

'To judge from what I've got here – and remember, I haven't collated it – people behaved in quite different ways.'

The peevishness, Lewis guessed, had now issued in a sort of challenge to Cheyney. Davies was trying to provoke him.

'You surprise me,' Cheyney said, refusing to be drawn. 'Give me two examples of the different ways in which people behave.'

He was *enjoying* this, Lewis suddenly saw. All this childish and academic banter amused him.

'I'll give you more,' said Davies. He fiddled with papers for another moment.

'The Home Secretary sent flowers – from the Office – nothing in that. But the Financial Secretary at the Treasury called. Why?

Richmond spent his last years at the Home Office. One would have thought he merited personal attention from them, but not from his former ministry.'

He was losing his audience, but he didn't seem to care. He was wrapping himself up in a world of his own.

'On the other hand, so far as I can see, he never received as much as a get well card from Clements, the Financial Secretary to the Treasury whom he briefed in the sad time of that man's party being in opposition, and with whom he would have worked had he got the job friend Fleming now holds. Now, of course, we know that Clements, in retirement, is himself a sick man. But a card, surely, is not too much to ask? Or, let us take William Howard, Minister of State at the Home Office when our Harry was there. Howard piloted a piece of legislation through the House of Commons – the Social Areas (Home Office) Fund Act, in case you want to know – and Harry was his closest Civil Servant on it. So far, no sign of a visit, no sign of a card. What do we learn from all this?'

Lewis intervened.

'Hold on,' he said, 'I'm getting a bit lost here. I'm confused by all these Secretaries and Ministers.'

Davies turned to him.

'It can get confusing,' he admitted. 'The Financial Secretary to the Treasury is a politician, one of several ministers at that Department. A Permanent Under-Secretary is a Civil Servant, hence the word Permanent: he stays in office whichever party is in power. Because of something I'm going to say in a moment I'd better add that there is often a social relationship between senior Civil Servants and opposition politicians. Sometimes it has been formed when the opposition chap's party was in power. These relationships have to be handled carefully, of course, so that the current government doesn't get suspicious. The other point here is that, in advance of a general election, the senior Civil Servants see a lot of opposition politicians. It's their job to brief the opposition party in case it suddenly takes power. All part of the smooth functioning of the British system. All clear?'

'I think so,' said Lewis doubtfully.

'Take your pick,' said Cheyney, good humoured again, 'what is it?'

Davies hesitated. 'I don't know yet. Somebody has something to conceal, and they will – experience tells this – conceal either by demonstration or by withdrawal. I prefer withdrawal. So we want to know more about either Howard or Clements.'

'You would prefer withdrawal,' said Morgan.

'I can give you demonstration, too. Why should an opposition spokesman – Richard Malone – visit a long-retired Civil Servant on his deathbed?'

Lewis thought it was time he said something.

'Were they old friends?'

'Not as far as I can see, yet. But, who knows. There are one or two others in the demonstrative category. Take Plumpton, for example . . .'

'You take him,' said Cheyney, and paused:

'I'm not being dismissive, Bob. I appreciate that I asked for a recap, and that you haven't had time to fill all the cross-bearings in. As soon as you can though.'

He turned.

'Tom, you know what to do. Make sure of the crematorium. Tomorrow the rest of us will be off to Brussels.'

CHAPTER TWELVE

BRUSSELS

Henri Le Marchand, Lewis saw, was short, plump, slightly officious and also, in some way, slightly anonymous. He wore a hat, a light raincoat, and heavily rimmed glasses. It was as though the glasses, his toothbrush moustache and his slightly prominent teeth were all artifices, devices of concealment and disguise, used to hide whatever might be revealing in his expression. But he came forward in a friendly enough fashion, shook hands warmly with both of them, and used his *carte d'identité* to speed them through customs and into a large and shiny yellow Peugeot parked outside the terminal.

It had been a silent journey. The Department's car, Cheyney already ensconced behind pipe and newspaper, had picked up Lewis in Battersea and taken them to the airport. Lewis was not sure what to expect, and had spent half the night brooding on their business, not simply out of interest or concern, but in case Cheyney wanted to talk. Cheyney wasn't surly, nor preoccupied. He simply gave a short and friendly greeting, indicated the newspapers piled between them, and got on with his reading.

At Heathrow there was time to kill. Cheyney refused airport coffee with an imprecation and relaxed quietly until it was time to get up and board. It was early – just before ten – but Lewis still wondered for a moment if Cheyney would order a gin and tonic on the 'plane: he was amused and entertained by Morgan's account of the Colonel's drinking habits. As it was, as soon as they had disposed themselves in their seats, Cheyney went straight to sleep, and Lewis drank his coffee as well as his own.

For a time Lewis looked across at the face of his companion. It was his first chance to study Cheyney in repose. The head was slightly inclined to the right. The fair hair was liberally streaked with grey. It was also, though short, untidy, and a lock, too short to dangle, tried to make its way down the high and broad forehead over the right temple. The eyelids were full and heavy, oddly, in so bony a face. The nose was thin – slim, Lewis thought, would be a better word – and slightly hooked, and the lips firm. As far as he could judge Cheyney was completely relaxed. There was nothing restless about his sleep. His hands lay on either arm of his seat, the long, brown fingers slightly splayed, cuffs of a trim Viyella shirt protruding from the sleeves of a grey tweed suit. What did he look like, Lewis wondered? What would one have thought he was if one did not know?

Lewis lit a cigarette, sipped his coffee, and contemplated. Not a policeman nor a spy, certainly. There was nothing of the combined furtiveness and authority about him that Lewis, depressed, often saw reflected either in his own mirror or in the faces of people he was talking to. Not a farmer nor a squire, Lewis, to his own faint surprise, concluded. The features and the hands were too fine for that and, besides, one could detect no bluffness, no heartiness there, even though the colouring of the skin and the clothes suggested a man accustomed to outdoor life. A gentleman – much abused word – certainly; but not only that.

It was a favourite game of Lewis's – a sort of detective practice, and one that experiment over the years had proved he was rather good at – to guess at people's professions and characters from their appearance, clothes, gait, without hearing them speak – voices were often a dead giveaway. If he now sensed a certain emanation of danger from the sleeping Cheyney it was only because, he told himself, he knew what Cheyney did. He could find no evidence for it in the man; nor evidence, even, of a soldier's life, though he knew that Cheyney had been a soldier for a long time. Lewis was trying to be objective, trying to shut out from his mind all he knew and had seen about Cheyney, and he was finding himself puzzled. Then they were coming into land and Cheyney came smoothly, easily awake, without a yawn or even the passing of a hand over the face and a rub of the eyes that usually attend a return from sleep. He turned his clear eyes on Lewis, smiled, and drew his despatch case onto his lap.

About Le Marchand – no one – or, at least, no other policeman – could have any doubts. His jollity and his courtesy alike were too studied. His eyes were a little too watchful, and he walked in that careful way policemen have the world over and which, in a man inclined to stoutness, is always particularly obvious to the trained eye. And there was, of course, that suggestion of disguise conveyed by the hat, the glasses, the moustache, and the teeth. A policeman, then. Obviously a policeman. But, equally obviously, a policeman of a special kind.

He and Cheyney seemed to know each other, but slightly, in the manner of distant acquaintances, or men who might have met once a long time ago, and perhaps have heard of each other and of each other's doings in the intervening years. It was Cheyney who introduced Lewis, and Le Marchand greeted him in a slightly, but not excessively, florid way. When they got into the car Cheyney sat by Le Marchand in front, and Lewis sat behind.

'I have established you at the Grand,' Le Marchand said as he drove off. 'That, we have found, is where Sir Henry Richmond always stayed when in Brussels. The assistant manager there is a most alert young man, and specialises in making himself available to and agreeable to guests. He knew Sir Henry: it seems quite well. So we start with that advantage.'

He spoke English extremely well – a relief to Lewis, who could manage French, but clumsily, and who had feared that he might be confronted with Flemish – and with only a light trace of accent. He drove with the relaxed care of an expert, his hands, shod in driving gloves, resting lightly on the wheel, a casual eye surveying the traffic. For all his slightly pampered appearance and air, Lewis thought, he looked like a man who would do many things well.

'You've been at work already,' observed Cheyney, his tone flavoured with compliment.

'Tom Morgan told me what you wanted to do, and gave me a hint of why you wanted to do it. I arranged for us to take a drink with M. Marceau this morning. Tom said that you wish to conduct this inquiry on as informal a basis as possible. There is – as yet at least – no suggestion that Sir Henry was involved in anything improper?'

'Not as yet,' said Cheyney.

Le Marchand chuckled. It was a jolly, throaty chuckle, with a suggestion of the well-mannered dirty joke about it. 'And *we* at least do not regard a little dalliance as improper. Except with the Flemish girls, of course. And that would be an impropriety of taste.' He chuckled again, more harshly this time.

'A talk with Marceau would certainly seem to be an excellent start,' said Cheyney evenly.

'And afterwards,' Le Marchand turned his head slightly to his left and gave something between a nod and a bow to Lewis, 'it would pleasure me greatly if you would both have lunch with me.'

'Delighted,' said Cheyney.

'Is there somewhere particular you would like to go? You know Brussels, of course?'

Cheyney turned his head to include Lewis in the question.

'Anywhere you pick suits me.'

They were passing the elongated grey-steel and blue sprawl of NATO headquarters, the flags of the allied nations fluttering out towards them with the prevailing breeze, the lounging sentries, the air of readiness.

'I used to come there quite a lot,' said Cheyney, nodding towards the buildings. 'And, of course, to Mons, to SHAPE.' He was thinking of that untidy, battered, charming town down the road where the first and last shots of the First World War had been fired and which now supported the spanking, brisk, automated, Americanised Supreme Headquarters Allied Powers Europe. He stirred himself from his memories.

'Do you,' he asked Le Marchand, 'take the same critical attitude to Flemish food that you take to Flemish women?'

Le Marchand chuckled again. He seemed to have an infinite variety of chuckles or; rather, a musical register on which he could play them up and down. This was a bass affair, reaching down from his throat into his chest, rumbling away happily behind his rib cage.

'It is not French, of course. But you can get French food in London. What had you in mind?'

'I suppose the *Taverne du Passage* is still in business?'

'Of course,' Le Marchand drummed on his steering wheel in

approval. 'An excellent choice.'

Cheyney explained to Lewis:

'It's quite a simple place, sort of family restaurant. Serves very basic Flemish food. But the stew is one of the finest meals I've ever had. Great bloody big plates of yellow stew and steins of beer. That lifts my heart.'

'Good. We will go there then. You will enjoy it, I think, Monsieur Lewis. As the Colonel says, it is primitive, a – how do you say it – *fundamental* dish of the Flemish people and the speciality of the *Taverne*. Indeed it is good.'

He took a hand off the wheel to rub his stomach in a circular way.

'Ah. Here is the hotel.'

'Leave the bags,' said Le Marchand as he climbed out. They went up the steps of the old hotel – sited just behind the horrendous EEC skyscraper whose outer face of glass and steel suggested the hushed, carpeted and air-conditioned offices behind it – and into the lobby. The interior of the Grand contained many suggestions of the comfort, darkness, and warmth of more leisured times – the faded but richly patterned red carpet; the sweeping, gigantically broad spiral staircase at the other end of the lobby; the chandeliers. But on this now tired comfort modern additions had been superimposed. An elaborate Formica and glass reception desk was there now. There was a porter's cubbyhole in teak. Instead of individual and mountainous indoor plants there were carefully arranged modern displays of smaller varieties. The tables in the huge lobby – and in the expansive cocktail bar that could immediately be seen as one entered – were attended, not by waiters, but by trim, pretty and efficiently made up waitresses. Here, and uneasily, Cheyney thought, old Brussels was coming to terms with its reincarnation as an internationalist city. He liked the Grand, and felt sad that the change had come.

A tall, dark, black-coated man with a pronounced five o'clock shadow and startlingly large brown eyes came towards them. Clearly, he had been waiting. He brought his hands from behind his back and extended the right to Le Marchand. This was Marceau.

'I've left the bags in my car, *M'sieu*. Where should we go?'

'Thank you.'

The accent was heavy, but the English perfectly clear, and suggesting a considerable command. From Le Marchand's hand, and into his own left, Marceau took the keys of the Peugeot. He advanced on the other two.

'Monsieur Cheyney? Monsieur Lewis? I am delighted to welcome you. I hope I may be able to be of service.'

Then he turned within the tiny circle the four of them made and spoke to Le Marchand.

'If you go into the cocktail bar *M'sieu.* I have reserved your usual table in the far corner. I will join you in a moment.'

He moved slightly round again.

'I will bring your registration there, gentlemen, if you will be so good as to follow Monsieur Le Marchand.'

And then he glided away from them.

Cheyney and Lewis followed Le Marchand into the big, rectangular, cool bar. Again, there was that faint impression of old and new put together in uneasy propinquity. The walls in pale grey with gold leaf frames arranged to little apparent purpose. The chandeliers. An ancient carpet. But a spanking new bar, all glass and glittering bottles. Half a dozen or so expensive looking customers. Low tables of glass and tubular steel legs. Little bowls of olives and nuts on each table. An attractive waitress, pale lipstick, heavily made up eyes, false eyelashes, a foundation and more than a foundation on her cheeks and forehead, a musky perfume, coming up to them as they sat down and waiting, attentively, smiling, for an order.

Lewis hesitated, and Le Marchand advised him.

'Take spirits. We have curious regulations in this country about where, when and in what quantities they may be sold. You may not always be able to get them during your stay. But you may have what you wish now.'

He chuckled again, almost a falsetto this time.

'Gin and tonic, then.'

'Calvados and coffee,' said Cheyney.

'Ah,' Le Marchand grumbled in appreciation. 'And for me, my dear.'

The waitress returned with Marceau. In addition to the drinks they had already ordered, she brought an ice bucket, a half bottle of champagne and a glass. She opened the bottle, poured for the assistant manager, smiled delightfully, and withdrew.

Marceau waited until they had taken a first taste of their drinks. Then he tested his champagne. He reached out and handed Lewis and Cheyney a registration card each. 'At your leisure,' he murmured. Then he passed over their keys. 'You are in adjoining rooms. I trust there will have been no mistake about the luggage.'

Then he sat back and said:

'How can I help?'

'I have told M. Marceau,' Marchand said to Cheyney, 'that you are anxious to reconstruct Sir Henry Richmond's visits to Brussels as far as you can and he is, of course, more than willing to assist. Indeed, I trust he has already made preliminary investigations.'

Marceau performed the difficult feat of bowing while reclining in an armchair.

'Right,' said Cheyney. And to Marceau, 'Well?'

'I am desolated that it should become necessary to investigate Sir Henry, almost as desolated as I was to learn of his – ah – demise.'

There was a subdued and effeminate theatricality about everything the man said and did. But he was direct enough, and evidently anxious to co-operate. Lewis wished that he could have seen as much willingness in English hoteliers on countless occasions in the past. Marceau was waiting.

Cheyney gave him no help. He, too, waited.

Cheyney and Lewis both – as they afterwards agreed – detected at this moment a suppressed, inquisitive, almost chortling air about the man. Marceau took a drop more of his champagne and shrugged gently.

'But you are not, of course, the first to inquire.'

Lewis heard himself say, 'What!' and felt his face dissolve, but he never before or again admired Cheyney so much as when he saw the bony, delicate face stay in exactly the same lines and the eyes retain their level look. He felt as though he had let the side down. Cheyney's silence forced Marceau, after a flickering glance towards Lewis, to continue.

'It was yesterday morning. Two men. Not, I am afraid, *hommes gentils.*'

This time Marceau bent his head well over his glass. It was as though he was putting words together. Then he looked up, and spoke to Cheyney.

'They sought to question the head porter, who came directly to me. I thought, M'sieu, that they were divorce detectives. They had, Maurice told me, such an appearance. And Sir Henry, although he has been here regularly for years, has not for a long time brought his lady. We are very discreet here, M'sieu.'

'I'm sure of it,' said Cheyney, and little puckered lines of concentration appeared along his forehead. 'Is everybody discreet?'

Marceau gave his delicate shrug.

'Maurice, certainly. Other of the staff who knew Sir Henry, I cannot say. But these men were here only a short while. And they have not come back. Maurice has kept watch.'

He looked down again, down and depressed.

'But I can promise nothing, you understand. M. Le Marchand did not telephone until last night, late. I had no reason to suspect anything except what every hotel manager must suspect.'

Lewis was becoming very impatient with the minutiae. 'Was there,' he heard himself say, 'anything to be discreet about? So far as Richmond was concerned?'

What was the look on Marceau's face? It was not discretion or deceit. It was not that veiled self-satisfaction, that delighted air of being about to spring a surprise, that had been there a moment ago. It was – Lewis saw it suddenly – uncertainty.

'There was,' he said slowly and carefully, 'the young lady.'

The breath came out of Lewis in a rush. Therefore, he almost spluttered. He drew it in again.

'*What* young lady?'

He was conscious that he had – and irritated with himself that he had – allowed his annoyance with the stately way in which Marceau was proceeding to get out of hand. He was angry. He wished he were back where he belonged, where his methods of questioning brought results, or at least stimulated reactions.

Cheyney quietly poured the remains of his Calvados into the remains of his coffee, swilled them round, and drained the cup. Le Marchand, silent so far, had already done the same.

'Well,' said Marceau, raising his hand. He waited until the girl appeared again. More coffee. More Calvados. More gin. No more champagne.

Marceau evidently enjoyed Lewis's reaction. He liked a gallery to play to, this man. Cheyney and Le Marchand were too remote, too distant for him. Cheyney was courteous, but withdrawn. Le Marchand was full of polite camaraderie; but it was studied. Lewis gave Marceau what he wanted, the kind of open and human and immediate reaction that he would never tolerate in himself. Lewis saw that he had given this reaction, and he resented it. However. He repeated:

'What young lady?'

'I tell you frankly, Mr Lewis' – Marceau was speaking directly to Lewis now: it was a kind of reward for his reaction – 'that she puzzled us. Or, rather, their relationship puzzled us. She called here, oh, perhaps three to four times. Sir Henry gave her dinner here one evening: we have excellent *cuisine.*'

He paused to let that important point go home.

'But they were not, how shall I put it?'

Marceau waved an elegant hand about and touched the top of his head.

'They did not seem *intime*. He did not hold her hand, or – shall I say it? – fondle her in any way. We thought she might be a niece. Or perhaps the daughter of a friend. And yet there was something else.'

On this note Marceau rested. He plainly felt that his major contribution had been made.

Le Marchand said:

'What did she look like?'

Cheyney said, at almost the same moment:

'How did he treat her? Describe them. Describe them together.'

Marceau's neat little hand inclined this way and that. He shrugged again, and tried to take both questions at once.

'She was young. Very young. Perhaps in her twenties. She was very clean, very neat. Not like a young person in that way at all. Long and dark hair. Very large eyes, brown. Not expensively dressed.'

He closed his eyes, as though he was remembering the girl; and perhaps he was.

'Cheaply dressed, in fact. But neatly. She was – is – very compact.'

103

'Good looking?' asked Lewis. 'Attractive?'

Marceau opened his eyes.

'How do you put it, Mr Lewis? Not my type.'

He looked at Cheyney. For the first time, and perhaps out of his own puzzlement, he seemed to be trying, honestly and hard.

'I cannot explain how they were together. Perhaps it is that when I see an older man, a distinguished client of the hotel with a young woman I expect . . . you know what I expect. He was very patient, very kindly with her. He was very *old* with her. It was not what I expect.'

He frowned. And then:

'Oh yes. She was a singer, I think.'

'A singer?' Lewis again, blundering away and unable to stop himself.

'Each time she came, except when she came for dinner, she carried a guitar. I believe . . . excuse me.'

Marceau got up, went into the hall. None of the others spoke while he was away. They sat there, digesting, wondering. He came back.

'I wished to check with Albert. My impression and his is that she always came for Sir Henry on Sundays, and that they went together to the *Parc National*.'

Le Marchand explained.

'Open air concerts. All day on Sunday.'

'It was always at a weekend that Sir Henry was here. For some time. After his business was concluded.'

'Tell me,' said Cheyney, 'and be frank please. What kind of guest was Sir Henry? Easy going? Difficult?'

Marceau looked at the fingernails of his right hand. Polished, Lewis noted with disgust. Manicured and polished.

'Not easy. He was not an easy guest.'

'But he was easy with this girl?'

'He was easy with the girl.'

And that was it.

'M'sieu Marceau,' said Le Marchand as they rose. 'I will send a police artist to see you this afternoon. I would be grateful if you, and anybody who saw this young lady, would help him to make a portrait of her. Also of the two men who called.'

Marceau nodded.

'I will arrange for that now. If you and Lewis want to change or unpack, Cheyney, I will meet you here in twenty minutes.'

Lewis a step behind, the two visitors trooped off to their rooms. When they arrived, Cheyney said:

'Come in a moment, will you?'

Lewis followed him in.

'You're unhappy, James. What is it?'

'Oh, shit. It's all too vague. That bloody fairy gets on my wick. What the hell are we doing anyway? Have we got anywhere? Answer, no.'

'Oh. I think we've come quite a long way, you know.'

Lewis stared at him. 'What have we found out?'

'Old Harry was his lovely self with the staff. And another self with this girl.'

Lewis was still belligerent.

'What does that prove?'

'It proves nothing. But it tells me something I had begun to suspect. There was more than one Harry.'

'That's typical of you lot. What the hell does it mean?'

Cheyney touched him on the shoulder.

'You're letting off steam. Go and unpack. You're doing very well.'

As a still potentially mutinous Lewis left Cheyney added:

'And be prepared for a pop concert tomorrow.'

CHAPTER THIRTEEN

CONCERT

It wasn't a pop concert. To Cheyney's and Lewis's relief, the open air music to which, it seemed, Harry Richmond and his friend repaired on Sundays was sweet and gentle. Le Marchand drove them as far as the gigantic steel and glass structure, built in the shape of an atom, which commemorated an occasion on which Brussels had been the site of an international scientific fair, and which now loomed over park and city alike. From there the three men, followed by four of the Belgian's officers, bore away to the left until they came to a clearing set among trees and surrounded by knobbly hills.

Here were perhaps two hundred people, mostly young, mostly scruffy, nearly all listening attentively to the plangent notes of a harpist seated at the other end of the clearing, on a raised platform. Lewis did not recognise the air; but Cheyney was surprised to find here, in the heart of a city as international as Geneva, the plaintive tones of a Western Irish lament. He was even more surprised when the harpist began to sing, in rich, sweet Gaelic.

Le Marchand led them to a seat while his men moved slowly through the crowd, walking and talking quietly, as though they, too, did not want to disturb the musicians with the dark errand that concerned them, on this clear, sharp and sunlit morning.

Indeed, it seemed to Lewis, there was an altogether superior technique of investigation at work here. He, Cheyney and Le Marchand sat quietly in the sun. The four members of the Belgian

106

police team were dressed like – to any but an experienced eye *looked* like – the people they were talking to. For a time Lewis watched them, filtering through from the outer to the inner ranks, moving in a meander towards the bandstand itself, where the harpist had been replaced by a young man in sweater, jeans, and a sharpened beard, playing a recorder. The member of the team would slip quietly down on his haunches beside a particular individual group. He would wait for the end of a tune. He would turn to the nearest of the group. He would speak. While the interval lasted, as the harpist flexed her fingers or the man playing his recorder blew through it and wiped the mouthpiece, he would produce the police sketch. Then – invariably as it seemed to Lewis – getting a brusque and bothered response he would wait through another number, and begin the talk again. It did not seem, though, as though they were getting anywhere.

Perhaps the technique was not that superior after all. Lewis would, himself, have done it differently. Either he would have sent one man Sunday after Sunday to infiltrate himself into the audience, find its constituent groupings, work closer and closer to the object, or he would have arrived with a team and a loudhailer, sought permission from whoever organised the whole affair, addressed the audience at large, and shown a blow-up of the police artist's picture. Either was routine. Either was the way one did such things. This was different. But . . .

Lewis dozed. It wasn't really the weather for it. But he dozed anyway. It was partly the sun, partly the fact that the three of them were shielded from any ambushing sharp breeze by the rock behind them, partly the almost mesmeric effect of the work going on below. He did not really sleep, but he moved into that half world between sleep and waking which has its delights as well as, occasionally, its horrors. The music pushed its way only a yard or two into his consciousness. It was a border to his reverie. It was not an accompaniment. It was not an intrusion either.

Lewis was not a musical man. A touch of Frank Sinatra, a little Billie Holliday when he was himself moved over some affair, Mary O'Hara when he wanted clean uplift. These were the points, the outposts, so to speak, of his position on music. At first, in the park in Belgium, he had thought, at least this music is quiet, not rackety. Now his soul of few tunes was responding to something quite different.

He noticed this. But it was, after all, part of the job. His mind moved gently upwards and away. It floated unsteadily and uncertainly over all this police work and music making. If Richmond's girl came here, if she played here, she couldn't be the tart of Lewis's original imagining. She couldn't be a dirty old man's plaything either. She certainly couldn't be a dirty *rich* old man's plaything. Not, Lewis supposed, that Richmond was rich. Nice alliteration that. But he would be rich to her. Again, he supposed. Part of the job.

But one of the nice things about this morning in Brussels was that he wasn't part of the job. Not really. He was a police sidekick, a police hanger-on, to Cheyney and Morgan and Davies. The excitement of Friday over his entry into their strange world, their strange language, their codesigns, all the things they knew about that he did not – like rules for retiring Civil Servants – evaporated in the sun. And he was not resentful. None of it seemed quite so exciting, so enticing, now, here with the music and the grass and the youngsters and the sun. And he wasn't, not really he wasn't, on duty. If he could put together the energy he would go and sit on the grass himself. Nevertheless, he had come to some perception of this girl. She had been, after all, his discovery, in a way. He had invented her and, lo and behold, she existed. Not as he'd thought she existed after seeing Sarah, not a nice bit of stuff for old Richmond to duck over here to, but a girl who played music in this park. The proof that she existed was the fact that those four men were down there looking for her and that that unshaven, nail-polished queer Marceau had dared to giggle about her.

Only they weren't down there looking for her. They were standing around the seat in a sort of hesitant half-circle. And Cheyney was awake and Le Marchand wide-awake. And Cheyney was looking down at him and grinning.

'Are you with us?'

Lewis very reluctantly agreed that he was.

Between the three men on the bench and the four men in the outer ring were two people, neither out of their early twenties. The young man was the one who had been playing the recorder. The girl was short, stocky, frizzy hair tied back with a scarf, long patchwork skirt, the feet of bare and unshaven legs protected by flip-flop sandals. They didn't look unfriendly. A little suspicious perhaps. But not unfriendly. Perhaps this technique of investigation really had merits, after all.

Why was Cheyney looking down at him? Of course. There was a woman there. Cheyney had risen to his feet. Le Marchand was doing so. He hadn't seen the immediate necessity, but he followed Cheyney. His politeness – that of it available – was to a colleague, not to somebody messy who happened to be of a different gender. In a way that combined embarrassment, anxiety to please and natural courtesy Lewis quickly followed Cheyney. That was over, then.

Cheyney spoke to Le Marchand and Le Marchand dismissed his men with thanks. The two youngsters watched the four salute and march away.

'Can I,' said Cheyney. There was no hesitation, no full stop, no difficulty in the way he said it. Le Marchand handed him the notes he had just been given. 'If,' said Cheyney, and moved his left hand slightly. Le Marchand said:

'If you could both join us for a *boc*? This is nothing official, you understand.'

The boy was American, the girl Australian. In their different accents they agreed and all five trooped away from the little park, around the corner, across the grass and into the building built like an atom. Still in silence they went through the weekend crowds – Le Marchand having bought tickets for all of them – up in the lift and into the bar.

'An extraordinary place, this,' said Le Marchand and asked them all what they would have to drink. While he was getting four tall beers and a Coca Cola for the girl the boy broke the business silence there had been. It had been telling on him: you could see that. It was telling on the girl too: her fingers were twitching at the patchwork skirt. The boy said, to Cheyney:

'What do you want with Jennie?'

'Jennie.'

Cheyney took out the sketch of the girl and looked at it. He put it down on the table between them, the calm eyes looking upwards and outwards at the boy and the girl.

'Jennie. That's her name? You're sure she's the girl we're looking for?'

The drinks came and the boy said, with an attempt at a shrug: 'She used to come here with the old man? Right? That's the one? Right?'

'Tell me about it, please.'

'What do you want her for? Jennie's done nothing wrong.'

He was uneasy now. You could see it. He took a swallow of his beer. He wiped his lip. Then he wiped his forehead. He glanced at the girl.

'I'm sure she hasn't.'

He convinced them. You could see that, too. Lewis sat there, trying not to look like a policeman. Le Marchand kept his glass in front of his face, adding to the disguise of his teeth, his moustache, his spectacles. Cheyney waited. Then the girl spoke, the twang of her voice emphasised by nervousness:

'She met him here. She's been coming for a year. She met him when he had his attack.'

'Tell me about that, please.'

'Well.'

The girl's hands left her skirt. She seemed to gain confidence as they came up to her middle and it all came out in a rush.

But before it could come the boy said:

'Two years, hon. Jennie's been coming for two years.'

'Yeah? Well. Anyway. A year or something like that ago Jennie'd finished and she was going home and this old fella collapsed and she went over to help him and, well, anyway, after that he used to come here, sometimes. With her, I mean. Dave'll tell you.'

A little, Lewis thought, affronted that the girl had spoken first, Dave took up the story.

'It's really about two years ago. We have this thing here, well, you saw it. Jennie came with one of the guys. She played the guitar a bit. Very nice. And there was this thing about the old guy, Carol told you. Then she used to go about with him.'

He sat back with relief. For him, for Carol, the story was all told.

Cheyney looked at Lewis and Lewis went for more beer and more Coca Cola. While he was away Cheyney fished out his cigarette case, offered it around – only the girl, Carol, took one – lit a cigarette and, just as Lewis came back, said:

'What was her name? Jennie, I mean.'

'Huh? Wilson. Wilson, I think.'

'Ah. Yes. But I meant, was she Jennifer or Jean?'

They looked blank.

'Was Jennie a diminutive? Was it short for something? Was it a pet name?'

Carol's face cleared and she spoke, again eagerly.

'Oh, I get it. No. Her name was Annabelle. She hated it, though. Annabelle Jane. And Wilson. Yes, that's right. Wilson.'

Christ, Lewis thought. Oh, holy jumping Jesus Christ. Anna.

Cheyney went on, slow, gentle, patient, considerate.

'You said she was going home when she met him, the old man. Where was home, please?'

'Look,' said Dave. 'Jennie hasn't been here for weeks. Months, really. What the hell do you guys want? I think it's time you told us.'

He looked almost endearingly truculent, his neat beard sticking out. He took a swallow of his beer and Carol reached out for his hand.

'I'm sure you're right. I will in a moment. But, just one more question please. Did you get to know the man, at all? The old man. What was he called?'

Dave meditated on whether this was a fair and diplomatic compromise. He decided it was. But, yet again, Carol spoke up for him.

'Harry. She called him Harry. He was a Sir or something.'

'I thought it might be. He's dead.'

Their young faces cleared. The death explained all to them. It explained the police. It explained these three. It explained the long thin man who was asking all the questions. What for Harry Richmond had been an ending, an ending of all things, what for Sarah had been perhaps a beginning, was for them, when it was reported to them, an easement, a justification, a relief, a closing of worry. They could relax now. The relaxation was almost tangible. It stood in the air. It could be heard in Dave's voice.

'You mean it's an inheritance or something?'

'Yes. That's the best way to put it. Something quite big. Only, you see, we must find her. Do you know where she is? Where's her home?'

They were wholly friendly now, eager to help, wanting to advantage their friend. But – you could see it in their clouded faces – they had nothing to help with.

'We haven't seen her for months. She hasn't been.'

Dave sensed the disappointment in the other three. He tried to repair it, make up for it.

'People come and go here. You know. They come and go. Jennie hasn't been around for months.'

Slow, again, Cheyney was. He was also careful.

'Can you help us find her?'

They looked first at each other. They were thinking at it. Carol spoke for them.

'Honestly, we don't know. No idea.'

Lewis was close to snapping. Cheyney went on at the same unwearying pace.

'I'm sorry. I don't quite understand. I thought you were friends.'

'Look.'

Dave came forward in his chair, bent almost double. He put his hands out to make a box. He splayed the fingers up and down.

'We just came together for the music. Some of us see one another through the week. But not everybody. We're remembering Jennie only because you asked. She was nice. She sang nice. And there was Harry. That was unusual. But I don't think, we don't think, there's anything else. We'd like her to get this bread but . . .'

He threw the splayed hands up on either side of his head.

'Tell me. What do you do? I mean, when you're not playing music?'

'Me? I work at Nato. Research. I'm a lawyer.'

'And – may I? – Carol, you?'

'I'm a student. I'm here on a grant.'

'Do either of you know what Jennie did?'

He had got them hustled up quickly over a hurdle or two, but if he expected any more information he was disappointed. They looked at one another, frowned, and Carol said:

'I think she was some kind of secretary.'

'But – forgive me, again. You said Jennie came here first with one of the chaps. Who? Is he still around?'

Their impenetrability, having foxed, was now beginning to irritate even Cheyney. Their otherness, and the otherness of their world, was beyond him. He wanted to turn to Lewis and say, you try, as one might speak to an animal trainer when one had been tried sorely by a recalcitrant beast. And he wanted to turn to Lewis only because Lewis was in his thirties, nearer in age to these young people than Cheyney himself, or Le Marchand. Dave was speaking.

'Look. I don't know. I don't remember. One of the guys, chaps, that's all.'

'I'm very grateful,' said Cheyney and stood up. They all stood up. Le Marchand took back his notes and told Dave and Carol that he might be in touch again: their addresses were at least known and available.

'Oh,' said Cheyney. 'Just one more thing.'

Polite, puzzled, they turned and looked back at him.

'Has anybody else been asking about Jennie?'

They looked at one another. They looked back at him. They shook their heads.

'And, just one last thing. Did either of you get to know Harry? Just my curiosity. I wondered what you thought of him.'

They looked at one another again.

'He seemed nice. He was just an old guy.'

And that was that.

CHAPTER FOURTEEN

CHELSEA

At just after nine that Sunday evening Cheyney's car trundled up Manresa Road and, at his instruction, stopped in the little private road outside his brother's house. Weary, depressed, lost, he grunted thanks to the driver and turned to the house. He almost stumbled into Charles's housekeeper, about to give an evening walk to the Invermuir spaniel, a friendly, jolly, bouncy, slightly overweight old thing but not, to Cheyney's mind, a dog at all.

Still, anything was better than his own company.

'Oh, sir. You're back.'

'Look here. I'd quite like a walk. Let me take the dog and you just drop my things in the house will you? Don't wait up. I've eaten, thank you very much.'

She was delighted. He could see it. She was relieved of the chore of the dog. She did not have to cater for Cheyney. And, after the trivial task of taking his things in she could go back to her comfortable basement flat and relax again. Desire was satisfied on both sides.

It was a long time since Cheyney had had a dog on a lead. Not since Bruce was in training. And then it was not a lead for taking a dog for a walk on: it was a thirty foot hemp affair, strictly for training only. So he took a few moments to adjust to the chain and leather affair he had in his hand now. Hand through the leather loop, fingers taking the chain, chain running down to the leather collar and the bouncing, excited . . . what was the animal called? . . . Bonny. Not a bad old thing, really, he thought grudgingly as

114

he waited for the housekeeper to get inside, but a casual dog, not a friend. Should get more exercise. Poor old thing, well fed, well looked after but, really, testimony only to Charles's unease in any house without animals. Not part of him at all.

Cheyney flexed the lead and thought about letting Bonny off for a run. But he didn't know the dog and he didn't know what she might do. He wanted a little air and something of a brood: she was an excuse. He didn't want to attend to her. So they set off and, in reparation to Bonny, Cheyney took her twice around the square before they settled down, a pint of bitter for Cheyney and – another gesture of guilt, this – a bag of crisps for the dog, outside the Princess of Wales.

He had not handled Lewis well on that trip. Most definitely, he repeated to himself, he had not handled Lewis well over in Brussels. Lewis had really wanted to have a go at those two youngsters. He had wanted to spend hours with them, going again and again over every detail of their knowledge of Richmond and – what was one to call her? – the girl. Le Marchand probably wanted to do the same. Cheyney thought he had stiffened a bit when Dave and Carol moved off. He had been distinctly gruff over lunch, in a pointedly painstaking way noting down what he would do to attempt to follow up the trail of Jennie. Jobs. Offices. Passport control. Please tell all you can about one Annabelle Jane Wilson, commonly known as Jennie. Perhaps, though, known to one aged man as Anna. What did it all matter? Reviewing what he had done Cheyney was convinced that the bait laid out for this girl – if she existed, if she was true – was already sufficient. He had not laid the bait. Harry Richmond had laid the bait. But Cheyney had set the trap.

For him – he realised now – the whole visit to Brussels had been no more than an attempt further to delineate Harry Richmond's personality by getting a line or two into the shadowy portrait of this girl. He had known she was there from the moment in the pub when Lewis had suggested her existence. She was a key to all the puzzles about Harry that Cheyney had been setting himself for four and a half days, give or take a few hours. He felt, in his talk with that wretched pair of youngsters, that he had got somehow closer to her, closer thence to Harry, closer, further, to the answer to whatever was the question.

115

She did exist. To prove it he lifted his left hand from the dog's friendly tongue and took the drawing out of his breast pocket. It was dark, but there was a lot of light from the pub behind him. He knew, as he looked at the sketch, that no artist, however good, could draw a likeness of somebody he had never seen. But there was something here. Long hair. That was agreed. Carol and Dave had recognised her and Marceau had described her. It was fair. That was suggested by an outside line of black around a white space before you got to the head. It was a good head, small and trim. Level eyes. Very level. Honest eyes. A slightly tilted nose. A good little chin. A daughter.

That was it. It was a daughter's face. Not the face of a wife or a mistress or a girlfriend or a plaything. There was, there, the impalpable, special, wondrous thing. Perhaps, after all, Harry had really hated Charlie because he wasn't . . . *this*. Hate? Too strong a word. Disliked? Disowned? Despised? Something there.

Cheyney pulled himself together. This was, after all, only a sketch by somebody of somebody the first somebody had never seen. He was confusing it with all his own questions and memories about and of Richmond. And of Charlie. Time to stop, now. There would be enough detail tomorrow, with Davies's report on the hospital and all the consequent interviews, enough detail to satisfy even Lewis. And, again, Cheyney remembered how silent and abstracted he had been with Lewis since the morning drink; and thought he should have handled Lewis better.

He got up and Bonny bounced around again with the will and energy and good intentions of a dog to whom every move is a game. Time to go back and telephone Rachel, Cheyney thought. To say hello, of course. To say he missed her. Perhaps even to chunter out all his thoughts about Harry and Jennie. But none of that could be done on the telephone.

'Bah,' Cheyney said aloud and shook himself. They started back towards the house, a minute at the most away.

Remembering Bonny Cheyney bent down to her. The poor dog had been an excuse. He recalled that he thought she should have more exercise. And, guiltily, he slipped her lead just as they entered the little road to the house. She did not, as he had earlier feared she might, run off. She did not even frolic at any distance. She stayed close to him, still bouncing up and down and chortling and sniffing. No damn good after all.

The lead still dangling from his hand, he put the key in the lock, shoved the door open and called her. She had stopped this time, her first gesture of independence, and sat on the top step whining and thumping her tail. Cheyney faced her.

'Come.'

She had, after all, given him a warning. The blow came from behind, just over the left ear and across the side of his head. Perhaps – who can know – some very deep sense of preservation had recorded the dog's warning and he had been hit over the ear rather than across the head.

As it was he fell to his right, steadied himself on one knee against the door and then pivoted around on his left foot to swing the chain with extraordinary and savage force against the face of the man who had paused to watch the effect of his own blow.

Short as it was, the chain wrapped itself around the head. In the move Cheyney's fist came within an inch of the chin. The chain laid abrasions all the way up the cheekbone and, through the hair, around the back of the head. The clip normally attached to Bonny's collar cut open the forehead all the way down to the right eyelid; and it cut through the eyelid as well. Now on both knees, keeping himself from being flat on his face with his left hand, Cheyney saw his attacker stagger right back, throwing his hands up to his face with the reflex of anybody, even a professional, hit around there. But, because he could not, given the reflex, use his hands for purchase or his arms for balance he went all the way back, falling, finally, but saved by the stairs. He sat down, eventually, on the last step, buttocks perched, head in hands, stunned, bleeding, unmanned.

But there were two of them. Cheyney was getting to his feet, blood in his left eye and in his mind, the chain automatically swinging when he saw the other man, a smaller one this, one who had left the rough stuff to his companion. Cheyney saw, too, a hamper across the hall. Still in shock he turned slightly to his left. Hit by panic and the unexpected the smaller man did the best thing he could. He could not fight. He did not run back into the house. He dashed past Cheyney and into the silent square.

Cheyney had meant to hit him. Indeed, he turned with the man's movement, bringing the dog lead over again. But his own reflexes were awry. It was a feeble turn and a feeble swing, and he came nowhere near the escaper. But he ended up in a momentary parody of a moment ago facing outwards, down the steps, looking again at the still bouncing, worried, somewhat frantic little spaniel. Nobody had heard or seen a thing.

Following the parody Cheyney, like a man coming home very drunk, put his left hand against the doorpost.

'Come.'

Bonny rushed gratefully in and Cheyney swung round to follow her. When he spoke his voice was very thick.

'Not such a bad dog, then.'

What he did, and how he did it, for the next three minutes must be put down to his state of shock. He was very lucky that the man who had hit him was not a real fighter. He did not get up. He had no guts left. He sat moaning on the stairs. Bonny trotted over to him, sheered away again with animal instinct, and bolted off downstairs. Cheyney very carefully closed the door. He moved across the hall – it seemed like miles – and picked up the thing he had been hit with. It was a foot long piece of stitched leather, loaded with lead. He held it in his right hand – the hand still holding Bonny's lead – and said, 'Hell.' Then he put his left hand up to the side of his head and found the blood.

Again – again it seemed miles – he started across the hall and opened the hamper. Charles's treasures were there. Cheyney was too broken to make an inventory. But he saw the Monet from the study. Doubtful attribution, he remembered. He saw the ivory and – carefully packed – the Chinese Buddhas. Burglary, then. Or the pretence of it. Richmond's house again. Cheyney seemed to remember himself, sometime long ago and very, very far away, making a distinction between burglary and housebreaking. But this was not burglary. This was another lie. Another lie. That was the thing to hang on to.

For some reason he could not see what was in the hamper with both his eyes. He squinted. He realised that he really could not see out of the left eye. He thought about this. Then he realised it was because of the bruise and the blood. The bruise and the blood. He could manage the bruise. He had to do something about the blood.

This brought him round again in a circle, facing the small

washroom off the hall. It also brought the man sitting on the bottom of the stairs into focus. He was a big man, but fleshy, not really hard. In the back of his mind Cheyney found something to regret in that. The life force, you see, was starting to move in him again. Something very deep in him had been starting to say that, if rusty, Cheyney was still very good, very hot stuff, very well able to look after himself. He now knew – if he had not known when the second man ran – that he had not had first class opposition.

That made him angry. And he still had to do something about the blood.

Quite steadily now he walked across to the stairs. The man who had hit him flinched as Cheyney swung the lead again.

'If you move I will kill you. Do you understand that?'

The man moaned.

'Do you understand me, bastard? If you move I will kill you. Tell me you understand.'

The man tried to say something, but he couldn't. And then he came forward from his haunches and came down on his face.

'Stay there.'

Cheyney went into the little washroom. He ran both taps and stood there for a moment, the lead still around his wrist. Then he laved his face with hot water, cold water, hot water, cold again. He got a towel. With a convulsive effort he tore it in half. He soaked one half and tied it round his head in a turban. Then he soaked the other half and went back into the hall.

'Get up.'

The man moved, but only to groan.

Cheyney swung the lead across his shoulders.

'Up.'

Very slowly he got himself to a sitting position.

'Here.'

Cheyney threw the half towel across his face.

'Upstairs.'

Silence. A moan.

'Wipe your face.'

It was horrible, now. Much worse than Cheyney's. The right eye was both closed and open. The lower part of the lid was shut, but between it and the brow there was a gap. Cheyney had hurt the man much more than the man had hurt Cheyney.

'Up. Upstairs.'

Cheyney knew he had to make the man more afraid of what he might do than he was of his present pain. Cheyney was also worried. He wished he had a gun. He was not sure how much longer he could last himself. That was the real worry. So, with his left fist he hit the man. Then he slapped him.

'Up. Upstairs.'

Somehow, they went. The attacker crawled. Cheyney shambled behind him, swearing. They got into the big living room. Christ, thought the man of property in Cheyney, there's going to be a hell of a bill for all this, the carpet's ruined.

'Floor.'

Glad that he was not going to be hit again the man sat down. Cheyney lurched around the corner. He poured a tumbler full of whisky. He sat down. The man was showing a sign or two of life. Cheyney thought it time to stop that.

'Move again and I'll kill you. Got that?'

Whatever that was might be assent.

Cheyney had sat by the telephone. It took a heroic effort to remember the Department's duty number.

'Cheyney.'

He listened patiently, stoically, while he was asked for formal identification. He even remembered his own number. When they had gone through this the operator said:

'Sir. Are you hurt?'

'Yes. Morgan there? Davies there?'

A flurry. A patter. A scramble. Then – thank God, thank blessed bloody God – Tom was there. Working late. Doing something. Hell, anyway. There. Tom was there.

'Allen, for God's sake, what's going on?'

Cheyney put half the whisky down. It gave him a few moments of perfect and immediate lucidity.

'Tom. I've been hit. Now. I've got one of them. I want you, a doctor, support, Lewis and Bob Davies. All here, at my brother's house. Now.'

Morgan knew when to reassure, not talk.

'Support in ten minutes. Me, doctor, the rest shortly after. Are you shot?'

'No. Hit.'

'Can you hold?'

'Until relieved.'

'See you.'

But Cheyney wasn't sure that he could. He needed ascendancy now. Also, the whisky and the shock were both hitting him. He looked across and down at his victim.

'If you move I will kill you. Understand?'

This time he got a nod.

'Say it again. Say that you understand that if you move I will kill you.'

And they went on like this, the man on the floor and the man in the chair with the chain dog lead, until, twelve minutes later, one of two young policemen rang the doorbell and Cheyney got down to let them in.

CHAPTER FIFTEEN

INTERROGATION

Two of them. Cheyney had made his way carefully down the stairs, his years and his hurt catching up on him. And he had got as far as opening the door. There were two young constables there, uncertain, not quite authoritative, wondering what they should do immediately about the tall man with the bashed up face, the blood streaks down his left jaw, the wet, torn and now also stained towel tied around his head in a species of turban. Not easy, their decision.

'Colonel Cheyney?'

All very well to be given and to receive a priority instruction — not just go and investigate a disturbance but, if you do and find one, be very nice, be particularly polite, to any member of the walking wounded who happens to be Colonel Cheyney. Difficult to follow, instructions like that, particularly if you just did not know who Colonel Cheyney was or what he looked like.

'I'm Cheyney.'

Just as he said it a little red Triumph did a racing turn in from Manresa Road. All three of them looked. Cheyney was back, leaning against the doorpost, the two young men not sure whether they should be watching him or looking at the car.

Lewis got out. As he came around the bonnet of the car he pulled out his identification and established himself.

Between the two constables he saw Cheyney.

'My Christ. Allen.'

'Just as well you're here, James.'

Lewis caught him and Cheyney's head fell on his shoulder.

'Upstairs. One man.'

The policemen started up and they found the man sitting exactly where Cheyney had left him. They waited.

'Relieved,' Cheyney said to Lewis.

'What?'

'I've been relieved. Held the fort and all that.'

Afterwards Cheyney found that it had taken Lewis just under ten minutes from hearing Morgan's call to get from Queenstown Road to Chelsea Square. Cheyney thought he had been very lucky to get Morgan. He knew he had been luckier still that Lewis was at home, and that Lewis had moved so quickly. Lewis might, after all, have had a girl to come back to from Brussels. He had been buying hard enough at the airport shop.

Within half an hour the situation had begun to change considerably. Morgan had arrived, with two of the men the Department kept on duty around the clock. The constables had been sent on their way with many expressions of esteem. John Gravell, the doctor who doubled an already substantial income, through the retainer for which Tom Morgan signed the chits, had repaired Cheyney (to some extent: stitches were in, a pad applied and secured, Gravell's pleas for his patient to rest and endure further examination dismissed, but a thing like a trip hammer was still going away like mad inside his skull) and had started to work, with even more cluckings, on Cheyney's victim. One man remained with Gravell, the others waited downstairs. Cheyney, Lewis and Morgan repaired to another room and Cheyney, grasping (against Gravell's orders and in spite of his prayers) another tumbler of whisky, was filling the other two in on what had happened.

'Well,' said Lewis as he finished, 'there's nothing in his pockets to tell us who he is. Wallet, fifty pounds or so. Loose change. Cigarettes. Players. A flash lighter. A torch. The other chap must have done the actual breaking.'

He pulled his brows together. 'I'll get one of your men, Tom – if I may – off with this lot and the weapon and see what finger prints can do.'

'Sure. But I think we'll have to aim to get more, and more quickly, out of our friend next door.'

Lewis and Morgan went out. Left alone Cheyney put his glass down, fumbled a cigarette out of his case, lit it, and laid his head back on the armchair. He closed his eyes for a moment.

Shock. Shock, he decided to himself. That above all made him feel so weak. It was, after all, a year since he had lived a life in which, however infrequent the irruption of violence, it was something implicit in the way of life, something you always expect, something that might lie around any corner, wait behind every door. He had, after all, then, been unstrung by that year away. He had suffered worse hurt than this before and gone on functioning without a pause. He did not at all like this intrusion into his consciousness of news of his own vulnerability.

But awareness was followed by a rising tide of anger and determination. That was in his nature. There was something there which invariably and inevitably rose against circumstances, against hurt, against opposition to himself and whatever he was doing. He gritted his teeth and swore to and at himself for some moments. Then he took a deep swallow of the whisky and forced himself slowly to finish the cigarette. Then he did some deep breathing and got slowly but steadily to his feet and set off to investigate.

Lewis was coming up the stairs carrying a tray loaded with steaming mugs of black coffee. He had found the kitchen, then. Cheyney stood on the landing, waiting for him, resisting the urge to lean against a wall and noting to himself that the housekeeper was presumably still happily sleeping through it all. He even managed to open the door for Lewis.

In the big room a flushed Gravell was arranging his patient in an armchair. The man's jacket was off and his shirt torn away. His head and eyelid had presumably been stitched, and were now bandage-covered. Gravell turned.

'Colonel Cheyney. I cannot be responsible if you will not take some further precaution. You should have an injection, an X-ray and . . .'

Cheyney lifted his hand.

'Thank you for all you *have* done.'

Flushed still, and irritable, Gravell left them.

Morgan laughed and began to speak, but Lewis cut in across him:

'I've got it. Tom Farmer. Tom bloody Farmer.'

The man in the chair groaned and opened the one eye.

'Tom Farmer,' Lewis said again. 'A *very* tough bird. Minder. Thug. Hard man. In and out for most of his life. I know the bastard.'

He walked across and stood over Farmer. Then he kicked him sharply on the ankle.

'Wake up Farmer. Wake up. It's the Old Bill.'

Morgan's eyes met Cheyney's and he grinned.

'He's been given a shot of adrenalin. Should take effect in a minute or so. It'll keep him awake and able to talk for a few hours. As long, of course, as there's no fatal internal damage.'

'You can't fatally damage this one.' That was Lewis.

Cheyney thought it would not be unreasonable for him to sit down now. He did so, carefully, placing his glass and an ashtray alongside himself.

'Does who he is tell you anything about what he is? I'm sorry. I put that badly. I mean about what he was doing here tonight? Who he might be here for?'

Farmer was wide awake now. He was twitching convulsively, probably the effect of the drug, and the open eye was rolling around the three men. He recognised Lewis. You could see that. Frank, full, unquestionable terror came into the eye when it rested on Cheyney. By God, thought Cheyney, he had worked that all right after the blows had been exchanged. Whatever force there had been in him had convinced this roustabout that he could and would do what he threatened. And he would have, he remembered, with a touch of pride that further revived his spirits and his energy.

'Not really. Hired cosh, this one. Or knife. Or gun. Anybody's, if the money's right.'

'It's odd, though,' said Morgan, also finding himself a seat. 'Our friends don't usually hire private and local labour like this.'

'Our friends?'

'Russkies.'

'I never,' stuttered Farmer from the chair. He had recovered substantially, that was clear, and he was following their exchanges. Whether it was the result of innate stamina or the effect of the drug they did not know. But, in pain though he was, frightened though he still was, he was coming round rapidly. It would be important to find out whether it was that the adrenalin had lifted him out of his abyss of pain and fear or whether something natural to his constitution was beginning to assert itself.

Morgan seemed to think so too. He got up and rubbed out his cigarette. He said to Lewis:

'James. If your training or your principles forbid anything of what follows you could get some more coffee.'

Cheyney remembered his coffee and swallowed some.

Lewis remained where he was.

'Can't make more of a mess of this nice room.'

Morgan stood looking pensively around.

'Attic,' said Cheyney. 'Used as a workshop.'

Morgan brightened. 'Lovely. Tools and all that sort of thing. Lots to stimulate the imagination.'

He went and stood over Farmer.

'Farmer, my boy. You and I are going to take a little walk. I'd prefer it if you were good enough to talk before you walk. Because every step away from that chair is going to make me madder. So it'll hurt more and more until you do talk.'

Then he walked away to another chair. Cheyney and Lewis watched the way Farmer's eye followed him: even the head was shifted around. But the fear seemed to be dying in the man's eyes now. Maybe he was going to make it hard for Morgan after all.

It was always a difficult question how professional bullies reacted to receiving their own treatment. Farmer was a big man, as tall as Cheyney, not as tall as Morgan, but about as broad. Obviously, and especially in his present condition, he was no match for Morgan. But that eye – again the question about the effect of the drug and the fundamental quality of the man himself – was ferociously alive now, hungry and vivid and aware and feverish. More often than not men like Farmer, who had held the crown of whatever road they had walked on all their lives, folded quite quickly. But there were exceptions. Farmer might be one of them. And Cheyney was conscious, from some impulse coming up from deep inside his brain, that their time was very short.

Morgan took his jacket off and folded it neatly across the chair. He followed it with his tie. Then he took off his shirt. It, too, was neatly folded and laid on top of the other clothes.

When he turned around the muscles rippled smoothly under his hairy torso. He looked powerful and menacing. Lewis shivered.

'Fuck off,' said Farmer.

He was looking right up at Morgan.

'We mustn't have you screaming and waking all the nice neighbours, must we?' Morgan asked thoughtfully. 'Let's see.'

He hit Farmer across the throat, not lightly, but not hard. Farmer gasped and gurgled and brought both hands up to his throat, retching.

'Cricoid cartilage gone, I should think. But you have a voice, haven't you? Otherwise you wouldn't be able to tell me what you know. Oh, and by the way, no rough language in my presence. You call me sir, always.'

With his left hand Morgan smacked the man sharply across the bandaged eye. Farmer tried to scream then, but it came out as a wail, hardly audible even in the spacious, empty, garden below them. If audible it would probably sound like a child's night time wail, the scared and somewhat hoarse product of a bad dream.

But there was a bit left in Farmer. He came out of the chair in something between a lunge and a lurch and groped for the tormentor. Morgan brushed down the left arm, sidestepped, took hold of Farmer's hair, rabbit-punched him twice across the kidneys and kneed him hard in the backside. He went down on his face, already half way to the door.

'Wait,' said Lewis, almost involuntarily.

'You know where the kitchen is if you want more coffee.' Then to Cheyney:

'The attic, you say, Allen?'

'The attic.'

'Up, you.' Morgan kicked Farmer again. The man got as far as all fours and Morgan hauled him up the rest of the way by his hair. Farmer tried to scream again, but again he could get out only the dreadful, gurgling, hoarse falsetto, absurd as well as horrible in a man of his size.

'Get. I've just started.'

Morgan pushed him forward. As he staggered Morgan went down in a sort of soccer sliding tackle and tripped him.

'Up, I said.'

'No.' The voice was strangled now not only by the result of the blow on the windpipe, but by the carpet. 'I'll tell you, for fuck's sake.'

Morgan reached over and slapped him again.

'No bad language. And 'sir' to you. On your feet.'

Even Cheyney felt some pity as Farmer struggled to obey. He knew, as perhaps Lewis did not, that this method of preliminary interrogation – called 'crash course' in the training school – was a judicious and tried way of establishing both physical and moral ascendancy over a man in shock and under drugs. It was less brutal than it looked. It was the effect on the victim that made it appear exceptionally cruel. It was a careful – a traditional, almost a ritualistic – combination of blows and orders. The stuff about Farmer not using bad language and calling Tom 'sir' was part of the package. Real physical torture was a much more bitter, vicious and prolonged affair. So was real brain-washing. But they took more time than they had. Looking at Lewis's strained face Cheyney wished he could explain all that to him. Somebody of Farmer's presumably robust physique and presumably low intellectual acuity (most toughies were so made) would take little enough time to recover from Tom's drubbing. His pain would start only if they didn't get what they wanted now.

Anyway, he got to his feet. Hands and knees first. Then one knee, one hand still on the floor. Then up. Then stagger. Then hands by his side. Actually, standing gave him an infusion of morale. He hesitated.

'Tell him, for God's sake,' said Lewis sharply.

Farmer yielded to that plea, as he had not quite yielded to the beating.

'Harry Moore it was with me,' he began in that strangled child's voice that was the only one he had for the moment, and added 'Sir', very quickly. 'Harry Moore and me did over the drum.'

'Cracksman,' said Lewis without being asked. 'Very good. Very expensive. The one that got away.'

'Get on with it.'

'It was a funny job from the start.' Farmer was almost resentful. 'We was to take what we could get and knock over this, eh, this gentleman here.'

'Kill him?'

'Harry on a killing?'

Lewis did not believe him.

'Kill him?'

It looked as though Farmer had called up judge and jury before his mind's eye at that moment. Then he looked at Morgan again and gave in. It was often like this. Once they started they could hardly stop.

'Yes sir. No sir.'

The second sir was for Lewis. The bully boy was obviously trying, even in his pain, to propitiate these terrible beings who had trapped him.

'I mean, sir. I mean Harry wasn't to know I was to, well, I was to, I was to . . .'

'Kill, ah, this gentleman?'

Morgan helped him out this time and Farmer looked grateful.

'That's right. Just a bit of rough stuff, see?' He looked at Lewis with, suddenly, an almost comically academic air. 'Harry's not above a bit o' rough stuff, see? Long as I'm around.'

Cheyney, at least, could see. Pity he hadn't managed to take the evasive, fast-moving Mr Moore.

'So.' Morgan was impatient now. 'You were to take what you could get in the house, kill Mr Cheyney and, presumably, get a fee on top.'

'Yes sir. Fee for me that is, sir. Harry just got the stuff. Christ, can I have a drink?'

'No. What was the fee?'

Farmer had one hand to his eye, one to his kidneys. He was almost prancing with pain. 'A grand.'

'Is that all I'm worth?'

Cheyney chuckled this time.

'Who,' said Morgan remorselessly, 'who hired you? When? Where? Who?'

'In the Skinner's Arms. Friday. Bertie Booth, it was, fuck him. Sorry, sir.' He almost came to attention.

'Grafter,' said Lewis as the other two looked at him. 'Only a few convictions. Sets up jobs.'

'Get him,' said Cheyney through his teeth. 'Get him here. Now.'

Lewis and Morgan hesitated a moment between themselves. It

was not a hesitation of doubt. It was a question about who would do what.

'You can find him?'

Lewis nodded and went to the telephone.

Morgan called, 'Smith,' and Smith came in.

'Take this, this fellow, away and keep him under wraps.'

Then Morgan went to stand by Lewis at the telephone. Cheyney sighed, long and softly. He thought that he had not yet telephoned Rachel. He thought he would do so in a minute. He took another swallow of whisky and one of coffee. He drew on his cigarette as he looked at Morgan and Lewis together by the telephone. Lewis would find out where Booth was. Morgan would get him. Nothing for Cheyney to do just now. So he drifted off into sleep.

They woke him just less than two hours later to tell him that they had found Albert Francis Booth, grafter, setter-up of jobs, dead.

CHAPTER SIXTEEN

SHE

'At least we begin to know what we are up against.'

That, Lewis recalled just before they assembled the next morning, was all of substance that Cheyney had said when they woke him up. He had politely and distantly responded to their mutterings and seen them off the premises, telling them that he would slightly delay their Monday morning meeting.

That was all. A team from the Department would, of course, see to the cleaning of the house. What Cheyney would say to its still invisible guardian they had no idea. That he would still have some protection Morgan sought to ensure by leaving a man, armed, in a car, outside the house. In none of this had Cheyney taken much interest. Once woken and apprised of Booth's death – cut down by a hit and run driver just outside the drinking club he normally inhabited until the early hours – he had seemed to drift off into some world of his own. And the only satisfaction Lewis and Morgan got from him was the assurance that he would be at the office the following morning.

Their meeting had been scheduled for ten thirty. Lewis had scarcely been able to sleep that night after they had left Chelsea Square. He did not know whether he wanted to get to the meeting bang on time, only a minute or so to spare, so that they could get straight down to business without his having to face the others or chat or talk to any of them before that business was reached, or whether he wanted to be there hours before Cheyney so that, if Morgan or Davies or both of them were already there he could

131

find out whether the fragile intimacy he thought had existed between the three of them a few days before was still alive. He wanted no chat nor gossip with Cheyney.

He could not explain his feelings. He was in too much of a turmoil on the drive home even to attempt to analyse them. He gave himself a stiff drink when he got in and sat down to the problem. It was with him most of the night and still there in the morning when he got up and made coffee and toast and looked out of his flat window into dear, battered old Queenstown Road. They were, perhaps, an attempt at a mix. There was all he had felt he had gained with these men up, at any rate, to Sunday night. He was pretty sure he wanted to keep that, with all its camaraderie and secrecy and hints of excitement. And, in repulsion, there was the horror of Sunday night itself.

Lewis was pretty sure he was not a softie. He had been hit himself. He had hit people. He had seen people badly beaten up and treated them with the same roughness that he had begun to use on Farmer. He knew all about brutal members of his own profession, men who wielded the truncheon too hard or who had roughed up suspects. He knew about them and, in a famous case, he had once helped root a bunch of them out. But he felt, most of the time, that he could understand what drove them, the sheer, terrible frustration of an over-worked, undermanned police force, a great certainty that you knew who the villains were and that things conspired against you when you went about nailing them.

But Cheyney's and Tom Morgan's violence was another thing altogether. He had been both disgusted and frightened by the way Tom Morgan had gone about Farmer. The expert, the clinical, way Morgan had made sure Farmer could still talk, but could not scream loudly enough to attract attention. The absolute lack of anger or hatred or viciousness or brutality of any kind in Morgan's face as he went about breaking a man already severely damaged. That was something altogether outside Lewis's experience, and it worried and scared him.

At eight o'clock Lewis poured himself another cup of coffee and put another slice of bread in the toaster. He was surprised, in a way, at his own repulsion. It was partly his police training, he supposed. That training had been offended, too, by the fact that while he had checked on Booth's hangabouts and likely whereabouts Morgan, as soon as he had finished, had taken over and actually sent the dogs out. In spite of himself, in spite of all that had been attracting him, Lewis did not like that at all.

And yet there was still the attraction. He bathed and shaved, trying to take himself through everything as slowly as possible so that events would make for him the decision about when he should get to Whitehall. For some reason there was a large part of him that wanted to be there as early as possible. It was perhaps the sort of thing that had made Morgan be at the office last night when Cheyney had telephoned. It was maybe the sort of thing that kept Lewis himself often very late at the nick when something was going on. Or maybe it was his concern about Cheyney. Curious, that. In his feelings Cheyney did not seem to be a part of whatever it was that was repelling him. He could just recall the dominant, coiled man he had gone to Brussels with and then the twisted, drawn face that fell on his shoulder and, later, the white, hammered face of the man sitting in the armchair. He wanted to know how Cheyney was.

Then, all his personal and household tasks were finished. And he had had another cup of coffee and a slow cigarette and it was still only nine o'clock. He listened to the nine o'clock news and there was, of course, nothing about Chelsea. There was nothing about Booth either. He just knew he could not stand the flat. Sod it, he thought. He put out his cigarette, washed the ashtray, and went down to his car.

Just about half past nine, just about an hour before they were supposed to meet, Lewis showed the pass they had given him at the entrance to the Department and, after it was checked, he was admitted. The truth was, he did not know what to do now. He took the lift and walked along the corridor to the set of rooms he and Cheyney shared. To get into *his* room you had to go through Cheyney's. To get to Cheyney's room you had to go past that nice-looking girl Morgan had parked on them. Outside her door Lewis stopped, undecided. Then he went in.

She was reading a newspaper. *The Times.* She stood up when he came in and looked a little frantically towards the inner door.

'Oh. Mr Lewis. Mr Cheyney is in there. He said – he asked – that nobody was to come in.'

This was an affront. Lewis felt it as such, and the sympathy he had preserved for Cheyney through his meanderings of night and morning evaporated very rapidly. Also, he did not like being given instructions like this by a pretty girl. A surly commissionaire, a tough NCO; either might have been acceptable. But not a girl.

On the other hand he didn't have anything to say to Cheyney. What did you say to a man who had been knocked about like that and was in the office in the morning before you were? If you had a great idea, well and good. But if you had got there only because you were restless, well, it just wasn't so easy. All Lewis's initial anger faded away. But he made a sort of comeback.

'He made it then?'

He was gratified to see that the girl looked, not surprised, but impressed. Lewis was checking on Cheyney. That was the message she had got. That was the message he instinctively wanted to convey. She was as impressionable as any WPC. Good.

'Good,' he said. 'I'll go along and see Mr Morgan, then. I suppose *he's* made it?'

Now they were sharing a joke. That was a successful move too.

'Oh yes. He did. Shall I show you?'

Meekly, prettily, she came out from behind her desk and showed him down a corridor, round a bend and into Miss Levison. Lewis almost quailed then, because Miss Levison looked very fierce. However, she asked him whether he wanted Morgan and showed him straight through. He had hardly a word to utter.

And then, to his delight, he found he did not have to pretend with Morgan. Morgan was sitting behind his desk and scowling, drinking coffee and smoking a cigarette. He did not look like the terrible figure of last night. He waved a hand at Lewis as though he was happy to see him.

'Come in, James. I thought you were the sort of bugger who'd be here early. Have you heard the Old Man's in? Help yourself to coffee. Over there.'

In an instant the tentative comradeship was re-established, hardened, almost set firm. Lewis got coffee and sat down.

'What's he doing? How did he do it?'

'I know. Looked bloody peaky last night, didn't he? Well. I got here at half eight. Cheyney had been here since seven, calling for half the bloody files in existence. He's sitting in there now, reading about Harry and Charlie Richmond and Zagreb. And he's reading all the current stuff about Moscow Central, you know, what the Russkies are doing in London now. Or, rather, what we think they're doing. I gather he created quite a flutter when he arrived, bandages and all that sort of thing. He's like that, James.'

'No doubt about it, then?'

'That it was the Russkies last night? I'd have said not. The only thing to be cheerful about, my dear James, is that we can take it as established that we know that. And we can therefore take it as established that we're on a trail. You haven't been wasting your time here.'

He gave his big grin.

'I never thought I had,' said Lewis, not really truthfully. But he felt rather confident. There were a great many questions he wanted to ask now. But he did not know which one to start with. He was forming one, but Morgan flowed on.

'The thing is, it might just have come off. But it was extraordinarily clumsy. You may have heard me say last night that they almost never employ local talent. If I had had any doubts that they'd done it last night they vanished with your little man Booth. Too many coincidences, certain evidence of enemy action. You know what I think, James?'

'No.'

That, at least was truthful.

'Cheyney knocked off in course of burglary . . .'

Lewis cut in, impatiently.

'I can see that, all right. Cheyney knocked off in course of burglary. You're supposed to think it was just that. Even if you don't you may not be able to do much about it. You may have your suspicions, but without Cheyney you can't do anything very much. *Ergo*, Cheyney's the key to this whole thing, whatever it is. *Ergo*, we have an investigator who is also the chief witness.'

'Right. If we knew what he's witness to. That's been the trouble from the very beginning. When we started on this thing it was a job to get him interested. But I've always been convinced that he was just what you say, the chief witness. Only the bugger can't remember anything about what he might be witness to. Why the hell d'ye think he came in this morning and asked for those files? He's trying to remember too.'

Morgan lit another cigarette. They were forged in comradeship now. They were excited, both of them. Lewis had forgotten his question. In unconscious reminiscence of Cheyney Morgan got up and rubbed his back.

'There's another thing, though. If Cheyney's the witness then it's all a long way back. Put that alongside the fact of last night's clumsiness. What do you get?'

'I don't know what you get.'

'One spymaster covering for another's operation. Look. Long way back Joe Bloggs – he may be Harry Richmond but I agree with Cheyney, I doubt it – is a traitor. His spymaster, the chap on the other side he works to, is Jack Brown. Long time passes. Brown goes to Siberia, retires to a *dacha*, I don't know. Bill Smith comes in. Bloggs may not even be operational now. But he's left successors. Anyway, Richmond remembers something. Cheyney remembers something. It's all about Brown's network. Smith must cover for Brown, fast. He hasn't got all the details, not immediately. But Richmond's dead, and he's told by *his* bosses that he must make Cheyney dead, PDQ.'

Lewis wasn't sure he captured all this in detail. But he got the sense of it.

'What have you done to protect Cheyney?'

'He's safe now. Once he got away last night, and came in here this morning, they'll guess he's rummaging. They'll know we guessed about last night. They'll suspect he's told things round here. They'll be worried that he's really remembered. I'll keep a watch on him. But after that operation last night there'll be a cut out. Now we don't have to worry about *Cheyney.*'

'Who, then? Who do we have to worry about?'

'Anybody connected with Richmond. That girl. That bloody girl. If she exists.'

The short hairs on the back of Lewis's neck shifted outwards. He was back with the terror of Morgan last night. Of course, he was accustomed to gangster threats to rub out witnesses. He had even known the threats to be fulfilled. But Morgan's words recalled Morgan's actions. Morgan's actions had been so detached, so clinical, so aseptic, so *complete* that Morgan's words now – though he was talking not of himself, but of the enemy – brought to mind homicide on a similarly complete scale. In this world, what life was safe? If the investigator was the witness, and the witness could be killed because he was an investigator, what investigator was not a witness? If Cheyney was now safe . . . But supposing Cheyney wasn't safe simply because he had looked at files? Or talked to any of them? If Cheyney wasn't safe, which of them was? And that poor girl out there somewhere? Lewis suddenly remembered his moment of happiness, of sheer joy and delight, his feeling – the detective's feeling – that he, having guessed at her, had struck gold in finding that she lived; he now thought that maybe he had sentenced her to death. He wished to his heart he had never thought of her. Richmond was lucky, being dead already.

'Are you all right, James?'

'Oh. Yes. Sure.'

He was picking up that damned elliptical vocabulary.

Morgan took their cups and went to get some more coffee.

Poor girl. Poor bloody, bloody girl. She might well be bloody pretty bloody soon. Bloody like Cheyney. Bloody like poor bloody Farmer. Poor bloody Farmer. Never in his life had Lewis thought even for a moment that he would have felt anything like this full-hearted sympathy for a man who had built his life on beating and maiming and even slaying. True, they had never got Farmer for a killing. But that did not mean that he had never killed, nor that they would not, one day, get him for killing somebody. But this – this was a way of dealing with business that was apart from anything he had ever known before.

'I wonder what you make of us?'

Morgan was quite gentle now. He had seen Lewis's turmoil. No. Too fine a point. He had seen Lewis's loss, and his fright. But Lewis was also a man. He was a man who had been pitchforked into something that, at the beginning, had looked like being at least interesting, intriguing, perhaps exciting. It had become a bit more than exciting. Then it had become a bit shattering, a bit frightening. But, whatever Tom Morgan had just seen in his face Lewis was damned if he would not make Morgan doubt whether he had ever seen it at all. So, mentally, he shelved the question he had been going to ask about Cheyney and, instead, did quite well by saying lightly:

'I don't know what to make of you. I was wondering where

Davies was.'

'In the bowels. Thrilled the old man came in early. Putting together his dossier on the hospital. You may have forgotten, but that's what our meeting this morning's supposed to be about. He'll have a speech ready for Allen.'

Morgan recollected.

'Sorry. I'm a bit strained myself. I don't want to seem to put old Bob down. He's the best there is. But at times like this, when I'm a bit strung up, and, damn it, yes, when I'm wondering what Allen's up to in that room, I play knockabout talkies. And I can't say I'm altogether pleased with Allen. He's taken over all my direct report system.'

He saw Lewis looking puzzled.

'It means he can ask direct questions of anybody who's working in the Department. Whatever they're working on. It also means that all reports go initially to him.'

Lewis understood that Morgan was irritated by all this. He also understood how big a man Tom Morgan was. Morgan was irritated, angry, felt useless in his own office, was glad of Lewis's company that morning.

But he did not really mind, perhaps because of what he thought of the old man, perhaps because of the job. Lewis was framing a question which might elucidate which when the buzzer on Morgan's desk went.

'All right,' said Morgan.

Then, to Lewis:

'He's ready now.'

It was just ten minutes past ten.

Neither Lewis nor Morgan were quite clear what they felt as they walked along the corridor. They did not speak, but there was a certain flow of thought between them. The flow was telling each man that he was the same kind as the other man. Lewis was vulnerable for the whole of this operation. Morgan had shown himself to be vulnerable that morning. But Morgan had not forgotten that Lewis had guessed at the girl; and Lewis had not forgotten how Morgan had behaved and what Morgan had done the previous evening. The scales were weighing down in Lewis's mind now. The horror and the fears had got together on a little train and were trundling away gently to the back of his mind.

There had, since, been the therapy of their conversation and there was, now, the anaesthetising effect of a walk down a corridor into an office for a meeting with a superior.

Lewis was beginning to rationalise his feelings and his instincts. A few minutes ago a scared voice in his head had been telling him that they might all be killed, that the girl might be killed, that he was in a war. Now he was beginning to see it, as he had seen it at the beginning, as something of an adventure for an Inspector of Police. It was not, of course, not now, a personal adventure, but something of an adventure of state. Equably, they passed the pretty girl and Lewis smiled at her, and they went into Cheyney's room. Davies was sitting there, table pulled over beside him like last time, files on it. 'Hospital', Lewis saw immediately, in big red letters. Teacher's pet, he thought.

Cheyney said, immediately:

'We've got the girl. Annabelle Jane Wilson.'

CHAPTER SEVENTEEN

ANNABELLE

After all, it had not been so difficult a task. The difficulty, the prevision, lay not in what they had done since Harry Richmond died, but in what Cheyney had done since Cheyney was attacked by Farmer. From Friday, two men had watched the crematorium. Four hours on, four hours off, in teams of two. It was the most unimaginably boring of assignments. To get to the job you had to drive through the Surrey town of Sutton, down a High street, turn right, and wait. Wait without being conspicuous. That was the rule. That was always the rule. The man in the car, parked the other side of the wrought iron gates and the tree from which dangled the sign identifying the garden of death, could at least smoke, even read a little. His companion who had gone over – or, in daylight, through – the gate, had to hunch miserably under laurels.

Then there was the problem of changing and spacing the cars. You could not, every day, have a car placed the same way, and in the same place. Yet, there was no cover for a car. When the rain started on the Saturday on which Cheyney and Lewis went to Brussels one of the watchers had to withdraw further up the road. He could pull into the drives or driveways of private houses beyond the crematorium garden. But he might be driven away. One woman rang the police. And the police, advised by Davies, moved the driver on to the next house. But it all lay, really, with the man in the laurels.

But a problem for you is always a problem for your enemy.

Again, Davies had taken up the point of Cheyney's instructions precisely. The hours at which the crematorium was open were themselves limited. The customers (Davies's word for the human being they were expected to find) could not come through the gate unless the gate was open. It seemed improbable that this customer would come over fences and across ditches. The man under the laurels had simply to follow the customer (specifications given) until he was sure he had the right one. Then, summon the car with the walkie-talkie and take goods back to base. No problem. Except a long, boring, pointless wait punctuated only by the exercise of ingenuity in placing motor cars and avoiding rain under laurels.

At six on Monday morning, though, Cheyney altered the instructions he had given before his trip to Brussels. (He had been at work an hour earlier than Morgan had imagined). This was, of course, after he had been attacked. He had been attacked after he had considered and found satisfactory a line of action which included the described methods of surveillance of a crematorium, and its garden. The fact of the attack was enough to redouble his efforts. He used the telephone, authority, good offices, anything that came to mind. The essence of what he did was, first, double the watchers – four men instead of two; and, second, send patrol cars from the three local police areas – including the Regional Crime Squad cars – touring round the roads and lanes that surrounded the crematorium. It is a matter of historical record that two cars with no satisfactory account of themselves to give were picked up. One driver and his passenger had to be released with a caution. Another driver and another passenger enjoyed diplomatic immunity. But from six in the morning to nine thirty, and in spite of the rain, there was a lot of activity on those roads, and two men under the laurels.

Just about the time Lewis sat down in Morgan's office, Annabelle Jane Wilson was driving her Mini against the traffic leaving the town for the city. She went as best she could through Sutton. Then she took the right hand turning and slowed the car down. She was looking for the place. She overshot it – even at twenty miles an hour. Then she realised what she had done, looked confidently over her shoulder, and started to reverse.

By the time she came back the gates were open. Having been

hampered by Sutton and annoyance with herself for having missed the place of the dead, she raced the car through the gates and pulled up only when she saw a building where – it seemed possible – she might find somebody who would tell her what she wanted to find out.

It was all of two hundred yards from the gate to that little building. Procter and Harrington tossed for it – quickly: they were professionals, even if both had been suffering the hospitality of the laurel bushes – and Procter lost. He ran a bit, and trotted a bit, and then walked a bit, so that he would not be completely breathless when he came up behind the girl who had driven the Mini. All the time, and with all his heart, he cursed the people who gave the orders. Even so, if the lady in the Mini had been attacked, if anything odd had happened, Procter would have been at least quite good.

It was a bit early for the caretaker, also.

Across twenty feet of gravel Procter watched the girl knock, look puzzled, pace about, knock again. He didn't want to upset her in any way. Walking across gravel might upset her. She might think he was the attendant she was looking for. He had to time his walk, though, so that he could hear her inquiry.

A man came out. Procter measured him immediately. About fifty. Well set up. Early retirement. Or redundancy. Doing a job. Makes up the mortgage or alimony payments. As he started to walk – the damn gravel afflicted his own hearing – he failed to grasp what the girl was saying. But he heard, well enough, what the attendant was saying.

He heard and he saw and he assessed the personality there. Man whose eyes flickered over and past the girl to see another customer, another inquirer, coming. Too much work this early on Monday morning.

She was – to Procter at least – the sort of girl who passes you in a street. She wasn't – Procter saw this too – a particularly tidy or a particularly pretty girl. She had long, ash-blonde hair, thrown back over a kind of cape thing with holes for the arms rather than sleeves, that she was wearing. Only when it moved slightly could he see her face. A bit too long for his taste. But clean, as best as he could see as he came across the gravel. The eyelashes were long. She was wearing trousers, so he could not see her legs.

What he heard the attendant say was:

'I'm very sorry to hear that, ma'am, miss. Oh, thank you, miss. You see, miss, the ashes were scattered. That was the wish of Lady Richmond. But there is a memorial here. I will show it to you, Miss. Just this way, please, Miss.'

Following him, she turned to her left.

It must have been a damn good tip, Procter thought. The attendant wasn't looking at Procter any more. As she turned, though, Procter saw that she was carrying, in her left hand, a very small bunch of flowers. Procter waited outside the little office until the attendant came back. He had had good work done for him, had Procter. So he was able to say:

'I want to pay my respects at Lady Greenwood's memorial. Can you show me there?'

He gave the man a pound. Indent for a fiver, he thought.

The morning was going to be profitable, Procter thought the attendant thought. The attendant took Procter to the memorial stone of another soul who had had ashes scattered all over this little park, a single thing left to show that they had existed, perhaps not left by their own will but by the will of others who had followed after them, and who feared they would go the same way and without memory.

Lady Greenwood's little stone was just beside Harry Richmond's little stone. And when Procter found himself a few feet to the right of the girl he – although he was a prosaic man – foreswore the fiver.

It wasn't because she was beautiful. Probably it was because she was young and crying. There was a fine mist of rain all over the place – and Procter had suffered from it under the laurels. It fell over and clung to the girl's hair. Her face had been very well made up before she had come here. But now she was crying and some rain at least was falling. The thing she had used on her eyes was coming down below them, right down her cheeks, in streaks of blue. The lipstick, at least, was indelible. That was still there. That could hardly be moved. As she stood there, though, her hair was becoming wetter, her face was becoming more streaked, she was sagging more and more. But her crying – quiet but still, almost uncontrollable – was becoming more vibrant. With the best will in the world – and Procter now had the best will in the world – it was hard to know what to do next. Especially when you knew of all those instructions from London, and all those cars about the place, and the gun under your arm, and your walkie-talkie.

Procter had watched lots of places and seen lots of ladies and become hardened to sorrow. But this morning, in this place, doing this watch, he felt troubled. He was a good man, so he reacted to trouble the way he had been taught to react to trouble. He checked his gun and its looseness in its under-arm holster. He looked all around the landscape. The girl wasn't looking. The attendant had disappeared. So he risked a scan with the little binoculars he carried in an inside pocket, a scan over all that area covered by the new instructions that had come early that morning. Then he put his bunch of flowers – still quite fresh, that must be the atmosphere – down by Lady Greenwood's stone. He walked away a bit from the girl, and employed his last weapon. He called Harrington on the walkie-talkie.

'I've got her. Can you come up and organise the support?'

'It is she?'

Harrington was bloody supercilious, even under laurels.

'Fuck off. Cover the whole area. Make sure we're guarded all round. I'm going to talk to her in five minutes. Remember instructions? Don't bully. But I'd like to see you up here with a uniformed constable in six minutes. Got that?'

The voice crackled back and Procter wondered if she would notice. She did not.

'All security, Max. Who's in charge here, anyway?'

'Do it,' said Procter.

It seemed as though she drew the flowers from her left side. It wasn't much of a bunch. When the crematorium attendant first saw her get out of her little car, and when he saw the little bunch of flowers, not held so much in the hand as held against her side, he thought she could not be worth turning out too fast for. He did not really know what to make of her. Even their little bit of conversation got him no further. The abstract, casual, indifferent way she cut short their discussion and put a ten pound note into his hand changed his mind about her. It might have changed Procter's mind in a way quite different from the way Procter's mind had been moving.

144

If she could give a crematorium attendant a ten pound note she could have bought a bigger bunch of flowers. She had not. She stood there, picking leaf after leaf off her little bunch of primula, a bunch so small that it could easily be concealed, or at least, easily unnoticed, from or by, anybody she had passed on her way here. Procter had left his bunch by Lady Greenwood's stone. Most people left their bunches by little stones, or by urns, just as people left things and flowers by graves. She picked the petals off and threw them out over the lawn. The wind was against her, and most of the leaves flew back. But she went on throwing them all the same, crying, and throwing, and looking. She had been told by the attendant how Harry's ashes had been scattered, and she scattered all her flowers as well.

And all the time she cried. Procter thought she might be aware of him. But she was aware of nobody. Even when Harrington and the stipulated uniformed constable came up across the crunchy gravel she did not notice. She wasn't beautiful. She wasn't dramatic. She was just doing something. She did not know when Procter and Harrington and the constable came up to her that their first instinct, their first duty, was to stop her being killed.

'Excuse me,' said Procter, 'can we have a word, Miss?'

'Yes?'

There were three of them around her just then. Procter could look into the big violet, tear-filled eyes. But Harrington and the constable could see only the smooth, damp back of her head. These two made shift to come round, so that it looked, eventually, as though the three of them were crowding in on her. They did not mean to. They just were.

'I'm sorry, Miss. You were, er, mourning Sir Henry Richmond?'

For a moment she looked as though she would take flight. She threw her eyes this way and that, as though she sensed not only the three of them but all the other men around her and around the place. She took in the policeman most of all, and most clearly. You could see that. Her eyes settled on him for a second or two longer than on the others, even on Procter.

Procter showed his card. 'I'm sorry, Miss. I'll have to ask you to come with me, I'm afraid. It's a security matter.'

There is no good way to do these things. Perhaps Cheyney himself might have found a different approach. Perhaps not. But on a wet morning in a crematorium garden Procter was doing the best he could. He had kept his voice low, soft, sympathetic, seeking to gain her trust by manner if not through words. He wished her no harm, no damage, no upset, even. He had felt her sorrow. He had not understood it. But he had felt it. He tried to get that over to her as he stood there in the drizzle, his card held out in its polythene sheeting for her inspection.

'Why?'

She shot the word back at him. It was an unthought defiance.

The trouble was, he did not know why.

Just before she got difficult the policeman, unexpectedly, took over. He could not have been much older than she was. They were both much younger than either Harrington or Procter. But he had a warm, exuding air that neither of the other men had. Also, perhaps, she was exhausted by her grief, and ready to be taken in hand, if it was done the right way.

'Come along, now, Miss. You come with me in our car, and one of these gentlemen will drive your car. It's just into London, Miss. Not really very far. Do you come from London?'

'I drove down from there this morning.'

'Well, you know it's not far, then.'

By now, his arm under her elbow, he had her turned round and walking. Harrington threw his eyes up at Procter and they began to follow, feet crunching the gravel, remembering their job, looking about them, seeing the curious face of the crematorium attendant. Harrington was thinking of asking for the keys of the Mini when the policeman stopped, took them from her hand, turned around, gave them to Harrington and turned away again dismissively.

She made a little last stand.

'What's all this about?'

She said it when he had got her to the door of the police car and had stopped his patter to open the door.

'I don't know myself, Miss. But I'm sure it's nothing for you to worry about. Just a few questions they want to ask you up in London. Look, this gentleman will sit with you too, I expect it's about the grave, Miss.'

He got her into the back seat. Procter got in on the other side. He seated himself very carefully, feeling she was unbearably fragile. The young policeman patted her hand. Patted her hand, thought Procter, not believing. He let it go back to her lap as though he was reluctant. Then he tapped the driver on the shoulder.

'O.K., George. Whitehall.'

CHAPTER EIGHTEEN

ARRIVAL

'Got her,' said Lewis, 'what do you mean, got her?'

'Got her,' said Cheyney. 'She came to the crematorium this morning. Procter and Harrington picked her up. Thank you, Tom. She's on her way here, now.'

Cheyney still had a patch over his left temple. It was nothing more, really, than a bit of cottonwool held together by a strip of Elastoplast. It was the little bit of evidence remaining from the night before. If he took it off the scar the blow had made, and the marks of the stitches, would be more crudely obvious.

'Oh,' said Cheyney to Morgan, 'I organised a meeting of the JIC for tomorrow. Is that all right?'

Lewis felt stupid. He also felt angry.

'What do you mean, got her?'

Cheyney turned his head.

'James. Haven't you grasped? Miss Wilson is on her way here, now. Bob tells me that Harry's sister was called Anna. But that's of no moment now. I thought you'd all want to hear.'

'I'd like to hear,' said Morgan, 'about the JIC.'

Davies got up, pushed his glasses back, gathered his files.

'Leave the files, please, Bob.'

Cheyney's desk was littered with files. It was probably true that he had pulled nearly everything out from the basement, the bowels, as Morgan called them. Davies put the 'Hospital' file down to join their dusty fellows.

'I'll look at that shortly, Bob, thank you. Meanwhile, I'd like

148

you all to be on parade when this girl arrives.'

'Thank you,' he added.

Davies had to cross the room to leave it. He put the hospital file on Cheyney's desk and then, in a kindly way, took Lewis's arm. They went out together, leaving Cheyney and Morgan in the room.

'What's the JIC?' asked Lewis as soon as they were in the corridor.

'Oh. Nothing to worry about. Joint Intelligence Committee. Tom's a bit upset because the old man has pulled together a committee that early. HIS and OIS will be there, of course.'

'Hang on a minute,' said Lewis, and he hung on to Davies's sleeve. 'Stay now,' he said as though he was speaking to a dog. 'Could you just tell me what's going on? You might even tell me what I'm supposed to be doing here?'

'Well, I don't know that exactly. What you're supposed to be doing here, I mean. I've wondered about that myself. But he took a strong line, you know, at the beginning, about having a policeman on the strength.'

He stood there in the corridor, bright eyes looking over his glasses, rubbing the toe of his right shoe against the calf of his left leg. 'Come and have some coffee, James.'

They went into Davies's office.

'Is he always such a shit?'

Davies thought about this. Then:

'You're thinking of the girl?'

'I'm thinking about all of us.'

Davies brought over some coffee. He shook his head.

'You're thinking of the girl.'

There was the truth.

Lewis had never thought of himself as sentimental. If anything he thought of himself as a tough guy. Yet, he felt protective of this young woman whom he had never met, about whom he had hypothesised, about whom he felt his new colleagues – and particularly Cheyney – were being callous beyond reason.

Davies said:

'Listen to a lecture.'

He was bringing Lewis a coffee at the time, and looking his engaged but detached self when he was doing it. He sat opposite

Lewis. Lewis realised that he had to say whether he wanted to hear the lecture or not. He nodded.

'The way Allen works is special to himself. You are confused about these things – forgive me – because you haven't seen much of how we work before. You are also confused because you've decided to be on the side of this girl.'

Lewis took his coffee, thought, and said:

'I'd certainly like to meet her.'

'That,' said Davies, 'was just a clever remark.'

'What do you mean?'

'My dear James. Your last was a defensive remark. You are thinking of two things. You want to know – as I want to know – whether this Miss Wilson has the key to our little story. At the same time you are intrigued by her. Why do you think you lost your temper in there just now?'

'I did *not* lose my temper.'

'Don't be silly.'

The trouble about Davies was that he was genuinely disinterested. Once upon a time he had watched birds for a living. With Lewis, just now, he was filling in time. Lewis, to him, was as interesting as Cheyney; or Miss Wilson. Treason had the same configuration of interest.

He did not sit behind his desk. He sat on it. He rubbed that toe on that calf again. Lewis was not accustomed to that kind of treatment. He had begun to have mixed feelings about these people again. He was – he confessed it to himself – missing the police station where an Inspector was treated with a certain amount of deference. He did not know why he was here. And when he saw Davies looking down on him, on the desk, rubbing his calf, he felt more than a little lost.

'You lost your temper,' said Davies. 'Nothing to be ashamed of.'

Lewis was almost tempted to confide in the man. He did not, of course, know that inside the bland face was as sharply striking a triphammer as inside his own head. Davies had schooled himself over years, partly from the natural inclination that came from the long years at the Edward Grey School of Ornithology at Oxford, partly from hopes and ambitions frustrated, partly from that cold bit of impenetrability in his mind, to deal with people like Lewis

150

just the way he was dealing with Lewis now. But nothing could conceal the fact that they were both waiting. Nothing, that is, except the fact that neither would tell the other.

And where, Davies was wondering, was Tom Morgan? At no stage since Morgan had succeeded Cheyney had Davies felt even the remotest twinge of jealousy. Still, now, he wondered where Morgan was. He wondered, not from envy, but from the burning curiosity that was the most important part of his nature. He wondered, not from jealousy or envy of Tom Morgan for being his boss, or for being in on things, but because Tom Morgan, not being in his room, might be having access to knowledge that Davies did not have. And, to Davies, knowledge was almost all. For now he had to get by with Lewis.

Davies's eyes had moved. Lewis saw this and thought of two things. When the eyes moved he thought that Davies wanted to know. He also thought that, after all, they both wanted to know the same thing. It gave him a fellow feeling with Davies, and cooled his temper, as he realised that Davies, too, wanted at least to see the girl. It would be hard to say whether they just wanted to see her or whether they wanted to see what lay behind her – what, if any, mystery she could unveil. But Lewis's grasp of the fact that Davies's concern was the same, exactly the same, as his own pulled a comradeship out of the fact that they were both in the same room. So, this time, Lewis got up without invitation and got coffee for both of them.

Davies did not like comradeship. He felt he had calmed Lewis down when Lewis was snapping at Cheyney. He disliked the way Cheyney had appropriated his files. He felt, for a moment, that he was not appreciated enough. Yet, the remark he made expressed not only his resentment but his curiosity.

'You're responsible, you know. Thanks. I'd like just one lump of sugar, please. You're responsible because you invented her.'

'Come off it.'

'No. Truly, you did.'

'Come off it.'

Just then Lewis was more confident than Davies. When they had begun to walk down the corridor together, after – he confessed it to himself now – he had both lost his temper and felt bewildered, he had thought of Davies as something of an uncle.

Damn silly word. There was nothing Davies could teach him. He had seen a great deal more of hatred and horror and suffering than Davies had. He was sure of that, just then. He also, and this quite suddenly, saw that Davies's part in the operation had come to an end. The files were no longer so important. He was disposed to be charitable.

The two men, thus, had come quite close to hating one another. Davies got off his desk, walked around, and sat behind it. Then there was a soft buzz from his telephone. He picked it up, listened, put it down.

He sat for a moment. Then:

'Let's go.'

In an instant incipient dislike, possible hatred, dissolved. They went, together, back down that corridor, paused and went into Cheyney's new room.

Lewis was immediately disappointed. For a start, Tom Morgan was not there. In an obscure way this lowered the value of the tableau. They should all have been there. She should have had a reception committee. As it was she just had Cheyney; and Cheyney was just giving her a glass of sherry.

For another, and more important, thing Lewis could not see her attraction. Her hair was both long and straggly. She was wearing a sort of shift dress. Across Cheyney's desk there was thrown a coat of some kind. Her face, Lewis thought immediately, not just with the observation of a man, but with the observation of a policeman trained not just to notice, but to remember, was all planes. He was reacting, now, to what Davies had told him was his invention. All along, of course, deep in himself, he had known that was true. It had been what he was most pleased about. Still.

Cheyney was courtly.

'Miss Wilson. I'd like you to meet Mr Davies and Mr Lewis.'

He took her left elbow and guided her towards them.

Her eyes were frightened, startled.

In an even voice Cheyney went on.

'James. Miss Wilson is going to help us. Would you look after her, please? Bob, I want a word.'

Thus it all came back to Lewis. He moved towards the girl, not sure what he would do now; not sure what he was going to do; seeking guidance, but either not daring enough or too proud to ask for it. His mind was pulled between worry at how to deal with her and triumph at the fact that Davies was clearly being taken away from it all.

The best thing he could think of doing was to follow Cheyney's example, take her elbow and move her out of the office. Just as he had got her to the door, Cheyney called him back.

'Please don't leave the building. Miss Levison will show you where you can take Miss Wilson. I'd like you back here in an hour or so.'

Cheyney frowned, then. As he frowned Lewis was aware, again, of the previous night. The frown seemed to him to demonstrate the enormous effort of will that was required to keep Cheyney on his feet. Lewis felt a surge of confidence. Last night this man had put his head on Lewis's shoulder. Now he was handing the job over to Lewis.

'I have told Miss Wilson that you and she should talk about Sir Harry Richmond.'

'Certainly,' said Lewis.

He and the girl – his hand still on her elbow – left. He would not, probably, have felt so good, if he had heard Cheyney talk to Davies immediately after.

'Bob. She is not to leave here under any circumstances. Matthews has already been on to me. Tom is trying to deal with them now. I only hope to God we'll have enough time.'

'You trust Lewis?'

'It's not a matter of trusting him. I think he may be able to understand her. We're on the edge now, Bob.'

CHAPTER NINETEEN

TRYON

It wasn't, really, a very long walk but, with Miss Levison ahead of them, they didn't speak. She took them down the corridor, down a flight of stairs, and into a comfortable room. It was, really, a living room; but it had the shabby character of such rooms in institutions rather than homes, not so much a drabness as an unlived in quality. In even the most structured, the most carefully tended, of family rooms, the rooms of even the most barren personalities and the most unhappy families, there are ever individual traces. The newspaper, though it may be folded, is yesterday's or today's newspaper, the almost invisible rip in the upholstery has been made by the cat. If there are drinks they will be an individual assortment, perhaps including an unusual liqueur, a particularly vile cheap wine, a favourite beer, a preponderance of some such soft drink as bitter lemon. There will be, perhaps, a photograph, a piece of embroidery, a souvenir. It is never so with rooms attended by caretakers, used only for business, even when, as in this case, some departmental designer has sought to introduce a measure of comfort, a measure of homeliness, to serve a particular purpose.

Lewis saw immediately the character of the room into which they went, and its essential falseness. He saw, as well, that the girl saw it. He was accustomed to conducting his interrogations either in totally featureless rooms in police stations, or in private homes. He saw, now, a couple of armchairs and a sofa, a sideboard with magazines on it – magazines just such as one would find in a doctor's or dentist's waiting room – a television set, a tray of drinks and a coffee jug bubbling away, a chest in a corner with a cloth thrown over it. There was no suggestion of dust or neglect about the place, no hint of carelessness or inattention. The furniture, if not elegant, was adequate, and solid, and respectable. The carpet was quite decent. From the door Miss Levison switched on three table lamps. A bit airless, perhaps, but still comfortable. But, despite the comfort, it was a dead room, a room made just for such meetings between strangers as was now taking place, but a room which, for all the thought that had gone into preparing it for such meetings, inhibited rather than helped their progress.

Certainly, its first effect on Lewis was to make him doubt his capacity for what lay ahead, and even question Cheyney's motive and efficiency. Of course, it was all clear to him in his head. His anger against Cheyney for the inhuman way he spoke about the girl had been deflected by, dissipated against, the announcement of the tactical decision that Cheyney had already made, that Lewis would be the better man, the younger man, the man whose profession had kept him closer to ordinary human feelings, than were Cheyney or Morgan or Davies, the better man to question the girl. But as they came together into the strange room Lewis really doubted it.

Still, his actions showed a subconscious deference to Cheyney's judgment. He said thank you in the most formal and authoritative way to Miss Levison and thus successfully dismissed her. He touched Annabelle lightly on the elbow and guided her towards the sofa. He got her seated and he smiled and he offered her a drink.

She showed the tip of her tongue for a second as she ran it across her lips. Her eyes moved around the room.

'I think a drop of brandy would do no harm,' said Lewis and turned away from her, showing her his back and giving her time to compose herself. Whatever strange story was working its sinister or perhaps just opaque way out here he was certain (as certain, though he did not know it, as Cheyney was) that he had no guilty party here, no plotter or spy or traitor or villain. But the fact that he knew or guessed that all he had was a sad and now badly worried girl was no help. People of her age reacted in the most curious and often defiant of manners to situations like this. She was vulnerable just now because she had been caught in sorrow, and the sorrow was still with her: this Lewis knew by instinct. He did not have to have been at the crematorium when the men came up to her and found her and put her in a car and took her off to London. He knew he had the edge for the moment because any fear or indignation she might be beginning to feel was itself still undermined by the feelings that had taken her to the crematorium in the first place. He now wished he had been there when she came. This could all have started earlier, and he would have had a better chance of finding out what it was she knew, and what might be useful, even if he was not yet certain what it was he wanted to or had to find out, or even how he should begin to go about asking her.

He gave her a stiff brandy in a tumbler and smiled – he hoped encouragingly – at her. Then he went off to inspect the coffee pot. He found that there was an array of cups and saucers on a small tray, a covered jug of milk, and a bowl of sugar lumps in which there was a pair of tongs. He shunted all the cups and saucers but two of each on to the sideboard surface and fuelled the tray. This he brought back and put it on the coffee table. He returned for the coffee jug itself and then sat down, the low table between them. He watched as she took a sip of the brandy, then a deeper sip. Then she coughed, found a handkerchief, blew her nose, and tested the brandy again.

'How do you like your coffee? I hope you don't want tea.'

'Coffee's fine.' She had a low and quite musical voice. There was a very slight sort of crack, a kind of huskiness, in it that would certainly limit her range as a singer but which, within a fairly narrow band of sentimental songs, would give her a warm, and perhaps even smouldering, appeal. He looked at her directly and straightforwardly for the first time, and tried to make some assessment of her, not the way a detective did of a suspect or a witness, but the way a man did of a woman.

She was not beautiful, and she was certainly not pretty. But there was a distinct sweetness about her. It was not too readily evident in her present condition. She had made up and then she had been crying. You could see that, and you could see what a mess it had made of her face, her appearance, though not of her character. The character could be seen in the even and large grey eyes, in the strong chin and in the fine bones of the slender hands cupping the brandy glass. He went through the motions of pouring coffee and consulting her about colour and taste – white, one lump – while he digested this first full impression of her.

Since she was still holding the tumbler of brandy he pushed the coffee towards her rather than handing it across. The alcohol had brought some colour into her cheeks. It also had begun to restore a fundamental deepness and firmness of temperament.

'Look. What the hell is all this about?'

'I'm sorry. It must have been very upsetting for you.'

'Of course it was upsetting.' She was beginning to get angry now. 'How would you feel if you were visiting a friend's grave and the fuzz started jumping all over you? Do you suppose they've done something with my car, by the way?'

It was a well-bred, clear, trained voice, still with that distant touch of huskiness about it. The touch of the common in the slang word about his own profession – about himself – saddened Lewis. It was all wrong, he knew, to let little things like that get to him just at a time like this. But there was nothing he could do to help it, really. He had not had his bearings, truly, since he had been sent off to team up with Cheyney, and if, if, there was starting, somewhere deep down inside him, a feeling that would shortly come rushing up his chest and all the way into his head, that he knew exactly how to handle this interview, and exactly what they wanted to know, it was not enough to give him his bearings back, certainly not when he was sitting facing this girl in the strange and hostile room, and when she had just spoken in the language of her heedless generation about the fuzz.

Still, there was a certain fellow feeling between them as they sat in the room.

He decided to plunge.

'It wasn't a grave, exactly, was it? Your friend's, I mean. How well did you know Sir Henry Richmond?'

He was not prepared for her shock. He saw the shock, the widening eyes, the horror she suddenly had of him and for where she was trapped with him. He saw, in a part of a second, how casually brutal his enthusiasm might seem. He saw, too, that he had made her angry – wildly angry – and defiant. And, above all things, he did not want her to be defiant.

She pulled herself together and she kept her temper. She put her tumbler of brandy down and pushed away the coffee. It was clear – so her movements said – that she would accept no hospitality in this room. She still had her handbag, and she took a packet of cigarettes from it. Lewis immediately offered her a light. She refused, and found her own lighter. She lit the cigarette, puffed at it a bit, and looked at Lewis again. Her hands were shaking.

'It was a grave.'

Lewis had still not quite got rid of the idea that he could charm her. In the back of his head he knew he could not do it. There was also the conviction seeping through him that he would get her to tell him what it was she knew. She pushed all the things he had given her further away. The brandy, and the coffee, went quickly. He and she realised at the same moment that, before he went for the coffee, in fact, just as they came through the door, and just after they had got shot of Miss Levison, he had given her a cigarette. The ashtray and the cigarette were pushed away, too. He looked, quite carefully, at the ashtray she was moving away from her.

'Look,' she said, 'I don't know who you are. I don't know what you are. And I don't know what you want. But I don't like it. I want to see a solicitor.'

Lewis made his decision very quickly.

'I'm sorry if I upset you. In a moment I'll tell you what all this is about. But I think you should know, first of all, that we picked you up the way we did this morning because we were afraid for you. You might have been attacked, kidnapped.'

The wide eyes looked back at him in straight disbelief.

'Who would want to kidnap me?'

'Take your coffee. Please.'

Reluctantly, she did that.

'Colonel Cheyney – the man you met upstairs – was attacked only last night. In his house. He was badly hurt, and he was very lucky to get away at all.'

At least he had provoked some interest this time. And she did – he could see it – believe his story about Cheyney. He took this little advantage in both hands, and he ran with it.

'Just before he died Sir Harry asked to see Cheyney. There

seemed to be something he wanted to tell him. Cheyney is retired now, but he used to run one of the country's security departments. He lives in Scotland and he came down to see Richmond. By the time he got here Richmond was dead. But all sorts of odd things started to happen. Richmond's house was burgled, for one thing. I'm just a straight policeman, and I looked into that burglary. So they teamed me up with Cheyney. We started to look into what Richmond had been doing since his retirement, and we followed the trail to Belgium, which is where we came across traces of you. For reasons I needn't go into, Cheyney was convinced you would show up at the, the grave. Believe me we had that place drenched with security men: he was afraid for you.'

She was looking at him as though he was mad. But, as he paused and she looked, she started to believe him. It was not out of any innate regard for authority, not out of any respect for the forces that had plucked her away from her mourning and swept her up to Whitehall. Either she was not made in a way that had built such respect into her or it was something the influence of her generation – or, perhaps, her way of life to date – had extracted from her. There was a vulnerability about her, even a sort of fear, but it came from her circumstances, not really from her character. That character was strong and true and determined. So, if even a part of her had started only a little to believe Lewis now it must be because of something she knew. Lewis stayed careful, stayed polite.

'I'll be perfectly truthful with you. We have scarcely a glimmering of what Richmond wanted to tell Cheyney. We're hoping you can help us.'

She shook her head with, Lewis saw in dismay, an honest finality. If she knew anything she did not know she knew it. His house of cards – Cheyney's house of cards – looked in distinctly perilous condition. But he stayed careful. He stayed gentle.

She began to speak herself. 'How . . .' She stopped and gave him a sort of half-shy smile. Then she retrieved the tumbler of brandy and took another sip. Come, this wasn't going so badly after all.

'How did we find out about you?'

She nodded.

He told her about the Bruges postcard and about Davies's

work on Richmond's travelling schedules. He told her of their trip to Belgium and their investigations, and she followed what was basically a simple and almost, even, an elementary piece of work with that wonder at witchcraft which outsiders tend to display in the face of policework. Then she said:

'I honestly don't see how I can help you.'

'You appreciate that Richmond wanted Cheyney to know something?'

'Oh, yes.' Her hostility was all gone now, Lewis saw with relief. Either the bedside manner had worked, or the simple revelation of Richmond's request had been believed and had reached her. Anyway, now she was co-operating, trying to be helpful, looking both puzzled and thoughtful behind her cigarette smoke, thinking hard, but coming up with nothing. He thought he would risk another tack.

'Tell me, if you don't mind, about Richmond.'

'I don't mind.' For a moment she looked shining with feeling and, despite the contemptuous instinct at the back of his head which afflicts every young man who sees a young girl lost to an older man, a feeling in which disgust plays no small part, Lewis envied old Harry.

'He was just very different from anybody I had ever met before. He was wonderful and considerate and very ...'

She could not complete the sentence. She blushed and cried at the same time. Full of amazement, Lewis could not contain himself.

'That wasn't his reputation, you know. It wasn't the view of the people he worked with. Fairminded, intelligent people. They thought he was a bastard.'

He wondered if he had made a dreadful mistake when he saw the flash in her eyes. But she was even and confident when she answered him.

'I guessed he wasn't popular. Or he told me he wasn't. It doesn't matter. I met him when he was ill – but you know that – and I fell in love with him. I don't care what he was like before.'

She saw, or thought she saw, something in his eye.

'There was no dirty old man stuff about it. We were in love with one another and I knew, soon after the first time, that he didn't have long to live. I was very happy with what we had.'

'You knew about his wife?'

'I knew he had a wife. And I knew they weren't happy. But we never talked about it. He suggested leaving her, but I wouldn't let him. I tell you, I was happy with what we had, even if it was only for a short time. You can believe that or not. *I* don't care.'

There was such conviction and passion and sorrow and defiance in her face and in her voice, all at the same time, that nobody could not have believed her. Lewis believed her; and he said so. What, he wondered, would Cheyney and the others upstairs think of this technique of interrogation? And would they be getting impatient with him?

'What did you talk about?' he asked, partly out of genuine curiosity. 'About his work? I mean, his previous work? Your singing? What?'

'No. I'm sorry, but I don't think I can help you there. We almost never talked about his work, his past. We talked a bit about singing and, you know, things and places. We used to go up and down the river at Bruges in a boat, and go to concerts and have meals. And, and, go to bed.'

'That's all,' she added hurriedly, embarrassed and defiant at the same time, half-sorry she had mentioned sex, half daring him to draw the obvious, the almost inevitable conclusion a young man would draw.

Suddenly, Lewis felt both great illumination and great sadness. Suddenly, he was completely convinced. He could see it all, all that they had been pursuing, all that this girl's slowly articulated sentences implied. He could see a man, old and hard and experienced, at the end of a life lived within the constraints of a world of power, influence and order, seeing and finding all that he had missed and finding it not so much in but with this wonderful girl with the violet eyes and the toughly shy air. He remembered Sarah Richmond and shuddered: it could never – not ever, not even in the far past – have been for Harry and her like it had been for Harry and Annabelle. Contradictory, impossible, absurd it might all have seemed to, say, Lewis, if he had watched them in the same boat in Bruges, but true it all was nonetheless. And he was therefore sad that they could have had so little of it. He was angry with Cheyney and Davies and Morgan for the way they had talked about Harry Richmond.

'What are you doing that for?' she snapped as she saw his shudder, ready to be angry, ready to defend.

'I was thinking of his wife.' He held up a placatory hand. 'I see all you mean about him and you. I'm on your side.'

She was placated, and even gave him a little more. 'He had a sister he was very fond of. Sometimes he talked about her. She was called Anna and she was killed in the war.' She shook her head, having said it with the wondering air of one to whom the war was so far away and so long ago that one had to wonder how it was that one knew someone who had been bereaved in its course.

'Did he ever mention his son?'

'Oh, he talked about him quite a lot. That's an exception to what I said about what we talked about, the things we talked about. At the beginning he talked about his son a lot. All that, all the things that he did upset Harry. I think he never forgot them.'

Lewis's hackles started to rise. His newfound sympathy for and understanding of Harry Richmond was rapidly endangered. Annabelle did not notice the warning note in his voice when he asked her what Charlie Richmond had done: she was absorbed in memory.

'Oh, you know, going over to the Communists like that. It upset Harry very much his son running away to Moscow. He said it made him give up all his own ambitions. He even went to tell the Prime Minister he didn't want some big job, at the Treasury, I think. He never got over what Charlie did.'

Lewis felt he was going mad. It was a very great tribute both to his experience and his self-control that his outer expression did not waver. But inside his mind was in a turmoil, a turmoil of triumph because, accidentally, almost casually, he knew he had stumbled across what they were looking for; but a turmoil of puzzlement also, because she had so immediately and directly presented to him what he knew to be the opposite of the truth. What to do now?

He poured more coffee and looked at his hand to make sure that it did not tremble with excitement. He thought he would invent a little.

'He talked a lot about it, you say?'

'Oh, yes. I think it nearly broke his heart. I used to try to get

162

him to forget it. But he said he's never talked to anybody about it before. He said he supposed he was too proud. Even when he pulled out of that job, when he told the Prime Minister about it, he wouldn't give a reason. He said that. He said he'd never talked about it to anybody except me, ever since the policeman came to tell him what Charles had done and how it had to be kept covered up.'

Carefully, Lewis, go bloody carefully, here. It's amazing. She really hasn't an idea. She's just prattling on about it. He forced himself to lean back in the chair and say with mock severity:

'He shouldn't even have told you about it. I suppose he even told you who the policeman was?'

'Oh yes.' Artlessly now, artlessly she spoke. She really hasn't an idea. 'He wasn't really a policeman, I think. You know, he was one of the mystery men, like you. Special Branch or something. He had a funny name and Harry used to keep repeating it and saying what a bastard he was, how he had almost enjoyed telling Harry.'

Lewis waited a few more seconds and she realised that he wanted the name.

'Tryon,' she said, 'Emmanuel Tryon. It *was* a funny name.'

'Yes,' said Lewis, and he stood up. 'Look. Stay here a few minutes, will you? There's something I must see the Colonel about. Help yourself to brandy or coffee. I won't be long.'

He patted her on the shoulder and walked out. In the corridor he paused and ran the palm of his hand over his hair. Then he straightened his tie, lit a cigarette and walked slowly, with his heart thudding, down the corridors towards Cheyney. Tryon, whoever Tryon was, had lied to Richmond about his son. It must have been an amazingly risky proceeding, even if the risk was limited. After all, Cheyney had only started to talk to Harry about Charlie on an impulse. But Tryon must have had a motive. Tryon must be a traitor.

Lewis came into the room. The three of them were there, talking. They stopped as he came in and Morgan, more skilful in the matter of expressions and the reading of them than Annabelle, whistled and clapped his hands.

'Well,' said Cheyney, and stood up.

Lewis forced himself to deliver a proper, if abbreviated,

narrative.

'I don't have it all yet, but I thought you'd want to know about this straight away. Richmond never talked about his past life to her, except about two things, his sister and his son.'

That was gratifying enough so far. Cheyney was puzzled by that.

'In the matter of the son he went over the same thing again and again.'

He took a breath.

'He was deeply distressed, and remained so up to the end, by the fact that his son had defected to the Communists.'

It was, beyond doubt, a spectacular triumph. Cheyney, whom he had always seen so wooden, and who had so perfectly retained his self-control in that bloody hotel in Brussels, who had come in earlier than everybody else this morning after that beating he had had last night, Cheyney was dumbfounded. He sat back down in his chair again and banged the palms of his hands on the desk. Morgan and Davies exclaimed and Davies came over from the window to look at Lewis as though carefully inspecting some rare wild animal. Morgan said: 'Well. Jesus.'

'How?' Cheyney began.

'He was told,' Lewis hurried on. Though anxious not to lose the floor he was also anxious to finish. 'He was told by somebody with some authority. She thinks it was somebody from Special Branch, but it could be MI5 or even, I suppose, this Department. But she said, and I believe her, that somebody told Harry Richmond his son had defected, that it broke Richmond's heart, and that as a result he pulled out of the running for some job at the Treasury. I suppose that was the PUS job you were telling me about.'

Cheyney was the first to regain his composure.

'And did you manage to find out who this individual was?'

He was not best pleased, Lewis realised, whether because of the drama, or the shock or because he had let his control slip. But Lewis was not to be denied.

'Tryon,' he said. 'Emmanuel Tryon. She kept saying what a funny name it was.'

For some reason this produced another round of amazement and shock. But, quickly, Lewis saw that it was not just amazement and shock. There was bewilderment there and – what was it? – *disappointment*. It was just as though he had come to them and told them that the girl had nothing to tell them and they had been convinced. He could not understand.

'What's wrong?'

The other three exchanged helpless looks, and Cheyney gave Morgan a small nod. Morgan said:

'James, I'm sorry about this. Emmanuel Tryon was a senior MI5 investigator. *Was*. He was killed in a car accident two years ago.'

CHAPTER TWENTY

WITNESS

After nearly forty minutes of expostulation, argument, expressions of principle, definition of responsibilities and, much more important, definitions of rights and privileges, all of which had gone along with, been supported or hindered by, and had come into conflict with, seedier and pettier refusals on the part of one man or another to make concessions to still other men around the table – after all this, Tom Morgan laid his trump card on the table.

'The fact of the matter is that we have the witness.'

That was the hard and difficult thing the others had to face. Meetings of the Joint Intelligence Committee had never been among Morgan's favourite gatherings. In the old days he had gone along once or twice as Cheyney's deputy; and he had also gone sometimes with Cheyney. He had tried for a long time, after he had started to go alone, because he had now succeeded Cheyney and was the boss of the Department, if not to get to like these sessions at least to regard them as being of some importance. Even this morning, the morning after Lewis had brought them the news from Annabelle about Emmanuel Tryon, the *late* Emmanuel Tryon, once MI5's top interrogator, before he died and before MI5 itself had been revolutionised, even this morning Morgan had shaved carefully and put on a club tie and a dark suit and made sure his unruly hair was smooth. But none of his concessions had ever won any favour at this meeting; and he was winning none now. Cheyney had refused to come along so, for the first time, Morgan was experimenting with Cheyney's tactics, the tactics he had once seen Cheyney remorselessly employ, and he was laying down the law.

'I think,' said Matthews, 'that yours is an absurd position. You have accused a dead man of what amounts to treason ...'

Morgan cut in.

'I don't like my words in a mince. I say Tryon was a traitor.'

When the big reshuffle had taken place the lines had been, at least theoretically, drawn between the intelligence services for the last time. All the MIs had vanished, as had the Secret Intelligence Service. Matthews, thin and elegant and with an enormously high forehead had, from a position in the SIS, become the chief of HIS, the Home Intelligence Service. Under him now came almost every operation within the United Kingdom, including military intelligence and the Special Branch. Across the table from him was Harrison, a great spy in his day, everybody said, master of all the dirty politics of South East Asia, but now a large and bloated figure running OIS – Overseas Intelligence Services – eternally competing with Matthews over the details of the intelligence budget, but allied with Matthews on one matter, that they should get rid of the last remaining rival Department, once Cheyney's, now Morgan's. Among their allies was that sandy haired little figure at the other end of the table, the figure with the pepper and salt moustache, Brown, the head of the Special Branch, nominally Matthews's inferior, perhaps, Morgan often thought, much cleverer than Matthews.

Cheyney had never been a good committee man and Morgan, by temperament as well as training, followed him in his distaste. He felt lucky that Patterson, who had become Minister of Defence just before Cheyney's retirement, had adamantly insisted on the survival of Cheyney's and Morgan's Department, responsible to him and to the Prime Minister alone. Morgan felt lucky at this not only for his own sake but because he genuinely believed in Patterson's principle that there should always be a devil's advocate (or, as he put it, 'a lot of clever buggers') inside the Whitehall intelligence machine. His resources were small compared to those deployed by Harrison and Matthews, but he felt that his people were more genuine (more 'saintly' as Davies had once said), anyhow, more dedicated than the squabbling crew he saw around the table every time the JIC met.

This business about Richmond had been – still was, by God still was – a complicated enough business. Too complicated by far to have these idiots barging around the table about it. And yet, Morgan at once thought with some contrition, they were not idiots. Their Chairman certainly was not. He sat at the top of the table, Sir Leslie Fowler, the only genuine Civil Servant – so ran the decree Patterson and the Prime Minister had drafted together – allowed, apart from the spooks themselves, all of whom were on the Civil Service establishment – to attend JIC meetings. Sir Leslie, very tall and big-boned and with large and black eyes, was also Secretary to the Cabinet, and had the Prime Minister's whole trust.

Fowler said very little at their meetings, yet there was something about him that made Morgan except him even from the hasty strictures he laid on his other colleagues. While he was trying to work out what this was, Matthews was going on:

'That's precisely the point.'

That's a very good trick, thought Morgan. Usually, when you want to be offensive in British committees you begin by saying 'With respect' or, if you want to be really offensive, you say, 'With the greatest respect.' But it's cleverer by far to take up something the other man has said, tell him he's precisely right, expatiate at length and, just when everybody else has begun to forget the initial point, to make your own request, and even appeal to him for support. You can sometimes carry a whole committee that way. But it wasn't Cheyney's way, and it wasn't Tom Morgan's way.

He hoped, glancing at Harrison, that it would never be. Harrison, God knew, had been in the field. He had been out there on the very sharp end of things. The hardest place Tom Morgan had ever been was Aden, and that was simply as a soldier. How could Harrison go along with this endless prating, and sit there nodding and smoking and twiddling his pencil as Matthews droned on, Matthews who had probably never seen a gun not designed for shooting clay pigeons?

Morgan knew that Matthews and Harrison – and Brown for that matter – all now knew what had happened to Allen Cheyney in Chelsea. That piece of suffering, in Morgan's view, and the admittedly vicarious suffering of those who had been with Allen so soon after it had all happened, including that really gifted policeman Lewis, even though he was a man lacking a lot of self-confidence, entitled his side at this meeting to make all the strategic decisions now. He still could not understand why Allen had thought that the JIC meeting should go ahead; and he could not imagine why Allen would not attend it.

To his horror he now heard Matthews utter a version of what was going through his own head. Matthews, starting again, was interrupted again by the entry of a messenger with a note for Fowler. The whole table waited while Fowler opened the envelope, read the paper inside, returned it to the envelope, shook his head at the messenger and returned his eyes to Matthews.

Matthews said:

'Let me start again.'

Nasty little shit, thought Morgan.

'With the greatest respect to Tom Morgan here, I have to say that I resent his point about his Department having a witness – or, as I believe he said, *the* witness. I freely confess that I am astonished to hear the accusations Morgan has made against the late Commander Tryon. But I am perfectly prepared – happy, indeed – to have those accusations investigated, indeed, ventilated.'

Christ, that's not a smile, it's a smirk.

'But, surely, we should do this together? Our committee exists to detect treason and espionage. We are all colleagues in the same cause. Even now I have to say – with respect – that Morgan has been very close about things. All I know, and for *all* I know all that Harrison knows . . .'

Harrison nodded. Too quickly. Too readily.

'. . . is that the late Sir Henry Richmond asked to see Colonel Cheyney, that Morgan looked into this request, that Davies – who, of course, I'm glad to see with us this morning – has been pestering my Department for files. That's all I *know*. And now Morgan says he has a witness and he will not let my people, or Harrison's or Brown's, talk to this witness. Is it male or female, Morgan? Really, this is not the co-operation I had hoped for when this committee was set up. This is especially so when Morgan makes these accusations against Commander Tryon.'

He waved little white hands in the air and put them back on the table. But, having been in full flow he was not quite finished yet.

'I am sure I speak for all of us when I say that we want to co-operate. But co-operation cuts two ways. Really, Mr Chairman, Morgan cannot ask for our files and conceal his witness. All this without telling this committee anything he wants to do or propose. I repeat: that is not the spirit in which this committee was set up.'

He paused and made a typical gesture. He flicked the nails of his thumbs against the inside flesh of his second fingers, the ones next to the index fingers.

'I want to make a motion, Mr Chairman.'

Oh, God, no, thought Morgan. The schoolboy obscenities rose to his mind. The trouble is, his thoughts ran, that I don't trust a single man around this table, except for Bob Davies. In the course of a few seconds he went back through the horror that had begun when Matthews had started his big speech. Of course it should have been right for them all to do it together. But it was not just Cheyney hurt he had seen. He had seen only a day before the copper Lewis taking Annabelle away to the Department's single safe house, a farm in Berkshire. Lewis and Cheyney and Morgan himself had talked to her before she started on that journey. When Matthews waved his little white hands and looked out of his piggy eyes, the pupils darting towards Morgan and Davies, towards Harrison, towards Brown, but most often they darted several times in a sentence towards Fowler – sitting bored and brooding up there at the other end of the table – he, Morgan, knew he would never yield that girl to an interrogation committee.

'I move,' said Matthews, 'that we appoint a sub-committee of this committee. The files of all Departments will be open to the sub-committee, and the sub-committee will also question Morgan's witness. Naturally, on matters of interrogation, each Department will employ its own interrogators, their activities to be supervised by this committee.'

I wish Allen was here, thought Morgan. He would know how to deal with this. He had been badly put out when Cheyney had told him, over breakfast, that he would not be coming to the meeting. But they had gone over, together, all the things that might happen to be brought up. The danger, at the moment, was that Morgan was drifting away on a fog of remembering all that he had thought and argued about Harry Richmond, and all that he had seen when Lewis and Annabelle went away to Berkshire, and that he was beginning to be hypnotised by Matthews. Snake and bird, he thought.

When he spoke, though, and whatever his thoughts, Morgan handled it well. Also, he showed a better understanding of the reasons for the survival of his Department and the constitution of this committee than did Matthews.

'Does anybody wish to speak to this motion?'

That was Fowler.

'Yes,' said Morgan.

This was the grand occasion for laying it on the line and tearing apart on a committee on which he had sat for a year. It was also a time for making, and earning, enemies.

'I have a few points to make. As I said earlier, we have the witness. I want to make it absolutely clear to this committee . . .'

He was enjoying this. He was going through motions himself, but he was enjoying it. The potential obscenities of the dialogue were now pure delight. Whether he won or lost he was batting for himself, and he was batting, also, for the cause he felt he shared with Cheyney and Lewis and Davies, and almost anybody outside this committee. He went on:

'I want to make it completely clear. My Department will not give the witness up to any other Department, nor share in the interrogation of the witness, except at the specific instruction of the Prime Minister.'

'So,' said Harrison, 'it's a woman. Always thought old Harry had one tucked away.'

In his mind Morgan flashed a signal of respect. The old field hand had got it. The careful asexuality of his remarks had been penetrated. But he did not respond; and he went on.

'There are two things my Department now want to do.'

He had all the attention now. It was, essentially, his determination, the determination of a man who was putting everything on the line, and the sense they all had of that determination, that won their total attention. At that moment Tom Morgan took down another thought from a shelf in his head. It wasn't quite like the thoughts he had had in Loch Hill in

Scotland. It was more a judgment thought than a fact thought or a guess thought. It was to the effect that everybody here except himself and Bob and, maybe, Fowler, was weak and could be bullied, whatever their interests. And once that thought had been taken down and inspected and found valid, there was no stopping Morgan.

'First, I want to see all the files Tryon made when he was vetting people. For his whole career.'

'I understand . . .'

He looked at Davies and Davies nodded. This was a move to convince Matthews and Harrison that he and Davies knew more than they really did.

'. . . that these files may now be divided between different Departments. I want to see them all.'

There was an absolute silence now. Morgan nodded again to Davies. Davies said:

'Sir Harry Richmond wrote a note to the Prime Minister, and a note to the Head of the Home Civil Service, saying that he did not wish to be considered for the post of P.U.S. at the Treasury at a time when he was one of two very strong candidates and one of three possibilities. Our Department now wants to re-open the vetting procedures on the other two men, and to reconsider the question of whether or not they were or are security risks.'

The meeting was now thoroughly petrified. Shit, Morgan thought again, was Cheyney always right about these things? He had predicted every move of this meeting, and every reaction except Fowler's, for Fowler showed no reaction at all so far. From his left Davies passed the two pieces of paper, heavy yellow paper with a red flag on the top right corner of each sheet signifying the momentousness of his request. Morgan had to sign each of these pieces of paper to make his request formal. It was a long way from an old man dying, and an old man and a young girl, and a tough young policeman struck by that same young girl: but it was reality. Morgan signed, and pushed the papers along to Fowler.

'Who?' asked Matthews, himself mesmerised by the paper and the flags of red.

'Sir Richard Fleming, who so regularly visited Richmond in hospital,' said Morgan, 'and Lord Holmwood, now retired.'

'There must be some explanation of this,' said Matthews,

172

unwilling to give up. 'My motion still stands.'

'I should make the position perfectly clear,' said Morgan. And he relished what he was now saying. 'With respect to Matthews, I want to give a deep interrogation to Sir Richard Fleming, who is, after all, the present Permanent Under Secretary at the Treasury. Evidently, we cannot interrogate Lord Holmwood. Lord Holmwood is not only retired, but senile, and in a home for rich old people. But I want . . .'

Matthews started to speak. Morgan held up a finger.

He held up more than a finger. He bent his head and picked up his pencil. Allen had better be right on this thing. In picking up a pencil and pointing it one was being really brutal, almost vicious.

Suddenly, Fowler raised a hand, and muttered as though he was going to intervene. Morgan raised his left hand and brought it down on the table with a slap. There were many things he could say now, especially things in hatred. Instead he said what Allen had asked him to say:

'Whatever this meeting concludes I will keep my witness. I have formally made requests for interrogations and files. I will leave those things to the committee. I have to repeat, I will release my witness only on the direct instructions of the Prime Minister. And further, I ask formally and again for Tryon's files, and the right for my Department to, ah, examine Sir Richard Fleming.'

Now, thought Morgan, you could get past Cheyney. Now you could make a stand of your own.

Morgan made that stand, suddenly and to the horror of Bob Davies. This sudden way of working was not Davies's way.

'I have to insist . . .'

'Gentlemen,' said Fowler, in that peculiar voice of his that, while it had some of the characteristics of a corncrake, contrived nonetheless to sound smooth, 'I have been trying to interrupt your, ah, deliberations for some moments.'

He lifted a piece of paper, the piece of paper, Morgan saw, that he had been handed just after he had entered the room.

'Debate is pointless,' said Fowler coldly. 'I have just been instructed by the Prime Minister that all Mr Morgan's requests are to be acceded to. His Department is to retain custody of this witness, and he and his people will conduct any examinations that the situation seems to require.'

'Christ,' said Matthews. He turned his face to Morgan again. The complete and precipitate nature of his defeat was apparent to him, but it increased rather than reduced the belligerence evident in his face.

'Is it permitted for your colleagues to know just who is going to conduct your investigation?'

'Colonel Allen Cheyney.'

Interesting to see what an effect the name still had. There was resentment in every opposing face except that of Fowler, who revealed nothing. But they were impressed, too, and perhaps, Morgan thought, even a little worried. He could see the rapid calculation going on behind their eyes and, not for the first time, deplored the kind of sickness he saw in that calculation, and was disgusted by it. It was a sickness that caused men to lose sight of the object of their work. Everybody here – perhaps even Fowler, though it was impossible to tell anything about Fowler or what Fowler was thinking – was now calculating about, not the value or importance of what Cheyney might discover, but how his work and his discoveries might affect their position. They had hardly yet had time to consider how Morgan had brought off this coup.

Morgan suddenly realised that he did not know how he had done it either. Then Fowler enlightened them all.

'The Prime Minister is fully aware that Colonel Cheyney has been, ah, assisting Mr Morgan on this matter. I understand' – he looked right down the table at Morgan – 'that there was an accidental but important involvement in the affair on Cheyney's part from the beginning?' Fowler was being deliberately ponderous.

'Just so.'

'In any event, the Prime Minister has particularly requested that all the files in other Departments which Cheyney and Mr Morgan want to peruse should be delivered to them immediately. That is, by this afternoon.'

It was Harrison's turn to protest.

'But that's bloody impossible. We don't even know what's wanted.'

Davies spoke for the first time, leaning forward, scratching the toe of one shoe against the calf of the other leg, 'I have all the requisitions here.'

In the moments of their being passed over Fowler showed how he was an efficient chairman.

'Obviously there is much to do,' he said, standing up. 'We'd better adjourn immediately.'

But he did not quite adjourn. The others left with Davies and he gestured to Morgan to wait. Then he walked down the table.

'I fancy that, in the circumstances, we should not consider it too early for a drink. Let me see, you're Scotch, aren't you?'

Morgan nodded. When they had their glasses, his of fine malt, Fowler's of sherry, the other man sat on the table and swung his leg. He looked down.

'Clever and daring man, your Cheyney.'

'He's all of that.'

'You didn't know he was going to see the P.M. this morning.'

It was not a question, but Morgan shook his head as though it had been.

'Ah, well. It was still quite a triumph. Your triumph, in the view of the members of this committee. It doesn't matter to them, ultimately, what stroke Cheyney pulled. It's you they'll blame.'

'I know.'

'May I ask a question? Please don't answer if you don't want to. Or answer as opaquely as you like.'

'Fire away.'

'How sure are you you're on to a winner? Cheyney's not pulling some stunt of his own?'

Morgan was stung.

'I had to drag him into this business.'

Fowler smiled a small and wintry smile.

'And, yes, I'm sure we're on to a winner.'

'You'll get somebody?'

'I'm less sure. Tryon being dead is a facer.'

'I can see that. There's something else I should tell you.'

Morgan thought he detected a trace of excitement, perhaps even of wonder.

'Yes?'

'Foreign Secretary's having the Russian Ambassador in this morning. Heavy if veiled warnings about activities of the Russian spooks at this moment. That usually works, doesn't it?'

'I was going to ask for it.' Morgan was relieved. 'Yes, in the present climate it usually slows them up. They arranged the attack on Cheyney, we've no doubt about that. Depending on the importance they attach to anybody who's left after Tryon we should get a few weeks' grace.'

'Good.'

Fowler stood up and emptied his glass.

'May I give you a piece of advice?'

'I'd welcome it.'

'If this goes wrong your neck is in a noose. Neither OIS nor HIS will ever forgive you. So ...'

'Yes?'

'I hope for your sake your man Davies requisitions everything in sight. You may need everything you can get to muddy the water.'

As he left Morgan felt mixed triumph and disgust. He and Davies had taken the precaution Fowler had advised. But he was triumphant that Fowler had offered the advice: that showed both which side Fowler was taking and which side he expected to win. That realisation was the source of Morgan's disgust. Like everybody else he had lost sight of the objective, discovering and defining Harry Richmond's heritage, and had his eyes now set on the distribution of power that would follow whatever occurred. Again not for the first time, Morgan wished he was out of this jungle and back in the Army.

But he was whistling when he rejoined Cheyney in the office.

CHAPTER TWENTY ONE

FLEMING AGAIN

'I think I should make it clear, Colonel Cheyney, that I am not accustomed to this kind of treatment. I have been here for five hours now, and our conversation has gone in circles. There are many pressing matters awaiting my attention and I cannot, for the life of me, see where we are going.'

He was angry and tired and it showed. After much reflection Cheyney had decided to meet him at nine on the morning following the JIC meeting, and in Tom Morgan's office. Fleming had, of course, been positively vetted before. But he had not for a long time been treated the way Cheyney was treating him, ducking in and out of aspects of his history like a lightweight boxer moving around, and under the guard of, a heavier and clumsier opponent, polite – most of the time – but remorseless; sometimes sarcastic, often deliberately uncomprehending.

The character of the investigation and the personae had changed. Lewis had been despatched with the girl to a safe house in Berkshire. He had gone grumbling and irritable, but also, in a paradoxical way, half-pleased and a little excited by the girl, whose guardian he was to be until they were finished. Davies was in the basement. His eyes gleaming, he had seen to the unloading of almost innumerable files from a series of vans all through the night. His computer had been linked and it had been instructed to answer all his questions. Tom Morgan came in and out of his own office from time to time and listened for a while to the conversation, but had never, so far, interrupted.

That left Cheyney and Fleming, sitting opposite each other, divided by the desk loaded with files, papers, scribbled notes, Cheyney's ashtrays regularly emptied into the tin wastepaper basket beside him, soiled coffee cups around them, a fug of smoke in the air, Miss Levison typing furiously next door and convinced that the world had set itself right again, now that Colonel Cheyney was in his office.

'What I still can't quite grasp,' said Cheyney, 'was exactly what sort of man Harry Richmond was. You must have some idea of that. Obviously you were friends. Nobody visited him more often in hospital.'

Fleming pressed his lips together tightly. He ached for a cigarette, but had so far successfully denied himself one. He burned with humiliation and fury and inwardly cursed that long-ago telephone call. But he would not yield now.

'Are you going to answer my question?'

'You didn't ask a question. How long is this rigmarole going to go on?'

'Ah.'

Cheyney stood up, walked to the window, rubbed the small of his back, turned around.

'We are satisfied that Tryon was a traitor. Does what I have told you so far convince you of that?'

Fleming debated whether to answer or insist on an answer. He tried to compromise.

'It certainly seems odd that he lied to Harry about his son.' Then, while Cheyney waited, 'Yes, I suppose he must have been.'

'There you are,' said Cheyney in a friendly and comforting tone. 'We must find out who Tryon was protecting. Now, you knew Tryon too: he was on your last vetting team.'

'Are you suggesting . . .'

'I'm not suggesting anything. Not at this stage, at any rate. Tryon ran the rule over all the candidates for the job you eventually got.'

Fleming attempted what he thought of as reason.

'Look here, Cheyney. I've done my best to help you. But I have a lot to do, and I've been here for five hours . . .'

'Good God. So you have. And I never thought of lunch. Look, I'll have it sent in straight away. Meanwhile, have a drink.'

Fleming was grudging in his acceptance, but he did feel he needed that drink, and he had it in his hand before he realised that he had let past the possible objection about lunch, and was now virtually committed to eating in this bloody place. Cheyney certainly moved fast. As Fleming was taking his first swallow, he muttered something and left the room.

Fleming had begun to formulate something else in his mind when Miss Levison came in. She carried a tray over to the desk and Fleming's spirits rose slightly. He had expected sandwiches, but was offered a very decent looking chicken salad, and half a bottle of white wine. He set himself to be composed and, after a while, he pulled his chair up to the food. He was hungry, and had finished in twenty minutes. There was no sign of Cheyney.

When five more minutes had passed Fleming allowed himself a cigarette. He got up and walked around the room. He had a peer at the papers on Cheyney's desk, saw no more than indecipherable hieroglyphics, and did not dare touch the files. He fetched up at the drinks table and found himself inspecting the bottles. After a good deal of hesitation, he poured himself a stiff brandy. Then he made another aimless tour of the room. He had given up trying to guess ahead of Cheyney and was now trying to make his mind a blank, trying to still its seething, choking off anger and annoyance, striving for perfect composure. After a while, and with something of the sensation of a guilty schoolboy, he helped himself to another brandy. Mustn't over-do this; but, God, it was a relief.

Cheyney was away an hour. He bustled pleasantly back into the room with armfuls of paper under his arm. He nodded, and went straight to the drinks.

'Ah. You've given yourself a drink. Wise man. Another?'

Fleming was quite irrationally furious that Cheyney had caught him out. There was no reason to be furious, he told himself. He was perfectly entitled to a drink. After all this bloody business, anyway. However, he declined another. Cheyney gave himself a generous Scotch. Miss Levison came in and took the tray away. She came back with another bloody coffee tray. Fleming, sweating slightly now, excused himself and set off for the gents at the end of the corridor. He relieved himself, washed, and leant his forehead for a moment against the cool tiles. Really, it was absurd that he was allowing himself to get into a state over that rude bastard.

'Friends,' said Cheyney as he came through the door. 'You and Richmond were close friends?'

'No,' said Fleming as he sat down. 'Colleagues. Not really friends.'

'But you visited him in hospital more often than anybody else. You even brought flowers. Every time.'

'I thought it my duty.'

'Oh, come. Don't be so stiff. No other colleague did that.'

'Well, *I* thought it my duty. He was a good and a loyal colleague. And he was very ill.'

It was absurd how readily a miasma of suspicion could be created. That, he supposed – he knew – was how these dreadful people worked. Everything was twisted, everything turned out of shape. Fleming felt a growing and helpless fear. Who was Cheyney, really? How much power did he have? The Prime Minister, no less, had telephoned Fleming for his co-operation, a request that could not be evaded, let alone denied. What the hell was going on here? What web was being woven? A combination of frustration and fear made Fleming burst:

'Look. I can't expect you to understand this, but I have a certain view about what is owed to people. I have – had – served closely with Harry Richmond for many years. I would as frequently visit any sick colleague I knew as well.'

'Lord Holmwood?'

'What?'

'You don't visit Lord Holmwood at all.'

'How the hell do you know that?'

'No visits recorded in your office diary. Do you go in your free time?'

The implications of his confidence sank in. Fleming came as near as years of discipline would allow him to spluttering. 'My diary. How . . .'

'You know what powers the Prime Minister has given me. Come, now. Do you visit Holmwood?'

'No.'

The admission was reluctant, not because Fleming did not have a case, but because the blanket nature of his just-made assertion weakened the case in advance. He felt himself slipping into the chains of a dialectic, a dialectic that had nothing whatever to do with the merits of the case, his understanding of what was going on, or his appreciation of and hostility to Cheyney.

'Holmwood is senile. There would be no point in visiting him. Harry and I talked a lot.'

'Not on the last occasion, apparently.'

'Oh, for God's sake. Harry was dying then.'

Fleming was almost shrill now.

Cheyney stood up and took his glass to the window. He rubbed the small of his back again and spoke over his shoulder.

'You don't like us much, do you?'

'What? Who?'

Cheyney came back and sat down. 'The Security Services.'

Fleming looked back at the cold eyes and the long fingers playing with the glass. Overstrained, he blurted again:

'No. I don't, damn it.'

'Why, I wonder?'

Fleming waved a hand.

'Oh, all this? But I'd have thought you'd put up with us because of the work we have to do. Or perhaps you're not interested in security?'

Had there been something in that brandy? In the wine? Even in the food? Fleming felt light headed, insecure, and yet oddly assertive at the same time.

'Your work and your methods seem to me often to bear very little relationship to your task. Of course, I'm concerned about security. But the orderly function of the Civil Service does not, as you seem to think, depend on people like you. It depends on people like, like, well, like myself and Harry Richmond. We've far more to get on with than espionage, I assure you. And let me tell you this . . .'

Fleming stopped and his eyes danced.

'Do you understand the kind of task this country is facing today? The Empire's gone, you know, Cheyney. The Great Game is not being played any more. The domestic responsibilities of government are enormous, and their successful discharge depends on hard work on industrial and financial policy, on the money markets, on economic relations. Not the sort of thing your imagined enemies would be interested in. Not secret papers stolen in the night. Not the plans of the new missile. Hard, grinding work, the kind of work I do. That is what will pull Britain through.'

He spoke with faith, perhaps even with fanaticism. Cheyney looked at him for a long time. Fleming thought he was about to take up the challenge. But instead he said:

'Did Richmond agree with you?'

'What?'

'During your years together. Did Richmond agree? When you had all these talks at the hospital. Did you discuss these matters? Did Richmond agree?'

His voice was very quiet, not intense, but serious. Undoubtedly serious. Relaxed by his outburst Fleming felt if not genial, at least co-operative.

'We rarely discussed it. We differed. Harry had quite a thing about security.'

'Really? I confess that surprises me.' Cheyney took a pull at his whisky. 'In one of our very few conversations he expressed views very similar to yours. More abruptly, almost violently, in fact.'

There was no mistaking the genuineness of Fleming's frown of puzzlement.

'You surprise *me*. In the old days he was for ever going on about spies.'

Fleming frowned. In a sudden change of gear and the mood of their exchanges they were having a real conversation. Fleming's tidy, interrogative mind reached out for the inconsistency Cheyney had reported, and started to fuss at it, poke it around, turn it over.

'I was trying to tell him about his son.'

That startled Fleming. 'You mean, he knew, whenever it was, that . . .'

'No. That's the damnable thing. I was going to tell him how bravely Charlie had died, and he cut me right off.'

The two men sat for a few moments in silence, drawn together suddenly and unexpectedly not only by the drift of the conversation, but by their mutual contemplation of what might have been, and how things might have been done.

'Until you told me this morning,' Fleming said, all animosity departed, 'I didn't know anything about the boy, or this fellow Tryon. But I did know that Harry – I suppose about that time – was most dreadfully cut up about Charles.'

'I never knew it. According to Charlie, he was a very devil as a father.'

'The boy may not have been reliable as a witness. And Harry certainly didn't demonstrate affection very easily. I suppose I only talked about his son with him three or four times in twenty odd years and, to be frank, one of those times we were both somewhat drunk. But he cared. I assure you he cared very deeply. I didn't know he'd heard the boy had defected, and, of course, not that Charles was dead. But it smashed up something in Harry. I'll always believe that was why he pulled out of the competition at the Treasury. At the Home Office, of course, he just worked out his time. All his flair had gone.'

'But you know,' said Cheyney, 'that was what I had begun to suspect?'

Their silence this time was protracted. Cheyney was going through the papers he had brought back with him after his disappearance. Fleming realised he looked worn, almost ill. A certain flicker of sympathy touched him. He felt quite generous, and still high on the brandy. He thought he would break the silence in a companionable way.

'You may have misremembered how Harry put things to you, you know.'

'You say,' said Cheyney, without looking up, 'or you imply, that you take little interest in security, or at least in espionage matters. But I see here that your evidence was material in putting Gibney away at his court of inquiry.'

'I suppose that's true. But it was a different kind of thing. You see, Gibney had betrayed the *Service*.'

He suddenly realised what he had said and what he had revealed. He wanted to explain it all now, the whole philosophy which underpinned his nature and his training. But the words would not all come out, and he was no longer very sure of his ground anyway. So he thought he would try to say something fairly light.

'Harry was interested in espionage generally. Mustard keen, once. Even had his doubts about ministers. Do you know, he was suspicious of Tom Clements, Lord Clements?'

'Is that so?' asked Cheyney, and started shifting through the papers again. Then he leant back.

'You know, I feel I know Richmond less well than when I started all this. I feel bewildered and strange at all the different facets of the man. I've uncovered too much and too little.'

He stood up.

'Sir Richard. Thank you very much. I'm sorry to have discommoded you, and I'm sorry to have been rude. All necessary, or so we like to think.'

'Is that all?'

Fleming was suddenly bewildered, now that it had all come to an end. He almost regretted it, almost felt an anger that ran counter to everything else he had felt during that long day that it was absurd.

'That's all. I don't think we'll have to bother you again.'

When Miss Levison had taken Fleming away Cheyney sighed very deeply. He called for Davies and Morgan and went to recharge his glass. They found him standing in deep gloom at the window.

After an hour Morgan said:

'So it's Clements?'

'It must be,' said Davies. 'Everything fits. Richmond was on to Clements and they decided to distract him. The thing is, security were undermanned at the time. Clements was to go to the Treasury as Financial Secretary, and Tryon wangled it so that he did the vetting alone. Clements sailed through. Richmond pulled out of the competition for the job of Permanent Under Secretary.'

'Detection's really easy,' he added.

'But there's more than that,' said Cheyney.

'All the co-relations fit,' said Davies. 'Tryon had vetted Clements before. That's very bad practice, but a long time had elapsed. It happened. We can only suppose that Richmond confessed his suspicions to Tryon. God, what a mess.'

'HIS is going to suffer for this.' Morgan was grim.

'The thing is,' said Davies, 'there's a lot more work to be done. We've fixed the relationship. Fleming's confirmed what I've worked out on paper. We've evidence enough for a court *in camera*. But we're a long way from a trial.'

'How do you suppose the Russians felt,' said Morgan, 'when Clements had his heart attack six months after he took the job? What a mess from their point of view too.'

'And what,' said Davies, 'are we going to do about an ex-minister who hasn't been in politics for nearly ten years, has hardly been to Westminster or Whitehall, and lives in seclusion in Devon?'

'What indeed,' said Morgan. 'Everybody in the story is dead or crippled. Richmond's dead. Tryon's dead. Holmwood's senile. And now we end up with Clements, nearly dead of heart disease. What the hell are we going to do?'

Cheyney stretched.

'Oh, I know what we're going to do,' he said. 'Remember what we said about treason, Tom?'

Cheyney walked up and down the room for a minute or so. When he spoke his voice was reflective. What he said was self-incriminatory.

'Do you remember, Bob', he said, 'what we talked about before Lewis and I went off to Brussels?'

He didn't want an answer. He wanted – they saw that – to talk aloud, largely to himself.

'You hadn't had time to complete the hospital files. But you knew them well enough. You raised the whole subject of who had visited and who hadn't. Who was close to old Harry and who wasn't. You even mentioned Clements.'

He stopped and gave a short, harsh laugh.

'Court *in camera*. Ha. All we could produce would be our suspicions and connections. If he was still in office, if he was still active, we could smear him, the way Skardon smeared Philby. But now?'

He paced again.

'Where I went wrong in all this was in concentrating on the inessentials.'

'Oh, Allen,' said Morgan.

'No. I did. I got too interested in Harry, and that whole business of the girl. Remember, Bob? I dismissed the politicians. I should have noticed – I remember now all right – that Harry briefed Clements before his party came to power. But, just like bloody Fleming, God help me, I thought all the time about the service – our service, the Civil Service, the Russians' bloody service. We'd – Bob would have – got round to Tryon in the end. But, instead of taking the whole thing coldly, and looking at everything in the round, I chased off like some boy in an adventure story. An adventure of state.'

He turned to Morgan and stared at him.

'Anyway, Tom, there's something gained. Go on with that work Bob has just described. Do it carefully. At least you'll have all the damned files now. That's useful. And let Bob be your guide, not me. There may be a lot of things – a lot of people – to be found yet. And don't, for God's sake don't, forget the politicians.'

Then, he said:

'But I'll help start the clearing up.'

CHAPTER TWENTY TWO

THE FINAL ACT

The house – a large cottage, really – nestled in a fold of hills. It had perhaps half an acre of ground, simply laid out in lawns, dotted with trees and bushes, bearing a slightly untidy look in daylight, a look wholly in keeping with the fact that it was tended by an underpaid gardener from the village. Lord Clements was not a wealthy man: he could afford little more.

Here he had lived for nearly ten years. He lived with his wife and his dog – an Old English sheepdog – and they had the gardener and a cleaning woman. He had a small study, looking out through French windows on the slopes leading from the back of the cottage up to the hills. He repaired to the study most mornings, while his wife busied herself with good works in the neighbourhood, and in so far as he had mental or physical energy that day, he would potter among papers and books and try to add a sentence or two to the treatise on political economy he had been writing since he was a graduate student.

When the weather was fine Helen would take him for drives around the countryside. He would get out of the car, sometimes, and sup beer at a local pub – nothing stronger was permitted. He took only the mildest interest in anything that happened in the country, though when he had sat for the constituency he had been the busiest and most conscientious of members. And he was still under sixty.

Most of the time Helen, a bustling, cheerful and uncomplaining woman, left him to his memories. It was reasonably safe to leave him alone. The doctors thought he might live for many years yet, with care, though they fussed sometimes about his lack of interest in things. He was still a big, fine-looking man, though with the gloom of unhealth around his cheeks that bespeaks the heart patient. He looked after himself, brushing his hair each morning for as long as would a girl. It was fine, longish, silvery hair. As long as he rested a lot, took his pills and watched his temper he might go on for a long time. And, in a curious way, he wanted to go on for a long time, though why, or what he was waiting for, he had never articulated, even to himself.

From about an hour after Cheyney had decided, the house was covered. There was no evidence of this, but Clements sensed a change in the air. He had that hypersensitivity to atmosphere which often comes with serious and chronic illness, and he knew that something had changed. He felt, not dread nor fear exactly, but change and suspicion, change in the even and deadly tenor of his days, suspicion at what portended.

So, when Cheyney's telephone call came he was not surprised. The call was made from the village: Cheyney did not want to be too far away when he gave his warning. Clements listened for a long time in silence and then spoke, in a slow and heavy voice that was a shadow of the rumbling bass that had once captivated political audiences.

'Could you come about seven, Colonel? My wife will have gone out then. And I think we should be alone.'

Helen prepared him a simple meal and laid it for him on a side table in the study. Though she was both affectionate and responsible, she had made a life for herself in the last decade, and he insisted on it as much as she did. Then, taking the dog in her car as she usually did, she set off for her meeting. When it was over, she would telephone him to check. Then she would go on to dinner. When she returned, about eleven or half past, he would be in bed in the little boxroom off the study. That was how it was and how, now, it seemed it always had been: stairs were not to be risked.

As her car disappeared down the road Morgan started the Rover. There were four of them, Lewis having been recalled for the last act. No triumph sat on them, or on their faces. Morgan brought the car up to the gate.

'Are you sure you want to do this alone, Allen?'

'Yes.'

Cheyney got out of the car, tall and straight, and opened the gate. As he did so Clements opened the door, and stood in the light from his hallway. He was a big man and, despite his illness, not at all run to fat. In the distance he even looked powerful. Only as Cheyney came up into the light could he see the sickness, the veins in the cheeks, the pouches under the eyes, the careful, valetudinarian, manner of the stance. It had all gone for Clements a long time ago. Here was no traitor, no threat: he was a prematurely aged and very sick man.

'Come in.'

Cheyney followed him into the little study. Following his host's gesture he sat on one side of a small and burnished mahogany desk and took in the booklined room in a sweeping glance.

'Colonel Cheyney. I keep drink here for the occasional guest. Yours is Scotch, if I remember?'

Cheyney accepted a tumbler of neat malt, almost half full. Clements had trembled a little in the pouring, and some whisky had run down the outside of the glass. It was wet and sticky to his fingers. Clements lowered himself carefully into his chair.

'Well,' he said at last, 'the hunter has come.'

'Yes.'

'Have you any questions? I will answer if I can.'

'Who thought up the ploy about Harry Richmond? It was brilliant, but very risky.'

'Not so risky. It was brilliant, though. That was Vishinsky.'

'Ah.'

'You wonder why he was not killed? Oh no. That would have been much more risky.'

There was an odd serenity about the man, almost a complacency. It was as though having had nothing to exercise his personality on for so long he was enjoying this interview.

'And you? You did not defect?'

'I never wanted to leave England. It was England I was working for, you see.'

After a pause, he added:

'No. You don't.'

'You destroyed the reputation of a very brave man in the eyes of his father. I find that the most unforgivable thing of all.'

'Oh, come. You killed the boy, not me. Or Vishinsky.'

That was a bit too close for comfort. Clements had lost none of his shrewdness. He was going on:

'However, I recognise your right to care about that more than anything else. A single betrayal always seems so much more heinous than a multiple betrayal, does it not?'

There really was very little more to say. A devilish curiosity had prompted Cheyney's behaviour, but he saw now that it would remain forever unsatisfied. However prolonged the conversation he would learn nothing new from this man, no light would be shed on treason or its roots now. All that he knew and all that he wanted to know he had told Tom Morgan over dinner. There was nothing else.

Misinterpreting his look, Clements said:

'You'll never try me, you know. Not that I care a great deal, except for Helen — my wife. But the ticker won't stand up to arrest.'

Cheyney reached into his pocket and took out a small automatic. For a second a shadow of fear and entrapment passed across Clement's face. Then he recovered.

'Ah,' he said, 'pistols in the library.'

'If you want to put it that way. There is a price to be paid.'

'There is always a price to be paid.'

'And this will spare your wife . . . something.'

'No doubt.'

Clements reached over for the gun and Cheyney misunderstood him.

'Shooting me will achieve nothing.'

'My dear Cheyney. I had not the slightest intention. But this is the end of our conversation? No grilling? No whys and where-fores? This is all?'

'All. There is the price.'

'There is a bottle of brandy over there. I think I will have a last one. A very stiff one, please.'

Cheyney obliged and Clements inhaled, drank deeply, spluttered and sighed.

'Where am I supposed to have got the gun?'

'That doesn't matter. It is untraceable. And there will be no inquiries.'

'How thoughtful.'

His strange, sick face and wide, staring eyes looked across at Cheyney. Here was the traitor run to earth, here was the end of the line that ran from the National Heart Hospital to Devon. Here was something unveiled after ten years, and it made a true ending, for there was nothing that could be uncovered from Clements now, just as there had been nothing to uncover from Tryon. Spies and traitors too were subject to the twists and turns of ordinary life and to the evidence of mortality that lay at its end.

Cheyney was merely the instrument of that somewhat peremptory mortality. He was there to see that a line was drawn under something. The drawing of the line was greater than revenge or punishment, greater than hatred, greater, even, than loyalty or treason. The drawing of the line was the end of all things, and it was Cheyney's job to draw the line. That was all. There was no more now. Just a great anti-climax, and an emptiness armoured against all feeling, even sadness, even curiosity.

Clements was speaking again:

'I suggest you finish your drink and wash your glass. There's a loo across the hall. Then we can do our business.'

Five minutes later Cheyney left the house and walked to the car.

Morgan jumped out.

'Allen. What's happened? There was no noise.'

'I went to wash a glass, to leave no evidence. He was dead when I got back. Heart. Here.'

He gave Morgan the gun and they got into the car and sat with the others for a moment. Davies having wound down his window, he and Lewis knew what had passed.

'The thing is,' said Cheyney, 'I still feel no closer to Harry Richmond, and I would like to be.'

'And I still know nothing about Zagreb,' said Morgan.

'I'll tell you tonight, Tom. After I 'phone Rachel to tell her I'm coming home.'